AF435369

The
Titanic
Connection

CHRIS JOHNSON

The Titanic Connection

First Edition

Copyright © 2024 Chris Johnson

DEDICATION

To my wife Katrina and my daughter Harper.

And to you, Awesome Reader. Thank you for buying this (or borrowing it from your local library).

Your support means the world to me.

Other Books

The Craig Ramsey - Occult Detective series

Deja Two (2022)

Dead Cell (2016)

Demon Blade (2018)

The Universe Crack'd (2021)

ChronoSpace series

Bootstrap's Journey (2017)

The Paradox of Buck Nowlan (2023)

The Time Traveller's Heart (2023)

The Titanic Connection (2024)

Standalone Books

Twelve Strokes of Midnight (2016)

While He Was Sleeping (2020)

The Trick (2016)

Grantley's Last Laugh (2023)

Read more at Chris Johnson's site *https://payhip.com/ChrisJohnsonAuthor*

"We all have our time machines, don't we? Those that takes us back are memories… And those that carry us forward , are dreams." - H.G. Wells, The Time Machine (1895)

"Time is a sort of river of passing events, and strong is its current; no sooner is a thing brought to sight than it is swept by and another takes its place, and this too will be swept away." - Marcus Aurelius, Meditations (circa AD180)

"Time is but the stream I go a-fishing in." - Henry David Thoreau, Walden (1854)

Chapter 1

**Electronic Diary of Anthony Nowlan
Apricot Corporation, Yeppoon, Queensland.
Australia.
2pm, 4th April 2019.**

I sat alone in the front office, my thoughts a restless mix of nervousness and anticipation. Something in my gut told me my time-travel invention was more trouble than I had imagined. I had already encountered too many twists, including the revelation that my wife was from centuries past. Now, I braced myself for what would come next.

The ring of the doorbell altered the feeling of disquiet festering in my stomach. The time I was dreading had come. The eleventh hour.

I should have felt in control. It was my own building. But something nagged, telling me this meeting should take place elsewhere. Somewhere neutral like the restaurant. Even a park bench by the beach.

But was anywhere truly safe from the man waiting outside?

I hesitated, wondering if I should open the door. Erin, my wife, had already told me about meeting this man, a ghost from my past. He had arrived at our home's doorstep a moment before she went into labour. *But this time, he is different,* she had told me. *How different,* I asked. *You'll see,* she said.

The time had come.

My eyes flicked towards the security monitor as I reached for the door lock release. Stunned by what I saw, my fingers trembled as I pressed it. The door buzzed, and I pulled the door open to see him standing there, a briefcase in hand.

Erin was right. He is different, but not entirely so. Erin was used to knowing the young version, a man in his thirties-or-forties, unlike the older, grizzlier version I first met in 2038 -- just shy of twenty years in the future. At that time, I was studying at Central Queensland University and working on my personal projects. He had befriended me, showing an interest in my passion for time-travel. This led me to show him my prototype ChronoSpace. When he learned I needed funding, he had the solution. But this couldn't be the same man from the future; he had died. This had to be the younger one from the present. Yet the puzzle remained: how had he aged twenty years in less than a year?

He removed his Ray-Bans and regarded me with the same familiar piercing, steely eyes as I take in his professional air. His charcoal suit, tailored to fit him like a second skin accentuates his lean physique. And the way he grasped my hand, shaking it, reminded me of my grandfather's handshakes. Strong and firm. Granddad would have called it a mark of good character, yet my experience made me wonder.

"Mr Nowlan," he said, his voice carrying a low, commanding resonance. "I trust you are prepared to discuss matters of utmost importance."

For a moment, I stood there, lost, taking in his features as I remembered the day I last saw him at his current age. In 2042, moments before I jumped back in time to 2017, he had pointed his pistol at me. We had fought, and he grabbed me just as I activated my ChronoSpace. When we landed in the past, he had held me at gunpoint and I think he would have killed me if fate hadn't intervened, killing him thanks to a bug in my time-travel device's programming. The man in front of me should not have existed.

"Are you going to let us in?" he asked, and I returned from memory lane, aware of the silver tie clip that glinted subtly in the sunlight against his crisp, white dress shirt. A movement from behind him caught my attention and I noticed two other people -- a man and a woman in similar attire to him.

"Of course," I replied, standing aside to let them inside. He thanked me as he stepped into the foyer. The other two followed, giving me barely perceptible nods as I greeted them. Although their eyes remained hidden behind their sunglasses, which they still wore, I knew they were checking out everything inside.

The door shut behind them. Its automatic lock snapped in place.

"Follow me," I said, taking them through to the small meeting room within.

Cutter followed, his gaze sweeping across the modest room with a subtle austerity. The small kitchen table and six chairs, remnants of a local secondhand store, seemed to echo a utilitarian vibe. As he assessed the space, a flicker of disbelief crossed his face, leaving me to decipher the unreadable nuances of his expression.

"We concentrate more on our work than niceties at present," I explained, wondering why I had bothered to say that much yet.

A slight smile crossed his face, then disappeared. My baby son Connor does the same sometimes, and Erin tells me its just wind. Maybe Cutter had wind too.

The other two agents drifted in soon afterwards. Were they doing something else in the hall, I wondered -- taking photos or something. They ignored my gaze as they passed and sat in chairs opposite Cutter, sitting on the longer edges of the table. As I sat at the table's head, I realised the position of power was eclipsed by their apparent posture of surrounding me.

"Would you like something to drink?" I asked, pointing to the empty tumblers and the carafe of water, its surface dripping with condensation. They nodded, and the female agent poured glasses for them. Something about her chin struck a familiar chord, but I couldn't place it.

"How are Erin and your baby?" Cutter asked, a question that prickled the back of my neck. On the surface his words were congenial and pleasant, matching his tone. But this same man had posed a threat to me when I arrived in this time-period, and before that too.

"Doing well," I replied, pouring my own drink and taking a sip. "Thanks for asking. So, Gary Cutter," I said, sitting back and facing my past nemesis, a man who I was beginning to think would be dogging me until time ended. "How can I help you?"

"Yes, Mr Nowlan, thank you for seeing me today." My visitor indicated his companions. "These are ASIS agents Liam Park" -- the male agent nodded -- "and Sofia Nguyen." The woman made no movement, plainly watching me with a stonewall face from behind the Ray-Bans still masking her eyes. Although unnerved, I pointedly fixed my gaze directly between and slightly above her eyes. A few seconds later, I turned back to

Cutter.

Cutter placed his briefcase on the table, flicked its locks open, and retrieved an A4-sized manilla envelope from inside. As he slid it towards me, I imagined another copy existed somewhere with the words TOP SECRET stamped on its outside. This one was blank. With a slight tightness in my chest, I brought the folder closer and opened it.

I extracted its contents, about a dozen photos, some colour, others black-and-white copies of what appeared to be older pictures. The top one grabbed my attention as I recognised the day it happened.

It showed me at the front door of my beach-house on Lammermoor Beach. It was from my wedding with Erin as I greeted arriving guests. Eyebrows crinkling, I lifted my gaze to Cutter. The bastard had still been watching me.

"Snaps from my wedding?" I said, feeling a touch of anger heating my neck. "Is that all you're here for?"

Cutter's tone remained calm and confident, speaking with greater wisdom than I remembered from his younger self. The contrast struck me with further questions as he said, "Beautiful photos. Your photographer agrees it was a lovely wedding." He paused, glancing towards Agent Nguyen, then back to me.

At that moment, I realised where I had seen her before. We had hired an ASIS agent to photograph our wedding!

"You owe us a larger blowup for the deception," I grumbled to the female agent. Her lip curled slightly at the corner before resuming its previous state. She said nothing. At least she has a sense of humour, I thought to myself.

"Deception," Cutter interrupted, "is a term I feel you are well acquainted with, Mr Nowlan. Don't you agree?"

Ah, here it goes, I thought to myself. This was going to be a repeat of the conversation he and I had in the restaurant in Yeppoon, soon after my arrival from the future. After breaking into Apricot Corporation where he beat up my friend Professor Stockwell before leaving with a copy of a video from my landing in 2017, he had tried to get me to admit to my ability to travel time. I thought we had already dealt with that and thrown him off the scent.

"You're not flogging that old horse again, are you?" I raised an eyebrow at him. "I told you before that I don't have a DeLorean."

"You said it was a little blue box, I understand." The response came so quickly, it made Formula 1 racers look like they run in reverse.

I hesitated, perhaps from guilt, wondering if that is what originally happened. Hoping he hadn't noticed, I changed the subject and asked what was on my mind. "Tell me, why do you look twenty years older in the past two years? Stressful job?"

Cutter snorted in amusement. "Droll, Mr Nowlan." He took a sip of water, the first sign I'd seen of him since he arrived. "All in good time; I will answer for you in due course. First, let's cut the bullshit."

Reaching into the opened briefcase, he removed something that made me utter a curse. He placed it on the table and regarded me with a mixed expression. As my eyes passed over the familiar object, taking in the familiar metallic oval shape that shone like brass, my heart beat faster.

"Familiar, Mr Nowlan?" Cutter asked, the twitch of a smile on his lips as he watched me closely. He reached across to the photos before me, lifted one to reveal a closeup of one of my descendants at the wedding. A similar, if not identical, object sat on my guest's belt buckle. "Care to guess how I got it?"

I sighed. There was no point continuing the charade. The smug bugger knew the truth.

The object in front of me was the ChronoSpace. Not just any ChronoSpace model. It was the original, for I recognised the scratches on it. A big dent in the edges of its casing reflected a distorted image of my face as if it were laughing at me. I guessed it must have come from when it fell down the chasm at Black Mountain. Just the same, I had no idea how he knew to go there for it, or survived the expedition.

When I didn't answer, Cutter added: "You gave it to me a little over a year ago."

My eyes bugged at that, awakening a hint of scepticism. A year ago? How could that be? "I *gave* it to you?" I asked, my brow crinkled as I considered everything. It was lost, and I never retrieved it. "Why would I do that?"

I reached for the device, which I had thought completely lost. Professor Stockwell had told me that he and Tenner had managed to track the errant time-travel device through quantum markers to three or four different points in time and space on the planet. Each of those moments were in the past. And that's how Claire came to find me lost in time to return me to the present era.

The chair creaked as Cutter sat back in his chair, resting his elbows on the armrests. Across steepled fingers, he gazed at me, a knowing smile playing across his lips. "I was surprised at first too, but he... I mean you... said I should also give you this." He reached forward with something and dropped it in my hand.

Stunned, I turned over the second familiar object. But this wasn't a device from 2019 or even the past. It came from 2042, or around that time-period. It didn't fit anything before 2038 because that's when it was invented for mainstream usage. In fact, this one came from someone else I knew from the future --- Keli Blankenship, the lady whose program helped me survive in Australia 1606. It was customised with a cat's photo -- one of her many cats, she had told me.

"Why?" I asked, sliding the device into my shirt pocket for later. "Why did I do that?"

"Isn't it obvious?" Gary Cutter asked, a tinge of surprise in his own voice as he spoke. "You needed me to trust you. Now I need the same in return. It's some kind of loop, you told me at the time."

A moment of déjà vu overcame me as I looked him in the eye. He looked the same as when I knew him in 2042 before my trip into this time-period, not the young man of 2017. Only then he wasn't acting friendly. We had fought, even traded blows before my ChronoSpace activated, flinging us back to this era. He accidentally died soon after, trying to kill me. Of course, this Cutter doesn't know that yet -- purposely.

Conflicted by my experience and the recent events, I could only shrug.

"I understand." He interlaced his fingers, leaning on the table. "You're wondering why I look much older than I did a year ago." He stopped to give me a questioning look.

Well, yeah. Besides the other things, that question still burned my brain.

"Something like that," I agreed and cleared my throat.

"Then let me explain, Mr Nowlan." He pointed to the photos from the envelope I had almost forgotten. "Check the next picture."

I did. At once, my eye bugged at what I saw.

It showed what looked like the interior of an English pub. Perhaps it was Christmas because we all seemed to be wearing those wrinkled paper hats. The tree in the background and the decorations on the cornices added to the atmosphere. Although the subjects in the photo were familiar, very close to me, I knew this hadn't happened. At least, not yet. Seated around the table, each of us lifting what could have been a pint glass to the camera, we smiled. Erin next to me, then the Lawson twins and Jasmine... and Cutter. Only he looked younger.

"Did I give you this photo too?" I asked, flipping to the next picture.

"No. The original is in our archives at ASIS. It's dated 1945."

Now that caught my attention. I looked at him, my jaw dropping as I studied his expression, searching for any clues or hints of deception. My brow crinkled as my thoughts raced. The year meant something to me because the Professor had told me my ChronoSpace had been to London of World War II. But I knew I hadn't. At least, I couldn't recall it. "1945?"

He nodded. "You showed it to me before taking me there to London during the Blitz and, later, another time before that." For a few seconds, he remained silent, letting that soak into my thoughts before adding: "And even stranger, you told me it was in our archives first, even insisted I check first."

That meant the photo was taken some time in my personal future timeline. My eyebrows formed a question mark as I took that in. "Right," I answered thoughtfully and focused upon the next photo.

A picture of the two of us, my eyes caught directly on my wife's image. Adorned in a gown that whispered of Edwardian sophistication, the delicate lace and satin draped gracefully over her slender figure. Her attire accentuated the graceful curve of her neck. The silhouette of the gown reflected her beautiful figure, a result of her devotion to yoga and Pilates, although the people aboard the ship would never have guessed that. She was the silvery moon beside me in my own suit of the era.

But this hadn't happened. Was the picture real or a damned good Photoshop trick?

"You told me that was taken in 1912 on the Titanic," Cutter explained, peering over the edge of the photo at it. "Erin looks beautiful as always. Amazing how the old fashions can further enhance us without revealing so much flesh."

Yes, my wife was beautiful in the photo, as always, but what was she doing on the Titanic with me? I had no desire to be back on that ship again, risking the prospect of clinging to an iceberg as the liner sank into the icy depths forever. It was no place to take our son either, but I didn't see him in the photo. What did that mean?

Cutter's face remained hard, unreadable, as he gazed back

at me. Even the other two agents remained quiet. Only the sound of a drip from the tap in the nearby kitchen sink and the buzz of the electric clock's motor reached my ears.

"I have a question," I said finally, remembering that this was my office. "You're in these photos too. What's your game?"

My visitor's face twitched, and something in his eyes told me volumes as he drew a breath to answer.

"Mr Nowlan --- Buck," he said, taking a slightly softer tone as he used my middle name. "I was hoping it was obvious. But someone close to you told me it didn't work the first time."

"First time? Who?" I interrupted, but he raised a hand to silence me and turned to agent Park.

"You and I have... One moment, this is confusing to me too." He paused to consider his words before continuing. "I have time-travelled with you, and you're going to travel with me."

"Bull dust," I responded in disbelief. "And the last I heard, you were associated with the Russian Mafia here, using their money to fund Sam's work." I held back that I had found out his future self would do the same for my work in time-travel, the prototype of my ChronoSpace.

He paused, caught off-guard by my revelation. To his credit, he kept his composure as he leaned forward. "They are a means to an end for us, something you will appreciate in time."

"When?" I asked, but he ignored it, continuing what he had apparently come visiting to tell me.

"Another thing. I'm not sure if I should show you this or not." He went to hand another picture to me and changed his mind. "But first, this didn't come from you. It came from someone else related to ASIS overseas. In Egypt. An archaeologist there found an ancient tomb. While examining one of the bodies, she found something that astonished her enough to report it. Our agency has kept it out of the mainstream media, but you may see it on social media at some time."

I took the photo and examined it. Another shock rippled through me as I took in the details. The mummified being was male, but I could only guess at the build. The face was desiccated, tanned, but otherwise recognisable in part. A tightness in my left pectoral muscle took me, making me lift my other hand to massage it. For there, in the photo was a man whose features resembled mine, but the greatest shock came when I recognised my jeans and Converse shoes... and the ChronoSpace on my belt!

"What the --?" I muttered as the blood drained from my face.

"Now that I have your attention, Mr Nowlan," Cutter said as I stared at the image, calculating the paradoxes, "we need your assistance. Not just for your family, or for your country. The whole world as we know it needs you."

Chapter 2

Erin Deering-Nowlan
Lammermoor Beach
1:45pm 4th April 2019

"Is something the matter, Erin?" Susan asked as Dan drove the car home from the Apricot Corporation office.

Erin shifted uncomfortably in the backseat. Between two children --- her infant son and the father of said boy --- the cramped position wasn't the most favourable. "I just never thought this is what life would be like," she said, comparing the features of both sleeping babies. "It's hard to tell their family resemblance yet."

"The DNA tests confirmed it," Dan mouthed as he took the car down a side street. "Our baby is the younger version of your husband, making you the aunty of our son and our daughter-in-law."

"That sounds downright dirty," Susan chided him, giving him a playful punch in the shoulder. "Besides, Erin and I aren't really sisters. She was adopted. Not that you can talk much about incest, Mr My-Family-Came-From-Mount-Morgan!"

Dan pulled a face of mock hurt at the jibe. A small mining town just under two hours' drive from Rocky, Mount Morgan was often the butt of jokes in Rockhampton that hinted at how almost everyone there was related to each other. "Hey! That's below the belt," he complained, holding a hand to his heart as though wounded. "Your family came from a smaller town, so what have you got to say?"

They chuckled briefly at the joke, allowing the tension to

leave. Then Susan changed the subject slightly, apparently sensing Erin's contemplative mood. "Do you remember, Erin, when I used to say the worst day of my life was learning I hadn't been adopted?" she added, giving a quick glance to the backseat.

"Sure do. I remember the expression on Mum's face, too. That was so cruel." Erin's smile at the memory faded as her thoughts drifted to the day before and the conversation with Tony.

His confession had hurt. Their tears still shone bright in her recollection, and the headache of crying lingered too.

Tony had confessed about his initial attraction to Jenny while trapped in 1606. But he had resisted it, despite her strong resemblance to Erin. He had even told Jenny that Erin, Jenny's daughter, grown up, was his wife. But things happened in the form of tea laced with bush mistletoe by Jenny.

"I didn't even know what had happened until too late," Tony had explained to her, choking on his painful tears. "I'd never do anything to hurt you, Erin. Honestly. You have to believe me."

Yes, Erin believed him without the virtual reality journal he offered her. Despite her initial doubt, she recalled the beginning of their whirlwind romance. He had been a virgin, she his first partner, his first kiss, his first everything. She remembered how he had found out by accident about how she once dated a man destined to be his enemy. Although it had happened before Tony met Erin, the thought had hurt him to the core.

As she gazed out the car window, she remembered knowing on that day she could trust him entirely with her heart. Jenny, however, was a different story.

"Earth to Erin." Susan's voice cut Erin from the horrible turns of memory lane. "Are you still with us?"

Erin blinked, wiping her moistening eyes as she regarded her sister. "Sorry, what was that?"

"I was just commenting on how strange it must be, knowing you were born in the 1600s," Susan replied, smiling. "Does that make you my big sister now?"

Erin allowed Susan's question to hang for a moment as she wiped some chuck-up from Connor's mouth. Yes, being born nearly 400 years ago was a peculiar facet of an evidently unconventional life. But it reminded her again of the painful memory from the previous night.

"Ha! That's a can of worms," Erin replied, shooting a grin back at her. It was an effort. But would she get an Oscar for it?

"The part I'm unsure of is why Tony didn't just bring her back to the current time instead of dropping her off in 1987," Susan said, with a hint of conspiracy in her voice. Dan tutted at her, murmuring for her to stay quiet, but his wife didn't listen or didn't hear. "Doesn't that seem odd?"

Erin knew the reason. Jenny's seduction of Tony had left her pregnant. Feeling trapped by the woman's deception, his guilty conscience had tried to hide her, the sour fruit of their union, in the past. That's what someone like Susan might think if she knew the truth, Erin figured. Too bad Tony had another reason for it. He didn't want to shock Erin further by meeting her mother at the same age --- when she was just as attractive --- right now. He had avoided something worse.

"You know something, Sue?" Erin said, as Dan pulled the

car into her driveway. "You're one shit of a mother-in-law."

The abruptness in her voice killed the vibe in the car for a second. Susan's jaw dropped in shock, her embarrassed gaze shifting to Dan, then back to Erin.

"What?" Susan said with a slight stammer. "Where did that come from?"

Erin hastily unbuckled her seat-belt and began undoing the strap on baby Connor's capsule. Her fingers fumbled on the catch as she did. She cursed under her breath before finally succeeding. But she was still stuck. "Dan," she said, "can you open the door and help, please?"

Dan nodded, getting out of the driver's seat and coming round to open the door on Connor's side. He gently took the sleeping Connor and capsule out. Meanwhile, Susan huffed in the front seat before stepping out to meet Erin as she unfolded herself from inside the car.

"Erin, I was only joking," Susan said, her voice taking a softer tone.

"A joke?" Erin snapped, taking Connor's capsule by the handle. She shot daggers from her eyes as she faced her sister. "More like an issue."

"You've got to admit," Susan said, following behind Erin as she stormed towards the front door, "it's rather strange, isn't it? I mean, we--"

"We?" Erin couldn't believe her ears. She rounded on Dan, who was just extracting baby Tony from the backseat. "Do you have something to say about it, too?"

"Leave me out of this," Dan pleaded, turning pale as he looked at the baby sleeping in his arms. Then he nudged Susan, adding: "Don't forget, you're talking about your own son here. The poor kid hasn't even grown up yet. What does that say about how we've raised him? Or will raise him?"

Susan huffed, her face turning red. "I am not a lousy mother."

"Oh, for Christ's sake, Susan," Dan replied. "Put a sock in it, won't you? I didn't say you are. Why don't you listen to yourself?"

Susan stopped, her forehead crinkling in contemplation.

"I'm sorry," Dan said, helping Erin pull open the sliding door so that she could enter. Erin gave him a nod of understanding, grateful that it wasn't both of them ganging up on her. "If it means anything," he added in a calming voice, "I understand the whole thing, and I don't believe our son... your husband... would do anything wrong by you."

"The thing is..." Erin fell silent, thinking. Was this the right time to tell them? To hell with it, she decided and faced Susan. "How about you come inside, sis? You already know about Tony's time-travelling, so you may as well hear the rest of this. You too, Dan."

Erin, cradling baby Connor, stepped inside, leaving Susan and Dan momentarily in the wake of their heated discussion. The air inside was cooler, less muggy, as she carried Connor to the nursery. Gently placing him in his cot, she moved towards the window and fixed her gaze on the quiet backyard.

Behind her, Dan entered, carrying baby Tony in his own capsule. The nursery had two cots for that purpose, the future man of the house carefully placed in the second one.

Susan entered and stood beside Erin. "I'm sorry about what I said before, sis. You're right. I do have an issue, and it's about how you're coping with all of these changes." Erin turned to regard her, a mixture of exhaustion and resolve in her eyes, then looked back out the window. Susan added: "It's making our heads spin too, you know."

With a glance at her sister, Erin headed out the door. "How about a cuppa?" she called over her shoulder, focusing on remaining calm.

She sensed the unspoken words pass as if by telepathy between Dan and Susan. Yeah, they were worried. She got that, but that didn't give her sister the right to accuse Tony of cheating on her.

"You know," she said, filling the kettle from the tap, her hands trembling slightly. "Tony didn't cheat on me, and you're right about there being a baby with Jenny. But it's not the way you think," she continued, noting Susan's gasp of astonishment, her own eyes reflecting the weight of the revelation.

"Oh, Jesus on a motorbike," Dan muttered, an uncomfortable expression on his face as he sat at the dining table beside his wife. "We've got some work ahead of us."

Susan nudged him with her elbow, urging him to shut up. "What do you mean, Erin?"

As Erin recounted what she had learned the day before, a heavy silence settled in the room. Susan's eyes widened, her hand covering her mouth, while Dan's brows furrowed in disbelief.

"Shit, no wonder you looked awkward with Jenny when we read the DNA results," Susan said, empathy melting into view on her face. She looked as if she was about to say something else, but changed her mind.

"Look, I get it, and I'm fine with Tony. I forgive him," Erin said, happily surprised to hear the words coming from her mouth as she spoke. It strengthened her, helped her feel better to tell her sister, who until meeting Tony she had once told everything. "I just get a funny feeling about her. It's like she's trying to prove something to Tony after his saving her life twice."

"But is that all?" Dan asked, his eyes fixated on her. "You're worried about his time-travelling again, aren't you?"

Erin brought the boiled water to the table with the cups. She placed them and answered as she poured. "He says he's not time-travelling again, but I can feel something is going to happen at the meeting today with the government agents."

Dan leaned forward, obviously certain of her response. "And you know you can't stop him, right?"

Erin nodded, holding her hands around the hot mug.

"Do you love and trust him?" Susan asked.

"Yes," Erin replied, and she felt it.

"Then you know what you have to do," said Dan, glancing out the front window when a movement caught his attention. "Oh, shit," he said, and they all followed his gaze to see Jenny Horne parking her car in the driveway. "Did we say the witch's name three times or something? She's here now!"

Chapter 3

Electronic Diary of Anthony Nowlan
Apricot Corporation, Yeppoon, QLD, Australia.
4:10pm 4th April 2019.

My head was swirling still. After making sure Cutter and his colleagues had left, I made my way to the kitchen to clear my thoughts. Collapsing in a chair, I rested my elbows on the table and cradled my face in my hands.

In my childhood, Granddad often said, "You'll be in more trouble than Flash Gordon." By 2030, the character experienced a pop culture resurgence, allowing me to catch glimpses of the 1980 film. Though it didn't captivate me, I gleaned the essence of the saying from it and the vintage comics.

Now, it held a profound significance for me.

With my eyes tightly closed, I took a moment to contemplate everything, and was filled with a chilling sensation at the image of the mummified corpse wearing my clothes. The same classical Calvin Klein belt and Converse shoes. And my ChronoSpace. I wondered how I gained the privilege of having my remains preserved, though. The Egyptians saved that for royalty, nobility, and special people. If it was my body, how soon would fate call me? Years? Months? ... Days?

A voice chimed in from behind me. "A penny for your thoughts, Tony."

Startled, I turned to see Tenner standing in the open doorway to the computer lab. Green light from her large screen monitor backlit her with a glow, like an ethereal halo that highlighted loose strands of her black hair. Her earthy brown eyes gazed at me. "Considering inflation, a penny is probably not enough," she quipped. "Are you okay?"

I gave her a nod. "Yeah," I replied, blinking the worry from my face. "I just finished the meeting with Cutter."

"He wasn't alone," she stated in a matter-of-fact way, heading to the nearby counter.

"No. Two others were with him," I replied, assuming she'd picked up snippets from the other side of the wall. "How much did you catch?"

"Not a lot," she answered. "I don't trust them. The other guy with your friend came poking his nose around the back here."

The notion aroused my curiosity as I faced her. "What did he see?"

"Just me making coffee," Tenner chuckled, then added with a serious look: "But not before I saw him." She took something from the pocket of her cargo pants. Holding it up for me to see it was a small disc-shaped object with a thin, flexible wire aerial. It clinked on the table when she dropped it. "I microwaved it, so it's safe now."

Remembering a similar trick I played on Gary Cutter when he tried to blackmail me two years ago, I had to grin at that. "Nice."

"So I still have a job here?" Tenner asked, but she wasn't joking.

Surprised by her statement, I fixed my gaze on her. "What?" I said, curious about the origin of her thoughts. "From what I hear, you were a tremendous help in rescuing me from the 1600s, Tania." I corrected myself. "Sorry, I meant Tenner."

Her real name is Tania Kowalska, but she prefers her hacker handle. When I was lost in the far-flung past, she mysteriously appeared, claiming she was from present-day Tasmania. She had hacked my quantum supercomputer from 2041 to prove herself to Professor Stockwell and Erin before her grownup granddaughter from the future brought her here.

She poured her coffee, pulled out the chair opposite mine, and sat down facing me. A tendril of steam rose from her cup, drifting between us, casting her in a mysterious light as her brown eyes studied me. "It's okay," she said. "I like you. Call me Tania if it means I'm still working here."

"Of course," I replied with a friendly wink. "Erin has told me a lot about you. The way you helped decrypt that data from the sub-atomic marker in my ChronoSpace is awesome. A quantum computer still can't accomplish that feat in this age."

"I had help," she said, giving a modest shrug. She paused, and I could guess why before she added: "My granddaughter... great-granddaughter... I'm not sure what now told me."

"Ah, Jasmine, you mean." I gave a chuckle at that. "Yeah, well, she's really something. She helped me a lot too, and Erin told me about how you met. But what makes you think you're out of a job?"

"Now that you're back, I've fulfilled my bargain. You're back. Task complete."

"In that case, I'd like to extend your contract," I said, not even thinking I should consult with Erin or Sam first.

Her face lit up, making her brown eyes shine like polished stones. "Really?"

"Too right," I replied, giving her a fist-bump. "Not just because you microwaved a bug for me, either."

She giggled at that. It sounded like a young teenager. "That was a bonus."

"Ha! Seriously," I continued, thinking I should have a cuppa too, but not getting up to get it. "Sam is still working on his SkyShield, and he's already had a quiet little bitch-session with me about how he wants it done before time runs out. And you can assist me with the programming."

The tiniest hint of a smile appeared on her face. It heightened her beauty, and momentarily, I perceived Jasmine's resemblance. "I'd love that."

"So, are you interested?" I asked, already knowing the answer.

Her lips tightened, pressing together in a thoughtful expression as she reclined in her chair. Her arms folded as she looked up at the ceiling. After a short pause, she sat up again and looked me in the eye. "Same pay, same perks?"

"Is that okay?" I asked, half-expecting her to want more. And she did.

"Pop tarts," she said, her face straight as a poker player's. "I want more pop tarts."

Her dead pan expression remained until I burst out laughing as I realised pop tarts were her weakness. We both chuckled together for a few beats before I nodded. "Yeah, okay," I answered, wiping a tear. "I'll add that."

"Great!" Her face resumed its straight expression a moment later as she stood, mug in hand. "By the way, I have something to show you since I'm still gainfully employed. Come and see," she said, beckoning me along.

Curious, I followed her from the relatively brightly lit kitchen and into the darkened computer lab. The green glow from her computer monitor had changed to a screenshot of Zac Efron.

Tenner sat in her seat, flicked the mouse, and the screensaver disappeared and transformed into the green text from before.

"You know," she mentioned, glancing up from her screen as I pulled up another chair to sit beside her, "time travel can age you."

"What do you mean?" I asked, amazed that I had yet another issue to consider.

Tenner's face glowed green from the screen she was studying. Data whirled past too fast for me to read as her fingers danced on the keys. "You were gone for ten seconds from our perspective this morning. Yet the ChronoSpace took thirty-point-eight seconds travelling the 300-odd years back to 1687. You spent two hours there before travelling to 1992, taking thirty-point-eight seconds to travel." Her voice trailed, lips moving silently as she calculated it. "From your relative point of view, you have aged five hours in ten seconds. That includes your trips between time-periods and the times you were at each one."

She was referring to my time-jump earlier that morning. At the time I was tying up loose ends, bringing a baby Erin from 1687 to 19--- to arrange for her adoption to the family who ended up taking her. Then I travelled back to 1606, rescuing her mother Jenny from the snakebite by whisking her off to the Rockhampton of 1989 where she could receive antivenom treatment. I had my reasons for making it that year instead of 2019.

Tania's throat clearing brought me back to the present moment. I shook my head, replying, "But wouldn't others have noticed this?"

"Not necessarily." Tenner opened another display on her screen. This one showed the timelines for me. "Not to the same extent, anyway."

Tenner's slender finger pointed at the two temporal sequences next to each other. "This first one," she began, "is from when you were away from 3rd December 2018 until 15th March 2019." A pang of guilt slapped me as I absorbed the length of my absence.

Jumps to Titanic and Hindenburg lasted less than a day each. Pompeii was the same. But my time spent in 1688, healing my wounds, totalled two months; 1606 took three.

"It's almost half a year that you were in the past." Tenner leaned back in her chair, a pencil twirling between her fingers. She looked at the timelines with a mix of concern and fascination. "But for us, you were gone four months, so you've really aged faster by a month."

"Should I jump ahead a few weeks to make up?" I quipped, although I knew my wife Erin's response to that would be unforgiving. "Don't worry, I'm not planning on doing that again."

"You could have saved yourself the longer trip and been here for Erin's pregnancy." Tenner's voice held the tiniest hint of judgement there. Rather than ignore it, I took accountability for it.

"Yeah, I learned that the hard way."

The hacker's eyebrows rose for a moment, her forehead crinkling beneath a strand of her raven-coloured hair. "Have I mentioned what I learned from the data on

Claire's ChronoSpace?"

This time, I raised an eyebrow. "Not yet," I replied, masking my concern at her initiative. Was it a willingness to prove her worth to Apricot Corporation that made her check the data without being asked? Or something else?

"It is big shit, and somehow I think it's related to why you couldn't return with your own ChronoSpace."

"Someone hacked her device, too?" I asked with a concerned sigh.

Tenner shook her head and took a bite of a pop tart I hadn't noticed beside her. She answered while eating. "No, bigger than that... But close." She tapped at the keyboard, bringing up a graphical analysis to the screen, then moved aside so I could see it better.

She was right. This was big. Someone had placed a beacon at a specific point in time and space. The beacon reacted with any other quantum device at that date within a 4000 kilometre diameter range. As it linked, similar to a GPS, it activated a barrier.

"Someone's rigged it so whenever you hit Australia at that year and location, you're sent back in time again," Tenner said, swallowing her food. "But you found a way around that."

"And I'd guess that's what happened to my ChronoSpace," I muttered as I considered the revelation. "But why?"

Chapter 4

Electronic Diary of Anthony Nowlan
Lammermoor Beach, Yeppoon, Queensland.
Australia.
5pm, 4th April 2019.

My gut twisted for a second upon spotting the little white 1992 Ford Telstar AX leaving my driveway. It was still in good nick. Its white paint, although faded, was clear, and its engine a quiet purr. Only the circular rust spot on the driver's door gave it character.

Jenny, my mother-in-law, waved as she drove past me and around the corner. Her forced smile made me wonder what she had left behind with Erin in my home. Hopefully, nothing edible or laced with bush mistletoe. Barely a calendar day had ticked past for me since I had left her in the 1980s, her belly round with our baby. I kind of regret never seeing our child, despite it being a product of the mother drugging me. I've heard it's a boy. At least it still had someone to call daddy in that time, even if it wasn't me.

But now I have a child of my own, legitimate too, and the product of love --- not the spawn from something that should never have happened. Mental note: take time to myself to wrap my head round that.

It would have to be later. I had something to talk to Erin about. Something important. But if Jenny's recent visit was an indicator, even that might have to wait.

The crash of the growing tide reached my ears on the sea breeze as I slammed the Jag's door. From inside came the sounds of activity in the kitchen. Erin preparing dinner, either for us or for Connor. By the sounds, probably ours.

After dropping my ChronoSpace on my living-room chair, I held my breath with anticipation as I entered the kitchen. "Hello," I said, standing by the kitchen table.

My wife's face appeared above the open fridge door. My gut untwisted upon seeing her smile. Maybe the recent visit from the witch hadn't been so bad. "Hi! Connor's fed and sleeping," she said, head bobbing down inside the fridge. Above the sounds of dishes sliding across its glass shelves, she added: "My moth---Jenny was here."

Her voice was neutral when she said it. I lifted a brow in curiosity as I pondered what that meant. Plus, she had almost said *mother*. Erin knew about what happened with Jenny, her deception, and the product of that. Still, I couldn't help wondering what further complications lurked in its outcome. "Yes, I passed her." I refrained from saying she drove instead of using a broom.

Erin shut the fridge with her foot as she took vegetables to the sink and washed them under the tap. "She made and brought dinner for us."

I bit my tongue on replying about what could be inside the meal. "Then why are you making the salad?"

"After what Jenny did to your cup of tea?" Erin responded in a surprised tone. "Who knows what she would put in the food and what it would do to us?"

Her eyes bore into me as I fought to keep a straight face at that. Those were my thoughts.

"Don't act innocent, Buck," she said, emphasising my name. "I know what you're thinking." She gave me a wry wink.

"What did she want?"

Erin flicked a glance at the table. "She left a journal here. She said she had written it after you left her in 1987. It's all about what happened in 1688 when she first met you, then about the witch trial, your escape, and..." Her voice trailed off.

"Did she read the whole damned thing to you?" I asked, feeling a hint of my gut ache return at the thought of any lies it may have contained.

"Actually," Erin said, chopping into a tomato with hard thumps of the knife on the board, "she painted a positive picture of you. Not bad for a mother-in-law, right?"

I stayed quiet, checking the kitchen bin, and spotted the corpse of Jenny's meatloaf.

"She also told me about what happened with the rest. Confessed everything! Even how you saved her from the snakebite. How you returned to tell her what you said to her. But there is something I need to know," she said, carrying the completed salad to the table. "Have you visited your other son?"

I shook my head, picking up the sliced ham from the kitchen bench to put on the table. "Not yet. I didn't know what to do there. I'm pleased enough that Jenny had a husband to be the dad, if you know what I mean. Besides, I have Connor with you. You're the reasons I never gave up on returning."

We sat opposite each other, eating our meal.

"When did you last time travel?" Her voice was steady, almost calculating.

"This morning," I replied. "I travelled back to visit several of times during the pregnancy, which I missed. But I had to be careful you didn't see me."

For a moment, my wife's features softened. Wordlessly, she gazed into space, the hint of a smile curling her lips. Yes, she remembered the times. I had made enough jumps to let her know I was there for her. Once I had even kissed her soft lips as she slept. At least three times, I made her a cup of herbal tea and left it on the bedside table for her when she woke. Even cleaned the house. It aged me by about a week.

"I thought I had dreamed some of those times," she whispered with shimmering eyes. "Or that your ghost haunted the place."

Haunted? Well, I supposed it's possible to wonder that. I flashed a quick smile at that. "Then I travelled back to Jenny in the hospital to give her the means to support herself and the kid."

She could have asked to check my iBioPad's logs. I had them, but it didn't matter.

Erin reached forward and took my hand. "Thank you. That's why I love you." She squeezed it, and I returned the gesture. "But," she added in a firm voice, "no more time travel. I don't want you lost and Connor without a father, or me without you."

My gut twisted again at that.

"So," she said brightly, "tell me about your meeting with Gary Cutter."

I took a deep breath as I considered her future reaction to the news I had.

* * *

Erin Deering-Nowlan
Lammermoor Beach
6:45pm 4th April 2019

Erin's head spun as she saw the pictures on the table before her. A tingle ran down her spine upon seeing the photo of the mummy wearing Tony's clothes and ChronoSpace.

"Is that you?" She reached for her glass and gulped a mouthful of water. Tony offered a disarming smile, his forehead smoothing for a moment, but she didn't buy it. "It is, isn't it?"

"They look like my clothes, but---"

She interrupted him, her head filled with charging thoughts. "Well, that's settled. You're not travelling in time to die back in that era. This is exactly what I---"

"Stop!" Tony held up his hands to silence her. "Look, they haven't even tested its DNA against mine yet."

"They won't need to," she blurted, heart hammering in her chest. "If you don't go, you won't be there. History has changed already to how it should be."

Tony drew a breath, a deep slow one, and released it. "No," he said, his voice calm. "History doesn't change. At least, that's what Jasmine reckons."

Erin stopped to consider that. Yes, Jasmine, another woman he met while time-travelling during her pregnancy. "How does she know?"

He shrugged, shaking his head. "She said she had to be careful with how many times she visited an area. For example, you have to limit the number of time-travellers on the Titanic. Otherwise, their sheer weight would sink the ship, not the iceberg."

Erin's head hurt. She blinked it away to ponder the idea. Then her own birth history came to mind. "Didn't you change history by bringing me as a baby forward from the 1600s?"

"No." Tony shook his head. His expression still appeared uncertain to her, then he added: "I don't think so, anyway. It would still happen in some weird spaghetti bog kind of way. Destiny."

"Including the bush roofie my mother slipped you?" she asked, then instantly regretted it as Tony's expression darkened. He turned his attention towards the sliced ham, picking at it with his fork. "I'm sorry. Anyway, enough of that. Tell me more about what Cutter wanted."

Tony pointed to the pictures sitting between them on the table. "Apparently, we're going to be working with him. The photos show we've already done it, just not in our personal timeline yet. Destiny again."

"What does he want now?" Erin asked, eyeing a photo from their wedding with curiosity. *My God,* she thought. *These ratbags have been watching us the whole time, knowing our secret. What else do they know?*

Tony cleared his throat, bringing her back to the present. She muttered an apology, blinking, and asked him to repeat it.

"We're going back to the past to save an English professor from the Germans. Maybe even save the world," came the reply. The way he said it made him sound stronger, determined. His misadventures in time must have affected him more than she thought.

"Who?"

"Albert Cardnell," Tony said, pushing aside one of the

photos to reveal a copy of an old monochrome picture. Definitely old-fashioned.

"What's so special about him?" Erin asked, studying the subject's features. She marvelled at how young men often appeared older than their years back then, and so dashing. For a moment, she admired the strength in the professor's chin. How old was he really in the photo? "And what happened to him?"

"There's very little about him on the internet," Tony answered around a mouthful of food. "He was mostly a mathematician who hobnobbed with Thomas Edison and Nikola Tesla."

"Tesla invented the electric car, right?" she asked, a quizzical eyebrow raised.

Tony suppressed a smile at that, a twinkle in his eye lighting up at her words. Did he think it a joke? "No, but lots of other cool things that led to the technology you enjoy today," Tony replied, suppressing a smile. "Anyway, back to the story. Cardnell apparently created an equation. According to some archival information Cutter grabbed from British offices, it could have made even Einstein's Relativity Theory drool."

"Why?" Erin asked, leaning closer, watching Tony's enthusiasm build and grow. "What could it do?"

"Cutter's records are sketchy, still redacted in some places, but I gathered it could improve production in manufacturing and other areas."

Erin couldn't help pulling a face over that. "So what? Productivity increases don't mean much. Micromanaging bosses around the world are looking at that all the time. Even overloading their employees."

Tony held up a hand and shook his head. "In 1912, when relations between the English and the Germans were already getting cold, it meant more. Enough to frighten the crap out of the British, at least."

"But wasn't Cardnell one of them?"

"Sure. He considered it useful to produce food quicker, for example. Or to build roads faster to reduce congestion. But one commander in the Royal Navy saw something else."

Erin's eyes narrowed at that, the pieces clicking together. "They could also build ships quicker, weapons of war."

Tony nodded with an expectant grin, urging her to continue. She thought for a few moments and realised the problem. "And if the British thought that, so could the enemy. The Germans!" she realised, aloud.

"Spies were everywhere. Both sides."

Erin wondered what the rest of the pieces were that she missed. "How does that relate to you?"

"Professor Cardnell was supposed to travel to the United States to continue his research. But they had to get him there in secret without the Germans knowing," Tony said, using the dish of ham to represent America, and the salad bowl England. "But they couldn't send anyone with him in case it brought attention to his whereabouts."

Erin imagined herself back in the period, the world black and white like the old movies she had seen. Streamers flying from the ship to the docking wharf, bands playing, and the handsome professor on the unsinkable cruiser. Maybe he had an alias to misdirect things further. How must he have felt, alone and without backup? "Let me guess," Erin surmised. "He didn't make it. He died on the

Titanic."

"Gone." Tony gazed at her, his eyes gauging her as he leaned forward. "Without a trace."

Erin pointed to the photo between them, the one of them in early 20th century garb. "This was on the Titanic, or so Cutter wants you to think. And your journal mentioned you saw a Nazi officer on the ship and the other foreign spies. Something about a difference machine."

Tony's jaw dropped, then surprise turned to admiration. "You *did* read it, didn't you?"

"Everything," she said, injecting a mysterious finality into her tone. "I had to make sure there were no other girlfriends or flings while you were away."

She gave him a wink at that, but he still eyed her with curiosity, measuring everything. The poor guy. He hadn't realised that being a nice guy made him a target for some women. They felt safe with them. She did, and that's why she loved him.

"Back to the topic now," he said, his voice deeper and better controlled than before. "Cardnell never made it to New York. Neither did his formula. And we know the enemy was onboard from what I saw."

Erin couldn't help asking, leaning forward closer to her husband's face. "Did the Germans get it?" she said, her voice in a half-whisper matched by the crash of the sea on the breeze.

"The Allies didn't think so, but there are hints in history that they had something."

Erin sighed. Everything pointed to what she didn't want: Tony travelling through time again, and dying in the past. But if the opportunity to change that arose, she would grab it with both hands.

"If you're asking for permission to go play with Cutter in the past," Erin said, putting on her firm, motherly voice, "then the answer is no. At least wait until Connor is older."

"But---"

"No! Tony, the answer is no. For all we know, Cutter is setting you up for something worse." She locked eyes with him, daring him to argue. But he only glared back, something ticking in his head. "I don't trust him," she said. "And besides, you said you can't change history."

Tony's voice lowered a half-octave, firm, not quick as she remembered it when they first met. "It can't change, but the photos show that's because we were there to keep it right." He paused, watching her reaction, his gaze never leaving hers. "I believe we're destined to travel back, to stop disasters, preserving history."

"You also said time is relative, yeah?"

He nodded at that, opening his mouth, but she stopped him. "Good, so it can wait! I'm not losing you again, *Buck with a B!*" Erin stood abruptly from the kitchen table and stomped away to the bedroom before Tony could rebuke her with something she knew would change her mind. She was already close and couldn't give him the satisfaction until she had time to think. "By the way, *hubby-poo*," she shot back over her shoulder. "It's your turn to feed Connor his formula tonight. Be a father and think of our son."

Chapter 5

Electronic Diary of Anthony Nowlan
Lammermoor Beach, Yeppoon, Queensland.
Australia.
7pm, 4th April 2019.

A multitude of thoughts buzzed for attention. Since Erin's brief grumble before fleeing to the bedroom, I tried to make sense of everything alone. How lucky I hadn't mentioned Tenner's discovery.

I took care of the dishes, cleaning and drying them. Since Erin prepared dinner, it was the least I could do, but it also gave me the opportunity to reflect. The trouble arose when I finished and realised I still needed extra time.

I checked the clock: 7 PM. According to Connor's feeding schedule, his next feed was at 8 PM. How could I process everything I'd learned from Cutter with these constant interruptions?

A creak from the ceiling caught my attention---the cool night air contracting it. It triggered an idea. My gaze landed on my ChronoSpace, reflecting the kitchen light. It glinted as if winking. Of course! Why hadn't I thought of that before?

For a second, I hesitated. Hadn't this been how I got into trouble before? Maybe, but what could go wrong? I wasn't technically leaving the house. Neither was it likely I'd have to worry about Stan, who probably thinks me dead now, anyway. Erin couldn't get upset about that, right?

Well, better to beg forgiveness than seek permission, I guess...

Electronic Diary of Anthony Nowlan
Lammermoor Beach, Yeppoon, Queensland.
Australia.
8:15pm, 4th April 2019.

Connor is an easy feed. Arriving at 8pm with a preheated bottle of formula, I fed my baby son in the easy-chair beside his cot. He drank fast, burped like a pro, and we finished in less than fifteen minutes.

After rinsing the bottle under the kitchen tap, I set my new destination on the ChronoSpace with my iBioPad.

Electronic Diary of Anthony Nowlan
Lammermoor Beach, Yeppoon, Queensland.
Australia.
12:15am, 5th April 2019.

There, Connor's fed again. Next!

A sound from the bedroom caught my attention. It must've been Erin. I tensed, waiting until I was sure she wasn't getting up. The seconds ticked slower than a wet week. Then another snore.

I relaxed. Good. At least she wouldn't catch me in two places at once.

Next jump...

Electronic Diary of Anthony Nowlan
Lammermoor Beach, Yeppoon, Queensland.
Australia.
4:15am, 5th April 2019.

Damn, why hadn't I done this before? It's the best idea I've had since inventing time-travel. Well, I can improve on it still.

I finished washing the bottles, ready next time. My ears

stay pricked for any noise from the bedroom. Erin is my greatest obstacle, since one version of me is sleeping next to her while I'm in the kitchen.

Electronic Diary of Anthony Nowlan
Lammermoor Beach, Yeppoon, Queensland.
Australia.
12:15am, 6th April 2019.

Fed Connor again. I'm glad I remembered to wash the bottles beforehand.

His nappy was bloody messy, though. What else are we feeding this kid?

Electronic Diary of Anthony Nowlan
Lammermoor Beach, Yeppoon, Queensland.
Australia.
4:15am, 6th April 2019.

Another feeding complete! I'm the man!

Electronic Diary of Anthony Nowlan
Lammermoor Beach, Yeppoon, Queensland.
Australia.
12:15am, 7th April 2019.

Almost couldn't wake Connor for this one. Maybe he's ready to extend the feeds to 5-hourly?

Next jump.

Electronic Diary of Anthony Nowlan
Lammermoor Beach, Yeppoon, Queensland.
Australia.
4:15am, 7th April 2019.

I think I'm getting tired already. This is so bloody boring, as though I've been doing nothing but feeding this kid for... I guess it has been an hour or two straight from my perspective though, hasn't it?

Electronic Diary of Anthony Nowlan
Lammermoor Beach, Yeppoon, Queensland.
Australia.
8:15pm, 7th April 2019.

That's Connor fed again. I must have spoken to Erin about changing to 5-hourly feeds, and she agreed. The feeding diary was a good idea to keep me updated without giving him too much.

Electronic Diary of Anthony Nowlan
Lammermoor Beach, Yeppoon, Queensland.
Australia.
2:00am 8th April 2019.

Phew! My head spun at the moment of my arrival.

The house was in darkness, as it was every other time. I reached for the switch in the living-room where I appeared. Where the switch was, I touched paper.

Surprised by this aberration, I pulled it away, prepared to turn on the light, then stopped at the familiar yet unexpected sound. A faint thump. The kind made by my ChronoSpace.

In the dim light, I stole along the hallway, thankful for the concrete floor letting me creep in the gloom. A light danced ahead and from around the corner. Connor's room!

Was it this time-space's version of me, perhaps? With ears pricked, I listened from around the corner.

A male's voice whispered something indiscernible. It wasn't mine, but I had heard it before. My hand darted to the light-switch. Thoughts only on my son's safety, I stepped forward as the room blazed with life. My jaw dropped, blood chilling in my veins.

"What the--?"

Primal instinct fired. Adrenaline surged through me, coupled with the overwhelming need to protect my infant son. Every muscle tensed as I confronted the threat.

Chapter 6

**Electronic Diary of Anthony Nowlan
Lammermoor Beach, Yeppoon, Queensland.
Australia.
2:00am 8th April 2019.**

A man dressed entirely in black was bent over the cot. Startled, he turned. Prepared for the bright glare, I was fine. But not him. While he blinked, distracted, I grabbed the first thing I could---talcum powder---and tossed it.

White hit his woollen mask directly over his mouth. The cloud spread about his head. He gasped, coughing hard, fighting to breathe, and I lunged.

Despite his difficulty breathing, he fended off my first fist. My second caught his jaw hard. Needles of pain dotted up my wrist to the elbow. He grunted from the blow, and I screamed to ignore the pain. He stopped my third punch, but my fingers caught the device on his belt. I yanked it from his belt, stamped on his foot. The round gizmo clattered to the floor from my fingers as his shoulder shoved me.

I stumbled. The brick wall caught my head. Stars jangled around my skull as the bedroom window smashed. Through blurred vision, I saw the masked man scrape glass from the sill. He punched outward at the fly screen. Security screens stop people from outside, not inside, but it took him some time.

Blinking, I glanced at Connor's cot. He was still there, awake and screaming, his face red and contorted. Hungry or scared? I couldn't tell. I stepped between him and the stranger in black.

"Erin!" I shouted, fumbling for something else to throw.

My wife shouted from down the hallway. Her footsteps pounded as I yelled at the intruder. My fingers found something and closed around it.

"Hey, you!" I roared. Distracted, the intruder faltered, turning to me, and I flung my new missile at him before he knew what happened.

Through the slit in his mask, I spotted his eyes bulge with surprise a second before Connor's dirty nappy slapped across his eyes and mouth. The smell of urine and baby poo reached my nose. He cried with disgust, gasping, dry-retching. The sloppy garment flopped to the floor, leaving a glistening brown track on his woollen mask. Before he could recover, I barrelled into his gut.

Inertia carried us through the smashed window, security screen and all, and onto the brick-lined garden bed outside. We struggled against each other as the roar of the sea reached our ears. Other shouts filled the air and two figures appeared from around the corner.

An ominous click near my ear froze my blood. A pistol's safety. "Hold it right there," came a cold voice.

My opponent froze too, hands moving up. I relaxed, rolled away, looked up into Cutter's stony face. On the other side stood Agent Nguyen, her weapon aimed directly at the intruder's chest.

"How?" I asked, puffing. Blood pounded in my ears.

"You're about to arrive. Go, jump back!" The agent hissed in reply. He was about to say more when Erin's voice floated through the open window, uttering comforting words to our son.

Shocked still, I nodded. Fumbling for my ChronoSpace, I

pressed its home button just as I spotted another version of me appearing from around the back corner of the house. The ChronoSpace whined and---

Electronic Diary of Anthony Nowlan
Lammermoor Beach, Yeppoon, Queensland.
Australia.
7:45pm 4th April 2019.

My stomach swirled as adrenaline churned through me. The sickening sensation urged me to the toilet where I sat. Too much action, I guess. That and the occasional vertigo of time-travel.

Thumping in my chest forced drumbeats through my temples as I fought not to throw up. I had to settle my breathing, clear my head, and not wake Erin. It had only been an hour and a bit since our argument about time-travel.

The events replayed through my head, Connor's first scream of horror echoing in my memory. Worse things added themselves to the bloody chain. The what-ifs, things that made my heart pound harder with terror. What if I had done something different, causing the man to kill Connor? Or if my son had died? What would that do to Erin? To me? To us? A part of me cursed myself. I should never have jumped ahead in time. How stupid had I been? Then came the immutable truth: if I hadn't, Connor would have been worse off. The horrors would have played out to their terrible conclusion.

The crazy part is, I am going to experience that night again. Damned time-travel. Why did I invent it?

There was only one thing to do.

Chapter 7

Erin Deering-Nowlan
Lammermoor Beach
6 am, 5th April 2019

The upbeat melody backed by George Harrison roused Erin from a confused dream. Shielding her eyes from the bright sun reflecting off a nearby glass, she listened to the lyrics of "Here Comes The Sun." Normally, she loved the song. This morning, the irony of the title brought to mind Tony's silly Dad jokes. Instead of a smile, the thought revived something in her head.

She turned her head to see him sleeping. Although his mouth hung open like a Venus flytrap, not a snore came from him. But a long thin drip of drool hung from his bottom lip, swinging as he breathed. Its arc brought it into the sunbeam from outside, reflecting the light. But no rainbow.

The only reason she found Tony's sleeping face notable was because of one thing. Something she had to talk to him about in a minute.

Erin rose, planted her feet on the floor and padded down the hallway towards Connor's room. Yes, he was sleeping, dreaming whatever tiny infants dream. The gentle rhythm of his breathing brought a smile to her face as she watched him. She traced a tender finger to his button nose, the one he inherited from his father. It was too early for his feed, so she decided not to wake him. Not yet, anyway.

She made her way to the kitchen, prepared a cup of coffee in her home mug. Another gag gift from her sister with the message etched in bold: "Coffee spelled backwards is

EEFFOC as in I don't give eeffoc until I've had my coffee." After finishing, she headed back to the bedroom, a glass of water in her hand. Lifting it, she dribbled its contents onto her sleeping husband's unsuspecting face.

Tony sat bolt upright, his eyes wider than a dinner plate. He sputtered, spitting water from his lips. "What the hell?" he complained, an angry glint in his eye.

"Burning the candle at both ends, were we?" she asked, placing the glass on her bedside table.

The furious glint in his eyes softened to a puzzled look. "What are you talking about? I've been feeding Connor last night, remember?"

Erin paused, keeping her own anger at check enough to maintain some sense of humour. "Funny you should say that. I'm betting you were in two places at once, right?" Tony paused, his gaze drifting away to the side for a moment. His lips parted, ready to speak, but she cut him off. "You promised no more time travel, Tony. I didn't want you to do it. Still don't."

He ran a hand through his sleep-mussed hair. "I can--"

"That's irresponsible, Tony," Erin fumed then, realising she was getting loud, brought her voice down to avoid waking the baby. "What if you had been lost again? Do you know how I found out?"

Squinting, he offered a sheepish grin. "Well--"

"I woke through the night," she interrupted, not wanting to hear his mansplaining. "You were in the bed beside me, and the light was on down the hall. I went to Connor's room and stopped when I heard your voice from his room. You were in two places at once. Do you care to explain that?"

Tony held up one hand, palm towards her to hold back the torrent of words and anger. "I promised not to time travel without you," he said, and before she could interject, "so I didn't. Technically not. Every time I jumped, I visited a time and place where you and Connor were present."

Erin paused, trying to keep up with her husband's words. What he said sounded like garbage, but she still wanted to know. "Why?"

"To get all of his feeding done in one go. I've done all next week's nighttime feeding in one night." He wiped some of the water from his face, flinging droplets in a mini-explosion. His gaze spotted the sopping mess on his t-shirt, and she noticed a slight darkening on his temple.

"What's that mark?" she asked, peering closer at the blue-grey blemish. About the size of a 10-cent piece, it felt almost hot to the touch when Erin's fingers brushed it, a subtle contrast to his otherwise cool skin. She peered closer. "A bruise! When did you get that?"

Tony touched the mark and hissed in pain. For a moment, he seemed ready to tell her, then shook his head. "Can't say, babe," he replied. "Not yet, anyway. But I need to talk to Cutter about it."

"Cutter?" Shock hit Erin as pieces fell into place. If Tony was injured time-travelling to the future, there was only one reason he'd need to talk to their antagonist. Anger flared. Cutter was up to his old tricks again. "Did he do this to you?"

But Tony shook his head. "Hell, no. Look, just relax."

"I would if you'd at least tell me what's going on, Tony. Why do you need to talk to Gary Cutter about a bruise on your head?" Erin's mind was a battlefield of love for her husband and fear of the unknown. What was he getting into this time? Then, a smile appeared on his face, lifting the cloud.

"It's okay. Yes, something happened, but not that." He took her hand in his. It felt warm around hers. Warm and safe. "This," he said, pointing at the contusion, "happened when I was feeding Connor." She frowned at that, and upon seeing it, he explained: "But he's fine. I just tripped over my feet from getting tired, that's all. He was still in his cot, so no harm done."

He squeezed her hand, the warmth of his hands reassuring. Nevertheless, Erin's eyes narrowed in suspicion, her gaze fixed on her husband's face as he held her hand, searching for any sign of the truth he might be hiding. "Then why the mystery about talking to Cutter about it all? What else happened?"

His words flowed seamlessly, leaving little room for doubt. Yet, Erin couldn't shake the feeling something bigger lurked beneath the surface. "It knocked something into my head that I hadn't considered before," he said, then took a deep breath as though preparing to say something else. The unspoken words drowned out his pregnant pause, belying a secret just beyond mention. As their eyes met, a silent understanding flickered between them--a truth beyond words, promising revelations yet to come.

Chapter 8

Electronic Diary of Anthony Nowlan
Home, Lammermoor Beach, Yeppoon, Queensland.
Australia.
1am 8th April 2019.

I stretched, cracking my neck. My iBioPad's screen glowed in the darkness, revealing the time. An hour had passed since I had placed the piece of paper over the light switch in the kitchen. Remembering that was what had stopped me from switching it on, I figured it best to keep that part of history the same. Nothing should change, especially if I wanted to find out what was behind the events about to unfold.

The hardest part since Erin discovered my ruse with the time-travelling baby feeds was that she took longer to go to sleep. That is despite being tired still. Last night, I remembered hearing the sound as I 'popped' into the present from the past. It reminded me of being a kid on Christmas Eve, listening for Santa Claus to come. Only I never heard him as a kid because I always fell asleep. This time, to avoid changing history as I remembered, I had to stay out of other-me's way.

Erin heard it too and wanted to get up, but I stopped her with a whispered, "Curiosity killed the cat." To preserve history, I had taped the note to the switch for "past me" to find, and my warning to Erin was for the same reason. She had said if I told her what was coming, she'd relax more. So I told her to stay in bed. She playfully challenged me to "make her," so I did. Since I didn't hear anything the first time, I was sure "past me" didn't either.

The danger of "being caught" made it more exciting for both of us until I remembered the past with Jenny, Erin's mother, and the terrible trick she played on me. For a second, I almost stopped. But this was my wife, not her treacherous mother. Although I satisfied Erin, I lost interest soon after and said I was tired.

But that was last night. Now I was propped in the spare room's bed against the cold brick wall separating it from Connor's room. My ears were on high alert, as sensitive as if I were enjoying an online Playboy magazine, listening for any approaching steps. Only tonight, it's my iBioPad I was reading, checking subscriptions of old Phantom comics on www.phantomtrail.com.

A text flickered on the screen.

Cutter: *Sofia and I are in position.*

It brought back the previous night's fun with Erin to mind. I couldn't hold back my grin. Such a dirty mind I have lately. I wondered where that came from.

I reached for the metal water bottle beside the bed and took a gulp from it. The metallic taste of the water bottle lingered on my tongue. I replaced the bottle.

A shame the third agent, Liam Park, was away on leave. But having been in the future and seen what was about to transpire meant I knew he wasn't needed. I had to remember that. Trust it. I just had to follow my part of the plan.

I tapped back my reply: *All set and waiting.*

A shiver ran down my spine in anticipation of it all. In an hour's time, "past me" would leave the scene before I (present me) arrive. I had no idea how things would pan out. The realisation made my mouth dry again.

I took another slug of water from the bottle, returning it in time as Cutter's next message arrived.

Is Erin asleep?

Me: *Yeah.*

Cutter: *The drops worked?*

ASIS Agent Sofia Nguyen had suggested I give Erin some sleeping drops to keep her out of harm's way. We didn't want her wandering into the middle of the upcoming fracas. As helpful as the idea appeared, I initially refused. But the agent insisted. Shoving the small bottle in my hand, she said it would be best to protect Erin this way.

I never liked the idea. It revived bad memories of the bush mistletoe tea Jenny used to drug me. It was dishonest. Deceitful. Sure, I deceived people by time-travelling in secret, but I believed my cause was noble. Well, no, it was selfish. I time-travelled to feed my son so Erin could get more rest. It only turned noble because I discovered something else was afoot, something bound to happen at 2am, in just under an hour. Still, there's no reason to drug my wife. I could never do that.

Cutter's message flashed on my screen again, repeating the last note. Was it him or Sofia who wanted Erin out of it? I dug into my pocket and retrieved the unlabelled bottle, still unopened. Bathed in the iBioPad's light, it looked like the kind for eye-drops.

Shoving the bottle back in my pocket, I tapped back a reply: *She's asleep.*

Of course, it was a lie. I don't care. There was nothing they could do about it anyway, not without spoiling our plan and stuffing up destiny. Somehow, I doubted they would. But I can imagine Sofia seething behind her expressionless almond-shaped eyes when she finds out.

Cutter's reply flickered on my iPhone. He had noted my reply's delay, probably sensed something wrong. With a silent sigh, I replied that all was well.

All fatigue left my head with Cutter's reminder. My thoughts changed, going over the plan. I would soon have to leave this room to meet the ASIS agents outside. There, we would wait for the intruder's arrival. Despite knowing the outcome, I couldn't shake the anticipation building within me. The minutes ticked away in the gloom, each second a witness to my racing mind, questioning every detail to come.

Suddenly, the unmistakable scrape of a foot on the concrete floor of the hallway jolted me into high alert.

*　*　*

Electronic Diary of Anthony Nowlan
Home, Lammermoor Beach, Yeppoon, Queensland.
Australia.
1:30am 8th April 2019.

A part of me screamed at the idea. It told me to wait, to stay in that spare room.

Closer came the footsteps. Light and stealthy, they came down the hallway. I turned off my iBioPad's screen, covering it with the leather cover. And I waited. My pulse pounded in my temples, drumbeats steady but loud, almost blocking out the quiet noise of the feet. A joint creaked. Not mine.

The door handle moved. Stealthily, I rolled from the bed and tiptoed behind the door, arriving just as it opened.

A dark, willowy shape glided past me towards the bed. I

sneaked up behind it, grabbed the figure with a hand across the feminine mouth.

With a muted cry, she shrugged.

"Stop. It's only me," I whispered in her ear. Erin squirmed against me, but I held her fast. "Don't move. Something's about to happen," I explained.

A thin finger of moonlight passed over her eyes as they rolled back towards me. "Relax," I urged. "I'm about to let go, but stay quiet. Okay?"

I kept my grip until she nodded and relaxed.

"What the bloody hell is going on?" she whispered to me, and I hushed her.

"Stay put in here," I replied. "I'm going outside before my past-self arrives. You stay in here."

"But--"

I interrupted her. "I'm going to arrive soon. You'll hear me in the kitchen, and I'll walk past down the hallway towards the bedroom. I, that is he, is not meant to see you, or you change history, got it?"

Telling her that much was all I could do. Luckily, I had considered this before tonight. I didn't know for sure Erin was in our bedroom (or would be, depending on how you look at it). She could likely be in the spare room when "past me" calls.

For a few heartbeats, she gazed at me. I kept my tone and demeanour serious, to let her see I meant business. The worry in her eyes intensified.

"Do you trust me?" I asked her, and she nodded.

"Then stay here. Wait. And don't come until I call, no matter what you hear. Got it?"

The next four seconds stretched as I waited for her answer, anxiously hoping she'd hurry because time was running out. At last, it came. She reached for my face, pulled me down to her waiting lips, and kissed me. "I love you and trust you."

"Good, I'll see you soon." I kissed her again for luck, stood back from her, and tapped my iBioPad's cover. A moment later, I jumped in time, only half-certain of what would come next.

Chapter 9

Electronic Diary of Anthony Nowlan
Lammermoor Beach, Yeppoon, Queensland.
Australia.
1:44am 8th April 2019.

My stomach swirled as I adjusted to my new surroundings. With every step, the coarse sand slipped beneath my shoes and the sound of the crashing waves intensified, overpowering the faint noises of the night. The beams from the waxing crescent moon bathed the area, casting elongated shadows from the she-oak trees. The dips in the ground became elusive in the shifting play of light and darkness.

I checked the time. It was one minute before I had left Erin in the spare bedroom. Hopefully, she was doing as I said. Her stubbornness could take her straight to Connor's room, which would be bad. She might meet the intruder destined to arrive, and change destiny, making things worse. The thought haunted me as I picked my way up the dune towards the house and into the grove of she-oaks that cast shadowy figures like thin-limbed giants with feathery fingers. No, I decided. I couldn't think like that. When Erin said she trusts me, she meant it. I should relax and return it. Yet the doubt niggled at me.

Suddenly, something gripped my shoulder. Startled, I jumped. "Shh!" said a familiar deep, gravelly voice.

Turning towards the voice, I looked into Cutter's boot-black-polished features. His eyes seemed to glow from them. "Apologies for any disturbance," he whispered in the darkness, signalling I should drop closer to the ground beside him. "You must improve your stealth techniques."

My what? I crouched beside him, noticing a small stash of snacks beside a thermos and two cups behind a bush that obscured us from the house. "How long have you been here?" I asked.

"Two hours," he replied, peering through what I presumed to be night-vision binoculars at the house. "How many drops did you administer to Erin?" I paused, calculating his question, then realised what he meant before he continued. "Mrs Nowlan is conscious and in motion. It appears she's en route to your bedroom."

"How much can you see?" I asked.

"Witness it with your own eyes," he replied, handing me the binoculars.

My eyes opened wider in disbelief at the amount of detail they provided. Somehow, they were powerful enough to pick up my wife's body heat signature even through the thick brick walls of my home. The clarity amazed me. I could almost discern the wrinkles in her pyjama dress as it hung to her knees. "I would have witnessed your self-gratification if that had been the case," Cutter admitted with a hint of amusement as I watched my wife's delicious figure. The memory of earlier that night came to mind of love-making with her before 8pm.

I arched an eyebrow, studying Cutter's obscured features. "Two hours you've been here, eh?" The question lingered in the night air, the unspoken implication of what Cutter might have witnessed making me uneasy.

"No sign of your uninvited guest as yet," Cutter confirmed, taking back the binoculars to have another look. Watching the house through them, he went over the plan again with me. We would stay here, hidden in the shadows behind the thin shrubbery across from my house. Agent Nguyen had found another vantage point on the next-door neighbour's hill overlooking my backyard and Connor's side bedroom window. She was watching there and...

As if on cue, Cutter fell silent, his hand to his earpiece. "You've discerned a presence?" The reply was inaudible to me, but my unlikely ally gave a nod. "At the baby's side bedroom window? Confirmed," he said, reaching for his weapon and checking its magazine.

The ASIS agent tapped my shoulder and beckoned me to follow. Keeping as low to the ground and the shadows as we could, we glided through the moonlit gloom towards the house's front door. I had turned off the sensors earlier that night to avoid them being triggered by our approach. Once we were undercover, Cutter tapped my shoulder and handed me something small. He pointed without words, and I nodded, putting the earpiece in place. Instantly, I could hear Agent Nguyen's voice as she intoned a commentary of what she saw.

"It's a male," she said, concentration clear in her narration. "No others visible."

"What is his status?" Cutter replied, his voice barely a whisper.

"Standing there beside the window. Looks like he's scanning the bedroom," Nguyen's voice echoed in my ear. "Now he's checking his watch. Shit!" My blood turned to ice at her curse. "He's vanished! Where the hell did--"

My fingers were already in action, dancing on the iBioPad's screen. We had already discussed the plan. I knew it back-to-front. A second later, I triggered my ChronoSpace. The world blurred around me, and I jumped me from 2am to...

Electronic Diary of Anthony Nowlan
Lammermoor Beach, Yeppoon, Queensland.
Australia.
1:57am 8th April 2019.

Again, I arrived before I departed. My earpiece caught the hurried breaths of presumably Cutter and me as we had approached the house.

"Male. No others in sight," Nguyen's voice cut through, followed by Cutter's question about the prowler's actions. I stood at my bedroom window on the opposite side of the house, just out of Erin's view if she glanced my way. Tiptoeing along the exterior walls, I crept towards the back door. Since I knew our target wasn't heading there, I'd be out of sight as well.

Wherever Nguyen was, she obviously didn't see me. Once at my house's back door, I crept closer to my infant son's back window.

"He's vanished! Where the hell did--"

Her shocked words were my cue. But there was something else I heard: the telltale pop of displaced air.

My fingers dropped to my belt and pressed the button of a device Tenner had created. Our new secret weapon. If my hunch was right, it would do its job. Hopefully not too well, or history would change.

Connor's bedroom light flicked on, its glow emanating from the window. I ducked back to avoid being seen through the curtains. With the breath held tight in my hammering chest, I listened in partial shock as my past-self shouted. "What the--?"

Soon came the sounds of the fighting. Furniture bumped. Blows landed like a hammer on meat in an abattoir. In my mind, I relived the ruckus going on inside, biting my lip as I wished I could join in to help my other self. But I couldn't. That would change things, maybe for the worst. Suddenly my baby son's heart-wrenching screams pierced the air, each cry slicing like a knife through lace. Adrenaline punched through my body, ready to come to his defence. But I couldn't. Same thing. History might change. I had to remind myself he was safe. He'd survive.

A crash punctuated the events as glass shattered and scattered to the ground outside the side bedroom window. My other self shouted for Erin.

"Tony's putting up a damned good fight in there," Nguyen's voice said, intruding on my mind. "Here comes Erin. Good thing you didn't give her the drops."

"How did you know?" I whispered, aware now that my other self had thrown a nappy full of poo into the prowler's face. The intruder was now retching from exposure to it.

"You are a good man," came the whispered response from Cutter. "But how disappointing that you failed to take precautions!"

The puffing from their running reached my earpiece a moment before I heard the thud of the two fighting men's bodies hitting the ground. More punches landed as the sound of their scuffling disturbed the night's silence. Running footsteps reached my ears, followed by Cutter's voice. "Hold it right there."

The wrestling stopped. The sounds conjured my recall of Cutter's stony face in the night as he held a gun to the intruder's eye. Agent Nguyen was there too, with her weapon aimed at the man's chest.

"How?" my past-self gasped in surprise.

Erin called my name from inside. Cutter quickly urged my past self to leave. I held my breath, hoping my idea worked, and I sighed with relief as his ChronoSpace carried him away.

Good. I hadn't changed history with my disruption device. But now I was in unfamiliar territory...

Chapter 10

Erin Deering-Nowlan
Lammermoor Beach
1:49am 8th April 2019

Erin's eyes widened at the sight from the nursery door, her heart pounding with a mix of fear and concern. Red-faced, her baby son screamed, his eyes focused directly on her. His tiny arms seemed to reach for her as his legs kicked, desperately seeking her comfort. She hurried, careful not to slip on the overturned nappy bucket, to pick up the yowling infant. He had no visible injuries, just a frightened glare as he yelled loudly in her ear while she held him close to her breast.

"Tony?" she called anxiously, her eyes flicking from side to side. Then she caught sight of curtains blowing from the ocean breeze through the smashed window. Fear clutched her heart as she slowly approached the window.

"It's okay," came Tony's voice from outside. He sounded calm, confident, even relieved. "It's safe to come out."

Cutter's voice replied, catching Erin off-guard. "Stay back, Mrs Nowlan."

Yeah, right, Erin huffed, blowing the hair back from her eyes as Connor began to settle.

"Is Connor okay?" Tony asked, coming closer to the window. Erin's eyes lit at seeing him. She sighed with relief.

"Yes," Erin said, "He's just frightened. So am I too, buster. What the hell? You told me it would be fine."

"As far as I knew then, yeah," Tony replied, his voice

holding concern as he scanned Connor and her. "I couldn't tell you everything."

Erin poked her face around the edge of the window and spotted a masked figure on the ground. She spotted strange splotches of brown on the man's mask. A horrid stench of ammonia reached her nostrils, and she realised what had happened with the nappies. Meanwhile, a ripping sound reached her ears as an Asian woman tightened a zip-tie around the man's wrists. "Who are you? Who is that? Tony, will you--"

Erin's heart skipped a beat as the masked stranger's foot lashed out, connecting with Nguyen's knee. With a grunt, the female agent fell, rolling back to a crouched position. In that instant, the man had leapt to his feet and kicked the woman in the shoulder. As she fell back, he jumped and swung his bound wrists under himself like a skipping rope and landed with them before him. He twisted his joints. The zip-ties flew away with a snap, and he darted for the fence.

Before he could jump, a flash from Cutter's silenced pistol lit the air. The man screamed, his hand flying towards his backside.

"Move again, and I'll shoot the other cheek," Cutter's voice droned casually but menacingly with monotone precision. The other man had no choice but to freeze, despite the blood staining his pants further as it ran to the soil at his feet. "Restrain him tighter."

The female agent strode towards the stranger and struck him on the back of the head with her fist. He collapsed against the fence. With quick precision, she fastened new zip ties around the prisoner's wrists and ankles---double restraints this time.

No sooner had she done so than the man's head twitched. A garbled choking sound came from his mouth as he appeared to struggle for breath. He collapsed, convulsing violently as though battling for control of his limbs. Rolling, his pupils turned upward in their sockets to reveal the whites, which seemed to glow in the dim illumination. At last, his body went limp, relaxed, and remained still.

Cutter swore, kneeling beside the body to check the vitals.

"Will someone please tell me what happened?" Erin insisted, but was cut short as the woman uttered another curse.

"He's dead!"

Shock quivered through Erin as the pieces came together before her. Her knees went weak for a second, and she had to lean against the sill to support herself and the baby. She had never seen a person die before, and the reality pierced her with deadly precision, sending shivers down her spine. Her hand instinctively lifted to cover the sight from Connor's face. "Who is he?" she asked as Cutter pulled away the intruder's black mask.

A collective gasp came from Tony, Cutter, and Nguyen at the face. They exchanged surprised glances.

"Agent Park?" Nguyen responded, shock and surprise in her voice. "But he's--"

"On leave," Cutter cut in, completing her sentence. "A one-way trip. Poison pill."

"Hidden in his tooth?" Tony asked, startling Erin even though she had considered the same possibility. She realised how quickly her shock had faded. Now, her main concern was how this would impact her family---another situation she needed to manage.

"No. Those are too risky, and fictional means." Cutter pulled the mask back over the corpse's face, shaking his head. "I think he grabbed it from his belt, using his escape as a distraction."

Tony's face paled in the light shining from the bedroom as he looked from the sleeping form to the agents. "What's going on?"

"Let us investigate, Mr Nowlan," Cutter replied as he and Nguyen lifted the apparent traitor between them and carried him away. "You can explain to your wife the rest. I will call tomorrow to arrange a meeting with you both."

Erin's brow scrunched as she considered the ASIS agent's words. She didn't like the sound of it, but something told her events had taken an unmistakable detour. "Is this about the Titanic?" she asked, hoping she was wrong.

Cutter and Nguyen paused, the limp body causing some strain. "You know?"

Erin affirmed with a nod. "My husband and I have no secrets, Gary. At least, not now," she added, realising tonight's events were a surprise to no one but her. She swallowed, considering her next words. Despite the less than ideal decision, she acknowledged the urgency. Casting a glance at Tony, then at the baby in her arms, she glared back at Cutter. "If you want Tony to traipse about in time, I'll allow it on one condition," she declared, her determined gaze unwavering. Despite the possible consequences, she was set to face whatever might come. For Connor, for Tony, for the family.

Cutter's face remained placid, almost unreadable. Just a glance at Sofia Nguyen and Tony revealed what he didn't want to. "Condition, Mrs Nowlan?"

Erin took a breath, standing taller, and set her jaw. Was this the right decision? She stared ahead, thinking about Connor. Bad people had come, and like the ocean pounding the nearby beach, she couldn't turn her back on them. "I'm coming too," she replied, with hardly a tremor in her voice.

"What?" Tony exclaimed, staring at her. "Erin, are you sure?

She ignored her husband's reaction, staring back at the agents. "You know I will, anyway," Erin added to bolster her position. "You have the photos to prove it."

Cutter stared back at her, not looking away from her steady gaze. After a few moments of silence, he allowed a slight smile. "Very well then. We'll meet tomorrow."

* * *

Erin Deering-Nowlan
Lammermoor Beach
6:45pm 8th April 2019

On the following evening, Erin cradled the steaming cup of coffee between her hands as she sat on the back porch, watching the sun set behind the sand dunes. Sleep had evaded her, crowded by a mind busy with last night's events.

The back screen door opened. Although she didn't turn, she knew it was Tony. His brow furrowed in deep thought. Their earlier conversation had been sporadic, consisting mostly of fragmented sentences and shared glances filled with unspoken questions.

Aware of the dangers to Connor and themselves, neither

knew how to begin. Erin longed to escape it all, but that couldn't be. They had to face this head-on. She only hoped her spur-of-the-moment words hadn't landed her in something too big for her to handle.

An alarm rang on Tony's phone, the one that detected movement at the front door. "They're here."

Together, they entered the back door, locking it behind them. Erin briefly wondered if it was worth it, given their enemies could pass through walls as if they didn't exist. But what else could they do to feel in control of their security?

Erin boiled more water in the kettle before settling down. Tony was already at the front door, letting in Gary and Sofia. Their voices became louder as they reached the kitchen. When she turned, the ASIS agents were sitting at the table.

"We've confirmed the DNA and fingerprints," Cutter began, his voice low but steady. "Last night's intruder was indeed Agent Liam Parks."

Tony's eyes widened in shock. He shook his head in disappointment. "One of yours. That's comforting to know."

"Tea, coffee?" Erin interrupted to stop Tony from carrying on about the breach. She could see the shame on the agents' faces. There was no point fighting them when they probably needed their help. Best to keep the peace.

The agents gave their responses, and she went back to listening as she prepared the drinks.

"But how?" Tony asked, his voice tinged with disbelief. "How did he come across another ChronoSpace?"

"You wouldn't know about that," Sofia countered, her

voice calm and practical in the storm. Tony nodded at that.

"We have two ChronoSpace devices," Tony replied, measuring his words. Erin could hear the wheels turning in his head as he thought further, accounting for them. He had created a second ChronoSpace for Erin, hoping she would return to 2042 and live in the future with him. She vetoed that, saying she still had family in 2019. "Mine, the one you found and returned to me, was originally lost in North Queensland over 300 years ago."

"How did you get back?" Cutter asked, scrutinising with his steely gaze.

"A friend from the future tracked me," Tony stated, "and brought me home. But before you say anything, I can trust her." He shut up at that point. Erin guessed he thought he had said too much.

"One of your wedding guests, I presume." Cutter's voice trailed at the end as if waiting for a response. Tony nodded, and the agents exchanged glances. Their expressions spoke volumes about what they thought, yet Erin sensed more lurked behind them.

Sofia took over, leaning forward towards them, her voice steady. "Your mission, like it or not, will be on the Titanic. Despite the obvious, it's not going to be easy, but it's easier than the other alternatives."

Erin opened her mouth to speak, but the female agent held up a hand.

"You're going to go through basic training, six months, to learn defence. The people you're likely to meet play keeps. It's not a trip to karate at the Police Youth Club. These people are killers."

"But you'll be there, right?" Tony's question sounded like a statement.

Cutter shook his head. "We are sitting this one out. And before you interrupt, the reasons are simple. You both have an advantage over Sofia and me. Even disguised, we would still appear professional and easily noticeable. You two, being green, so to speak, are perfect for the role."

Tony drew a slow, deep breath and released it. His eyes filled with concern as he turned to look at Erin. "Do you still want to come?"

Erin paused to consider the situation. Although she didn't like the idea of traipsing through time into danger, the idea thrilled her. But there was Connor. Was this the right thing? She nodded. "I'm doing this for our family," she replied, despite the strange foreboding twisting her stomach.

Chapter 11

Professor Albert Cardnell
Southampton, England.
10th April 1912. 11:00am

Not one square foot of the area remained still amongst the excitement and bustle of Southampton port. Wagons and motorised trucks carried luggage to the docks, their horns blasting on their way to collect more. Dockworkers hustled about their business, shouting to each other. Newly arrived passengers of Titanic gaped in awe at the mammoth vessel that loomed high above them. Truly, it stood as a testament to human ingenuity and a harbinger of the luxurious journey that awaited its passengers--or some of them.

A lone man looked down at them from the top deck of the ship's stern. Arriving earlier had provided him the unique opportunity to witness the spectacle from this vantage point. Other early arrivals, from varying passenger classes, chattered amongst their groups. Closer to the Veranda Café sat the ship's band playing "The Sailor's Hornpipe", its lively and jaunty melody dancing amongst all within earshot.

Yes, it was a fantastic day that heralded the beginning of a new age, the man thought to himself while blending with the people. Behind his bright eyes and smile hid an important thought, something no one else could yet know. To everyone else, he was Albert Thornton, an architect. In a previous life, he was a Cambridge professor of mathematics and physics.

That was a secret now. No one on the ship could know his

name, his true purpose on this marvellous ship. Although he held many other secrets about himself, even from his most trusted friend Ernest Rutherford, this proved to be his biggest.

Cardnell leaned forward, his elbows resting on the railing, as he watched the people below. A tear welled in his eye at the thought of leaving everything behind him. Not only his connection with Cambridge University, the faculty there, and the long conversations with his closest colleagues, and his cousins. He would also miss the underground cafés, the life of checking the classifieds in search of coded messages, and the life of duplicity in a cruel world.

He wiped the tear with a handkerchief: a drop of sadness blended with an anticipation of his future. Absently, he regarded the moist spot on the linen square before returning it to its pocket.

* * *

Electronic Diary of Anthony Nowlan
Titanic, Southampton, England
11:00am 10th April 1912.

The first thing I noticed upon our arrival, besides the swirling sensation in my stomach, was that we were inside the ship. The floor felt odd, off-kilter, and I took a step back to steady myself. But my foot met empty air. In the next moment, a falling sensation gripped me, and I called out in fright. Before I knew it, I was up to my neck in the water.

At first, I thought the ChronoSpace had made a mistake and brought me to the ship's final night. Then I looked up to see Erin standing there, looking down at me, her hands on her hips. An amused smile appeared on her face as I floundered like an idiot in the filtered saltwater.

"I just can't take you anywhere," she tutted, reaching out a hand for me to grab. She slipped in after me with a tremendous splash and came up spluttering. "What the hell?" she cursed, coughing water. "You didn't have to pull me in too!"

Laughing, I pulled myself up, thankful that the ChronoSpace and my iBioPad were both waterproof, courtesy of a bit of preparation before starting this mission. "I didn't," I replied as I sat on the edge and offered her my hand. "Come on."

Luckily, our luggage was on solid ground. We would have dry clothes at least when we reached our cabin.

"This doesn't look like the top deck to me," Erin grumped, casting a gaze around the tiled walls and overall opulence.

"Excuse me, sir and madam," a male voice called from nearby. "You are not yet permitted in here until after we set sail."

We turned to face a uniformed ship officer. Despite the slight twinkle I caught in his eye, he maintained a stern authority as he helped Erin to her feet. I thanked him, removing a handkerchief from my inner jacket pocket in a feeble attempt to dry Erin's face. Her eyes dropped to the soggy cloth and opened wide in amusement before she laughed hard.

"Your luggage is here," the ship steward interrupted, observing our bags beside us. "But where is your porter? I trust you didn't carry this here yourself?"

Still rocking with laughter, I apologised and showed him our tickets. They were facsimiles of the original tickets.

The people who had bought the real tickets had mysteriously been overcome by a bad stomach bug induced by a 21st century drug in their tea. Since they were ill and unable to travel, their rooms in first class would not go to waste.

He took the tickets and read the room number. "Your cabin is on the higher deck," he said, handing them back to me with a polite nod. Catching sight of another gentleman, he called out, "Porter Smith! Here, lad, take Mr and Mrs Devereaux to their accommodation, won't you?" Smith dutifully loaded our bags on a trolley and pushed it towards the door. "Please follow him. Do you know the name of your other porter?"

We shook our heads, thanked the steward, then followed our luggage.

Porter Smith guided us through the opulent halls of the Titanic, our footsteps echoing against the polished wood panels and intricately designed wallpaper. Despite our displacement in time, the ship exuded an air of luxury matching a floating palace of the age that promised a voyage like no other. The aroma of the fine wood reminded me of my grandfather's woodwork as we ascended a grand staircase adorned with a wrought-iron banister.

Erin glanced at me as we did, silently mouthing the words, "This is where you were last time?" I nodded in reply, pointing at the exact spot where I had stood for the photo with Jasmine and the Thrill Seekers.

On the higher deck, we found our first-class cabin, a haven of refinement. The door swung open to reveal a spacious room with lavish decor that mirrored the elegance of the

Edwardian era. Deep mahogany furnishings gleamed in the soft glow of electric lamps, casting a warm ambience over the quarters.

Erin's eyes widened at the sight of the plush carpet underfoot, a tapestry of muted colours that complemented the ornate patterns of the curtains framing the porthole. A gleaming dressing table adorned with crystal perfume bottles stood beside an intricate carved wardrobe. The bed, draped in luxurious linens, beckoned with promises of comfort amid the rhythmic hum of the ship's engines.

The steward, having observed our awe-struck glances, explained the cabin's amenities with a practised grace. "You will find the en-suite bathroom just through there," he gestured toward a door embellished with brass fittings. "And should you require anything during your voyage, the ship's staff is at your service. Extra towels, perhaps?" he added, noting our soggy clothes dripping on the carpet.

I thanked the steward, and he waited there as though he hadn't heard me. Soon realising why, I extracted a one-pound note from my wallet. He eyed its wet condition, shrugged as if deciding money is money, even soggy, and took it. Both he and Porter Smith left.

Erin retreated to the en-suite where she began removing her day dress. Meanwhile, I realised the waterlogged condition of my suit's effect on my windpipe and struggled to remove the tie and loosen the button.

"I wonder how Susan and Dan are getting on with looking after Connor," she said, her voice floating through the ajar door.

"They'll be fine," I replied, cursing the tie around my neck, which refused to budge as I strained on it. "They won't notice, actually. The handy part about time-travel is, we can be back mere minutes after we left -- although we should be away longer."

"Not too long though," she said, drying her hair as she strutted by me in her bra and panties to open our luggage. After our six-month training with ASIS, basic training for the mission, her figure had toned up magnificently after childbirth. She caught me perving at her, and lifted her hands to her breasts, hooking the fingertips on the bra. "You're not getting your hands on these puppies until later. We're on a mission, remember?"

She pulled down the cloth, flashing me with a cheeky glance at them, and covered them again. A goofy grin crossed my face as I regarded the twinkle in her eye, then remembered. Yes, the mission. Find the professor and retrieve his formula before the Titanic sinks. And avoid the spies, who would kill to have it themselves.

Erin found a new day dress and began dressing in it. "Well, hurry up," she chided, seeing me still struggling with the tie. "We want to be there before the boat departs."

Chapter 12

Professor Albert Cardnell
Southampton, England.
10th April 1912. 12:00pm

Under the crisp midday sun of April 10th, 1912, Southampton's bustling port transformed into an intricate play of maritime marvel as the RMS Titanic, the epitome of opulence and engineering prowess, prepared to embark on its maiden voyage. Anticipation charged the air, and the crowd's excitement grew as they gathered to witness history unfold.

As the clock struck noon, the colossal vessel loomed majestically against the backdrop of the bustling port. The liner's sheer magnitude was awe-inspiring. Its towering smokestacks, adorned with billowing plumes of white smoke, reached toward the sky like a Titan's fingers. Sunlight glinted off the polished brass fittings and the ship's elegant hull, creating a dazzling spectacle that captivated onlookers.

The melodious strains of the ship's band filled the air, playing a lively tune that added a festive note to the proceedings. The ship's crew, donned in immaculate uniforms, moved with precision on the decks, attending to final preparations. Streamers and flags fluttered in the breeze, a kaleidoscope of colours.

Professor Albert Cardnell stood on the deck of the Titanic, his eyes scanning the horizon as the ship prepared to leave Southampton. A salty sea-breeze tousled his salt-and-pepper hair while he reflected on how the bustling activity around him contrasted to the open sea's tranquillity that lay ahead. Although reserved in nature, Cardnell couldn't help feeling a sense of excitement, eager to witness the unfolding journey.

The ship's horn blasted, startling him. He turned towards the sound and caught sight of something.

Amongst the passengers milling about, he spotted a young couple engaged in conversation as they advanced along the deck. His heart skipped in trepidation as he realised they would come close to him. Despite their intriguing manner, a nagging instinct compelled him to look away. Eye contact would attract attention, which his US contacts advised him to avoid for the sake of his safety.

"Good day to you, sir," the gentleman said as they approached. "Quite an auspicious day, isn't it?"

Cardnell looked away from the open sea and turned to them, adopting a friendly smile. "Good day to you both," he replied, tipping his hat to the feminine half of the pair. He momentarily paused upon seeing the man's easy smile that exuded a magnetic quality. "It's certainly a remarkable day for such an occasion. The Titanic setting sail on this historic journey," he added, glancing between them.

The woman, with her dark hair cascading in loose waves, returned the smile. "Indeed, it's a marvel of human engineering. My brother and I were just discussing the wonders of its design."

Cardnell raised an eyebrow, pleasantly surprised by her interest, yet something disturbed him. He had to tread carefully to avoid giving away his game. Adjusting his spectacles, he cleared his throat and glanced at the band playing at the nearby Veranda Café. "Ah, an enthusiast! Ship design is a fascinating field. Are you both architects, too?" He hoped to himself that he had chosen an occupation with which they were unfamiliar, amateur at best. If they knew more than he did on the subject, he could blow his subterfuge.

The delectable beauty's eyes lit up with enthusiasm as she exchanged a knowing glance with her male companion before responding, "Not architects per se, but I do have a keen interest in various scientific endeavours. The Titanic provides a splendid opportunity to explore such matters." Her gaze remained on him, capturing his eyes with hers of emerald.

Cardnell nodded, maintaining his amiable facade, and turned his attention back to the man. His mind raced, considering the possibilities of this voyage. While he had to remain cautious, surely there could be no harm in this brief encounter for the voyage's duration. "It's refreshing to meet like-minded individuals. I'm Albert Thornton, an architect by trade. I find inspiration in the melding of form and function."

The gentleman, a tall and imposing figure with a rugged charm, chimed in, "Architect, you say? Well, Mr. Thornton, I must admit I'm more inclined towards activities like skeet shooting or shuffleboard. But I do have a soft spot for chess."

A hint of a perfumed scent, sandalwood perhaps, wafted on the salty sea-air across his nostrils. For a second, Cardnell paused, lingering on a memory it invoked of past acquaintances. The woman's polite cough returned him to the present. "Chess, you say? A game of strategy and intellect. Excellent. Perhaps we could engage in a match later in the journey."

The gentleman nodded at the idea, crossing his arms. "I would be offended if we didn't."

Maintaining an air of innocence, the raven-haired beauty added, "Oh, how delightful! I'd love to witness a game between skilled players. I love watching a man who can manipulate a piece." She gave a gentle laugh, shaking her head as if remembering something once forgotten. "Where are our manners? This is my brother, Victor Hartwell, and my name is Seraphina."

The conversation continued, Cardnell skilfully avoiding mention of chemistry, metallurgy, and allowing a tiny word or two of physics per his engineering guise. Yet Seraphina's fascination with science persisted, leaning towards discussions of atoms, creating an atmosphere of camaraderie.

At last, Cardnell noticed the sun dipping below the horizon. Hues of orange and pink speckled across the ocean's waves. "It's getting late," he said. "Why don't we reconvene for a game of chess in the Grand Staircase Lounge later this evening? It would be a delightful way to pass the time."

Victor, with a subtle nod of agreement, replied, "An excellent idea, Mr. Thornton. We shall look forward to it."

With that, the siblings turned and resumed their tour of the decks as the ship embarked on its first leg towards Cherbourg, France. Watching the handsome couple from behind, something told him that his proposed game of chess would reveal more than just Victor's strategic acumen.

* * *

Electronic Diary of Anthony Nowlan
Titanic, Southampton, England
11:55am 10th April 1912.

The brisk wind swept across the deck of the Titanic as we stepped into the open air, squinting against the sunlight, even with our sunglasses. Excitement filled the air, borne by a sea of passengers bound for New York. Finding the professor amongst this crowd would be like the proverbial needle in the haystack.

I scanned the faces as they passed. There was the distinguished elderly couple, dressed impeccably in the latest Edwardian fashions, strolling arm in arm. His silver hair matched the pearls around his wife's neck. Another, a solo traveller in a well-worn leather jacket and weather-beaten hat, reminded me of Indiana Jones. He turned upon hearing the laughter of a pair of newlyweds, their eyes gleaming with excitement, still in their wedding clothes. They nearly bumped into a solo musician, who was playing a violin, totally lost in the melody, while a woman dressed in a mysterious black veil watched and listened to him playing. None of them matched the man we sought.

Our quarry was travelling alone, we suspected, and we knew from checking archives earlier that he was likely to be travelling under a pseudonym. If so, the chances were high that he had changed his appearance too.

"We'll never find him amongst these people," Erin grumbled, adjusting her wide hat to shield her eyes from the sun. She side-stepped a couple of young children, narrowly avoiding a collision as they ran past in their oblivious game of chase. "I wonder how Connor is," she said, watching them duck and weave amongst the other passengers.

"We'll be back before he knows we're gone," I replied, adjusting my spectacles against the glare of the sun. "Keep your eyes peeled, babe."

All we had to do was find the Professor, learn his suite's location, then find his formula while he was suitably distracted. Simple, right? But we'd be dodging the time-travelling spies I knew would be here as well as the spies of this era. And I had no idea if there were others I hadn't met.

"This might have been easier if we had backup from Gary Cutter," Erin replied, catching up to me as I forged a path through the first clear space to appear between the throngs. I harrumphed to myself. Yes, the ASIS agent said he would have gone, but he was concerned any time-travelling enemies would recognise him on sight. Erin and I were deemed unknown at this point. Although I know that at least some would meet past-me from my previous time jaunt to this era, this was all at the same place and time. I had my doubts about that. Despite his logic, a strange feeling told me that Cutter had met with a strange accident while time-travelling with me to the past that had affected him.

"You could have worn a pair of these," I said, tapping the frames of my spectacles. On the inner side of the lenses flashed a display of squares superimposed over the faces of the people before me. Invisible to a casual observer, they were focused on my retinas and programmed via my hidden iBioPad to detect known faces.

"They work for you," she replied, admiring the shape of the frames, "but I couldn't handle all that flashing."

"It'd satisfy my librarian fantasy," I quipped, dipping my glasses to waggle my eyebrows over them at her. "Rawr," I added in a husky voice.

She giggled at that, playfully punching my arm. "Eyes front, goofy."

The speakers in my spectacles' wings whispered an alert in my ear. Instantly, a red-lined square highlighted a gentleman towards the ship's aft. I tapped Erin's hand with my fingers as I zoomed in on the subject.

He was a man of early-to-mid forties and an average height for that time-period, roughly five-foot-ten. Although shorter than me, his lean and scholarly frame held the posture that reminded me of my own college professors. While still facing away from me, apparently having turned away towards the water. But my facial recognition software, courtesy of ASIS, had picked him up without an issue.

"Which one is he?" Erin enquired, pulling me down to her height so she could catch a glimpse of my lenses from the side.

"Easy on," I warned her, nearly losing my balance, and managed to point out a gentleman in a tan suit. "Over there."

The ship's horn blasted as the ship left the pier, pushed along by the tugs. Distracted, the man turned his head, and my glasses caught his full face.

MATCHED, the display flashed before my eyes, changing to a close-up of the man next to an archive photo. Ah, yes. His neatly trimmed beard was the right shape, matching his jaw, but it carried more spots of grey than the picture.

"It's him," I said for Erin's benefit.

"Let's go!" she said excitedly, almost with an over-eagerness, and moved ahead, dragging me along like a dog on a leash.

My heart jumped in my chest at the prospect of meeting a historical genius. Maybe he wasn't Einstein, but he was brilliant according to a letter Rutherford wrote about him. We were five metres away when suddenly my glasses flashed again. My ears stung from the dinging alert.

The inner screen of my lenses displayed two pictures: a man and a woman. I slowed my pace, holding back Erin as I read the information. "Oh, shit," I muttered, perhaps too loudly, as a nearby priest gasped at my outburst.

"Come on," Erin said, oblivious to my exclamation. "We can join the conversation."

"No," I replied, lifting my voice above another blast of the ship's horn. "We hold back for now."

Erin's eyebrow raised in quizzical concern as she stared at me in disbelief. "But he's--" she started to say, then stopped. Realisation flowered across her face as she turned back to the scene before us. "Those two are spies, right?"

I nodded. "Yep. According to the archives, she's Seraphina Hartwell, and he's Victor Sinclair. English, but traitors to the Crown. They disappeared in 1912, whereabouts unknown."

"We need to be careful," she said, the mental cogs twisting in her voice as she considered the options.

We waited, blending into the background while keeping a watchful eye on the professor and his suspicious company. Their conversation seemed casual, their body language telling me they didn't know each other. But that might not last long, and there was no telling the extent of their plans for him. Since my records indicated that the professor had never been seen since the Titanic's disaster, what did that mean would happen to him?

Chapter 13

Professor Albert Cardnell
Southampton, England.
10th April 1912. 6:30pm

The soft hum of the ship's engines reverberated through the air as the Titanic docked in Cherbourg. As the decks bustled with activity, inside the luxurious enclave of the Veranda Café provided a reprieve for Albert Cardnell. A man of habit, he always ate at 6pm without exception, a custom fostered since childhood. This trip proved no exception to his rule, although he knew he would bend it tonight for the main dinner at 8pm.

So as not to spoil his dinner, he opted for a smoked salmon appetiser, an Edwardian delicacy that showcased the ship's commitment to culinary excellence. Thin slices of silky-smooth salmon adorned the china plate, accompanied by capers, lemon wedges, and precisely cut toast points. Its combination of textures and flavours tantalised him, making him wish he could eat more. In the far corner, a solo violinist conjured a haunting rendition of 'Danny Boy' that segued to a newer number he didn't recognise. He spotted a couple at a neighbouring table, noting the male's copper-toned hair, and then the woman's meal: quiche Lorraine. That would be delectable if it weren't for his arranged meeting in the Palm Court.

Checking the time on his pocket watch revealed he had fifteen minutes. That was time to enjoy a fruit tart adorned with seasonal berries. The flaky pastry cradled a lovely pastry cream, of which each mouthful provided a burst of fruity sweetness that bloomed across his tongue. Such a shame the serving was so small. He dabbed his lips with a linen napkin and, dropping it to the plate, rose from the table. As he stood, the young woman from the nearby couple's table glanced at him. He nodded a greeting to her, receiving a pleasant smile, and left.

Where the Veranda Café was open air, the Palm Court presented as an enclave of refined elegance. Palms and exquisite decor provided the perfect backdrop for relaxation away from the bustle of the decks outside. He strolled through the simulated oasis until he spotted a familiar sight -- Victor Sinclair and Seraphina, engrossed in a chess game at a secluded table.

Victor, with his piercing blue eyes fixed on the chessboard, appeared deep in thought, contemplating his next move. Seraphina wore an enigmatic smile, her eyes dancing as he approached their table. His heart thudded in anticipation of spending more time with such intellectual individuals.

"Mind if I join in?" Professor Cardnell enquired, his eyes gleaming with a genuine enthusiasm for the intellectual challenge.

Victor, looking up, acknowledged the professor with a nod. "Certainly, Albert. I'm glad you held your word for this chess challenge. Seraphina was helping me warm up." He reached forward and moved his black knight before sitting back with a satisfied beam. "I believe that is checkmate, my dear sister."

The checkmate configuration was visually striking. The white king stood helpless, cornered by the black queen, bishops, and a well-positioned knight. With a seamless alliance, the black pieces trapped the beleaguered white king with no escape route. Such a symphony of calculated moves, the professor thought to himself. He relished the challenge ahead playing opposite such a strategic mind.

The professor settled into his chair and took a breath, taking the time to measure Victor's features as he reset the board. His opponent's striking blue eyes reflected the overhead electric lights. "Shall we begin, Albert?"

Cardnell nodded as Victor held out his closed fists. He chose the left, which his gaming opponent opened to reveal a white king.

"Your move," Victor confirmed, handing him the white king.

The polished ivory chess pieces awaited their players on the ornate board, a silent witness between the two opponents. Victor Sinclair, his eyes reflecting a strategic glint, and the professor, a connoisseur of puzzles now facing a mental challenge for supremacy of the game.

Their deliberate opening moves unfolded with elegant strategy. Victor displayed quick and decisive manoeuvres, launching efficient attacks while maintaining a balanced defence. Meanwhile, Cardnell, as Thornton, responded with clear-headed calmness, matching Victor move for move.

The mental gladiators settled into the intricacies of the game, oblivious to the hushed conversation of gathering onlookers. The chessboard became a battlefield of wits and strategies.

As the game progressed, the professor realised he was facing a formidable opponent in Victor Sinclair. The pieces' positions pieces on the board led to an impending checkmate. The tension in the Palm Court grew palpable, mirroring the intensity of the chess match.

Surveying the arrangement with a mix of apprehension and determination, Professor Cardnell, a seasoned champion, prepared for the challenge.

On the black side, Victor Sinclair's pieces stood with an air of confidence, poised to execute their next move. The black queen, a formidable presence, dominated the centre, flanked by bishops and knights positioned to shield their sovereign. The white king seemed cornered, surrounded by looming threats, and the professor could almost sense the impending doom.

White rooks, stalwart sentinels, guarded the edges of the board, while the bishops angled toward the centre in a defensive stance. The knights, the professor's daring cavalry, waited, ready to leap into action. However, the true potential lay in the queen, a potent force waiting for the right moment to strike.

As the professor contemplated his next move, the impending defeat loomed. He saw the precarious nature of his position, with the black pieces closing in, their shadows stretching over the white squares. In his mind's eye, he envisioned the imminent checkmate, recognising the peril of every step he took.

Victor shifted in his seat, his expression similar to a cat, its tail swishing back and forth, waiting to pounce on its unsuspecting victim. Cardnell spotted the tip of his opponent's tongue sliding across its lips, intrigued by the premise. Beside him, Seraphina gazed in to the professor's eyes, a gentle smile playing on her lips. He quickly diverted his gaze back to the board, hoping to find another strategy to avoid defeat. A way his fatigued mind did not see.

At last, with a sigh, the professor sat up and reached for

his king. His fingers had almost touched its ivory cross, to knock it over in resignation, when a voice cut in from behind.

"I couldn't help but notice your game," the stranger said, addressing them both. "But I believe you can win this match."

Both Victor and Professor Cardnell blinked in surprise as they turned towards the man. The professor's eyes lifted in recognition of the gentleman, the brown-haired man from the Veranda Café. He raised an eyebrow as the newcomer regarded the chessboard with open fascination. "Two moves will do it," the tall stranger added, his smile carrying a mix of bravado and uncertainty as he glanced at Victor, then back to the professor.

The audacious claim hung in the air, perplexing both Victor and Professor Cardnell. They exchanged puzzled glances, unable to fathom how such a swift victory could be achieved. The newcomer, seemingly unfazed by the scepticism in the room, awaited a response.

"Two moves?" Victor's eyes flickered with a mix of surprise and concern. He exchanged a quick glance with Seraphina, who gave him a shrug. His face turned pinkish as he challenged the third man. "I'd like to see you try."

The brown-haired man nodded, gesturing towards the chessboard. "May I?"

The professor nodded his assent, shifting his chair towards Seraphina, who placed a gentle hand on his arm. Distracted slightly by the gesture's intentions, he turned his attention back towards the young man.

The enigmatic stranger took his place at the chessboard, his fingers moving a piece with nonchalant precision. As the first move unfolded, a quiet hush fell over the Palm Court. The professor, Victor, and even the ever-charming Seraphina remained still, entranced by the unfolding spectacle.

Cardnell's gaze shifted towards Victor's throat, where a tiny bead of sweat had formed. It slid down the smooth shaven skin and disappeared into the collar's fabric. His opponent glanced upwards at the newcomer, the hint of a scowl receding as quickly as it formed, then back at the board. For a moment, he looked undecided about his next move.

The professor's eyes widened in surprise upon seeing the board before them. Of course! How could he have missed it? It was a slight comfort to know it had slipped past Victor's attention, too.

Only one move remained, save for Victor's resignation. He soon proved himself a man who would go down fighting. The black king moved a square, the ultimate piece of a trap he had designed himself.

In a stunning display of strategic brilliance, the mysterious chess player executed the second move, declaring, "Checkmate."

Victor, suppressing any signs of frustration, glanced at Seraphina with a subtle nod. She hadn't noticed as she gazed at the stranger with an expression of mixed awe and fascination. Maintaining his suave demeanour, her brother turned his attention to the stranger who had interrupted the game.

"Well, it seems we have an unexpected chess enthusiast in our midst," Victor remarked, flashing a charming smile at the small crowd that had gathered. "How about a game, my friend? I'm feeling a bit more warmed up now."

The stranger grinned in response. "That would be smashing. A friendly match it is."

"May I know the name of my opponent?" Victor asked, his tone slightly strained.

"Devereaux," the man replied with an accent Cardnell thought sounded like his friend Rutherford. "Anthony Devereaux." With a jovial grin, as though laughing at an unspoken joke, he reached forward to grip Victor's hand.

"I say," Cardnell said, taking his saviour's hand. "Your accent. You sound almost like you're from New Zealand like a friend of mine..." He stopped himself from mentioning Charles Rutherford's name, realising that could reveal clues to his hidden identity.

"No, Australian, mate." Devereaux replied, his hazel eyes crinkling with amusement. "Born and bred. Now, how about this game?"

Victor gestured towards an empty table nearby, transitioning the focus away from the previous game's outcome. As they set up the chessboard for the new match, Victor's face lit up. "I must say, I enjoy a game with a bit of excitement. How about a friendly wager?" Victor proposed, his eyes glinting with a mischievous spark.

Anthony Devereaux raised an eyebrow, intrigued. "A wager, you say? What do you have in mind?"

A confident smirk crossed Victor's face as she answered, "If you win, I'll treat you to a bottle of the finest champagne we have on board. But if I win, how about sharing a secret? A hidden talent, perhaps?"

The Australian, playing along, chuckled at the suggestion. "Deal. May the best strategist win, but we'll make it even more interesting again."

Chapter 14

Electronic Diary of Anthony Nowlan
Titanic, Cherbourg, France, England
7:35pm 10th April 1912.

No sooner had I mentioned a new challenge to throw Victor off his game, to give Erin time, than I realised the crowd gathering around our table had grown. With it came the anxiety that gnawed my nerves like a termite on a toothpick.

Stage fright, I thought to myself as the breath caught in my chest. That's what it had to be. I tried to relax the way my high school drama teacher had taught me, but it didn't work. Deep breathing? Nope.

"What challenge do you propose?" Victor asked.

Then Erin's voice whispered in my ear. "What's going on?" it crackled through the tiny speaker in my glasses. My reply caught in my throat as the professor and Victor regarded me with curious expressions.

"The Knights Tour," I stammered, sweeping a nervous gaze at my two chess companions: my quarry and my enemy. My brow crinkled as I realised something. "Where's the lady gone?"

"She has gone to lie down before dinner," Victor responded, his bravado beginning to return after I had helped Professor Cardnell defeat him.

"Ah, gone to her cabin?" I repeated for Erin's benefit.

"What?" Erin replied, distracting me again as I prepared to explain the Knights Tour to everyone else. I wondered if she realised the same as me: Seraphina was more likely to be heading to the professor's suite, which is where Erin was then.

"Not now," I hissed. "Just get your arse in gear. You're getting company soon."

"Well, go on," Victor chided me. "The unsinkable Titanic will likely sink before we start. Do hurry up."

A few people guffawed at the thought, a joke at my expense. My laugh was the only one that held irony.

"The Knight's Tour," I began, fighting to keep my voice steady, enunciating each word to avoid stammering, "is a chess puzzle that involves a knight moving to every square of a chessboard exactly once. Although we don't know its exact origins, the puzzle has a long history in the world of chess."

"What?" Victor exclaimed with surprise. "A puzzle? You're challenging me with a child's amusement?" Weakness made his voice shake, and that improved my mood.

"Do you wish to renege?" I challenged, gazing straight into his eyes. The spy's history as a vicious killer echoed through my mind as I did, and I fought to keep eye contact. Others turned towards him, most likely unaware of the killer he represented in their midst. He hesitated a moment, possibly calculating the situation, then shook his head.

"No," he responded. "I look forward to the change in mental stimulation."

* * *

Erin Deering-Nowlan
Titanic, Cherbourg, France
7:38pm 10th April 1912

When Tony had distracted the professor and his unsavoury company, Erin glided along the passages towards the first class suites. The cabin she and Tony shared was in the same section as the professor's suite, a fact that they had confirmed by following him after his meeting with Victor and Seraphina.

It made it even easier with the steward monitoring the section, too. Stationed at the end of the corridor, the uniformed man soon knew every guest in his care. He turned to her with a smile as she approached.

"Mrs Devereaux! Dinner is at 8pm," he remarked, removing the master key from his pocket as he walked her to her own suite: A48.

She laid her palm on her stomach. "I believe I have a touch of seasickness and am not hungry."

The steward tutted at the horrible news as he unlocked the door to her suite. "That is terrible news. Perhaps--" A commotion at the end of the hall caught his attention. A woman with two yapping corgis chastised them as her porter tripped and dropped the bags. "Excuse me," the steward said, hurrying back to investigate.

Erin scrabbled to find her copy of the skeleton key, one made on Tony's iBioPad 3D printer, and trotted towards A42. With a glance back at the steward, she unlocked the professor's door and slid inside. The door snapped shut behind her.

"I'm in," she whispered into the microphone hidden in a brooch on her dress.

* * *

Electronic Diary of Anthony Nowlan
Titanic, Cherbourg, France
7:48pm 10th April 1912.

Everyone present applauded Victor for being a good sport. I joined in, determined to pressure him into participation, whispering for Erin's benefit, "I hope you get what you need fast, babe."

I turned to a nearby steward and requested some stationery: pencils and letterhead paper. He soon returned with five sheets and three pencils. After thanking him, I swiftly drew a chessboard on one sheet and asked the professor to do the same on another. "These are to mark our progress. Could you please number the squares for clarity?" I held up the drawings for everyone to see. "One is my board; the other is for Mr...?"

"Hartwell," Victor responded.

I had to stop myself from giving away the game. So he was using Seraphina's name? Interesting. "Hartwell," I repeated, adding, "That's a potent name. Thank you for accepting this challenge." I then explained the Knight's Tour rules: moving the knight to every square of a chessboard only once. The twist was that we would do it blindfolded, calling out our moves in turn.

The colour drained from my opponent's face, which changed from smug to horrified. "I beg your pardon?" he said as others in the audience murmured their astonishment.

"Of course," I replied, confidence building in me as it left his heart. "That's what makes this a test for intelligent men, one that stands apart from being a child's amusement."

He glared at me, his eyes moving up and down my body, measuring me. I tried not to blink. To do so would show weakness, which I couldn't afford, given what I had read about him. Quiet fury lingered in his reddening cheeks. His hand rose, shifting inside his jacket, and I held an anxious breath for what would come. But instead of a revolver, he withdrew a navy-blue handkerchief and shook it out to make a blindfold. "Very well, but beware of the cost when I win."

I returned his bravado with contrasting quiet confidence, retrieving my burgundy-coloured silk and allowing someone else to bind my eyes with it. "We will stand with our backs to the scribes charting our progress."

"What is to stop you copying my moves?" Victor asked aloud from my left.

"Good question," I answered. "Will someone please call out a starting square for Mr Hartwell? And one for me, too."

"Mr Hartwell, 7." "Mr Devereaux, 42."

A hush enveloped the room. The first move was crucial, dictating the course of the intricate dance that was about to unfold. "Would you do the honours of the first move, Mr. Hartwell?" I called out.

"7 to 13," Victor called aloud.

"Cross out 7," I said to the scribes, miming the movements with my hand, "and circle 13, so all can follow."

"Get on with it," Victor said, his voice a thin mask of impatience and cunning.

"Very well," I responded, wondering how Erin was doing in our quarry's suite. "42 to 59."

* * *

Erin Deering-Nowlan
Titanic, Cherbourg, France
7:45pm 10th April 1912

The desk's position allowed a passenger to sit and gaze outside at the endless ocean while writing. Inlaid with brass fittings and intricate inlays, it reminded Erin of her father's woodwork, a hobby that amused him when not running the sheep farm. She ran her fingers across its polished surfaces for a second before pulling herself together. Her mission, she had to focus.

Erin opened each drawer, finding only a bible in the top drawer. Gideons were around this early in the 20th century? She blinked away the surprise and refocused on her goal.

Where was the formula? Where would the professor hide it?

Erin focused and checked underneath the desk, but found nothing stuck there. Perhaps under the drawers or on the backs of them? She checked each drawer again.

Meanwhile, the soundtrack of the Knights Tour (whatever that was) came through the earpiece hidden by her hair. Tony and his opponent were calling out numbers like a terrible game of rec room bingo.

"27 to 37," said Victor's voice, followed soon by Tony's response: "17 to 2."

Erin's mind floated back to a scene from a movie she had once watched, her eyes settling on a painting hanging on the wall. That and the numbers gave her an idea.

She headed across the room, reached for the painting and lifted it. Her eyes lit up at the discovery. The dial and handle of a safe faced her. "Tony, we have a safe here. Can you help open it?"

Tony swore under his breath, the sound like a hiss in her earpiece. "A little busy here, babe," he whispered back, his tone reflecting he was talking under his breath. "2 to 12."

"Okay, maybe later," she said, then caught her breath in surprise as she heard something outside the door. Her heart thumped harder as she heard scratching at its lock. "Shit, is the professor still with you?"

"Have you got that, professor?" Tony's voice answered, and she heard the man's reply.

"It must be Seraphina," Erin whispered, panicking as she sought a hiding place. "She's here, coming in the door now!"

* * *

Electronic Diary of Anthony Nowlan
Titanic, Cherbourg, France, England
7:53pm 10th April 1912.

"What?" I replied in a whisper, the mental representation in my head almost disappearing with the distraction.

"18 to 1," Victor intoned, his voice a mixture of trepidation and concentration.

Erin's voice carried urgency as it vibrated through my earpiece. "Seraphina's inside the room. Can't talk."

Someone cleared their throat, bringing my attention back to my current situation. Before me stood a crowd of eyes, some friendly, some not-so-friendly, all of them watching me in anticipation. Blindfolded, I couldn't see them, but I could feel their gazes bore into me. "It's your turn," Victor replied haughtily.

Through my earpiece came another whispered curse from my wife for whatever reason I couldn't visualise. If I moved from here, I could blow our cover, making things more difficult. But Erin had gone through the same six-months of intensive training from Cutter and the ASIS as I had. We knew of this danger when we took on the mission.

"Oh," I said, cringing as I heard something that sounded like a thump. A muted cry.

"Are you well?" the professor enquired from behind me.

"Are you stuck?" Victor replied, sensing a victory in the wake of his previous defeat.

"You wish," I replied, standing taller and taking a breath. "Follow this, if you dare." With that, I rattled off the remaining squares of my Knight's Tour: "45 to 39, 39 to 56, 56 to 62, followed by 52, 58, 41, 35, 25, 10, 4, 19, 36, 51, 57." Just one short of the final move, I hesitated, listening to the professor's gasp as I uttered the last one. "That leaves me at 42." I stopped there, releasing a sigh, and the mental image from my thoughts.

"He did it! By Jove!" The professor's exclamation filled the room. For a second, no one dared speak before one gentleman in the audience began clapping, joined soon by the rest.

"Wait!" I announced, signalling for silence. It was as much to listen for anything from my wife. The sound of heavy breathing came through my ears, then the sound of a toilet flushing. Still blindfolded, I turned to my opponent.

"Here's your chance, Victor," I said, turning all attention to him. "If you can complete your own tour, we may call it a draw. What do you say?"

"Very well," Victor replied.

"Just don't make a mistake," I warned him, "or you will have to reveal to us your deepest, darkest secret."

He drew a deep breath, his feet scuffling on the floor as he shifted his stance. We waited with bated breath. My heart hammered, uncertain what was happening for my wife after what sounded like fighting.

Victor started speaking, all of us watching him in growing anticipation as he spoke. "1 to 11, 11 to 21..."

The pulse in my temple pounded harder with each number he called with accuracy. With a furrowed brow, he named each move until he had ten remaining numbers.

"31... 16..."

I held my breath.

"6... 13..."

"Wrong!" called the scribe in charge of Victor's page.

"It is not!" Victor blurted. "It can't be. Check again."

The scribe shook his head. "You have already been on 13."

"Preposterous! You must have made a mistake," he declared belligerently. The sound of cloth moving reached my ears as he ripped off his blindfold. Before he could ruin things for me, I cut in... to ruin them for him.

"If I may help," I called, raising my voice, and sensed everyone turn to me. "I believe you meant to say 3..."

A pause fell over us as the scribe checked the paper. "Yes!" he cried, a gasp erupting from the audience as they realised something was afoot.

"Then you would, to win a draw, have said..." I lifted my hand to my forehead in deep concentration. "8, 14, 29, 46, 61, 55..."

The crowd hushed. Beside me, I could hear Victor draw an uncomfortable breath.

"Shall I continue?" I asked the crowd, who responded with a resounding, "Yes!"

"From 55 to 40," I added, receiving a small cheer as the scribe signalled I was on track. "30, 24... which brings me to 7!"

I tore off my blindfold to the hearty applause of an audience mainly composed of men. Some exclaimed, "He not only tracked his knight but the other gentleman's too!" Nearby women clapped as well, adding to the atmosphere. I took a gracious bow for everyone. I turned towards Victor, ready to shake his hand, but he spun about-face and quit the room.

My heart jumped to my throat as I realised where the doorway led.

Towards the first class suites.

Where my wife was in the professor's room!

Chapter 15

Erin Deering-Nowlan
Titanic, Cherbourg, France
7:58pm 4th April 1912

Erin's heart thudded in her chest as she darted behind a folding screen, her eyes scanning through a tiny crack in its hinge at the door. The room was dimly lit, shadows dancing ominously as the noises of deckhands and passengers filtered from the night outside.

"What?" Tony's voice echoed in her earpiece.

The door creaked open, and Seraphina slipped into the room like a silent phantom. Dressed in dark, form-fitting attire, she moved with a lethal grace. "Seraphina's inside the room. Can't talk," she whispered for Tony's benefit, then realised that could have been a deadly mistake. She held her breath, praying that her hiding spot remained undetected.

Seraphina's sharp eyes scanned the room, searching for any sign of the professor's documents. Erin watched, her mind racing for a plan. The gravity of the situation pressed on her. She debated whether to attack and seize the formula or bide her time, hoping Seraphina wouldn't discover her presence.

The ticking of a clock echoed in the cabin, each second stretching, making her sweat more. Erin, desperate to avoid detection, pressed herself further into the shadows. She glanced around, hoping to find something -- anything -- to defend herself.

The raven-haired beauty, unaware of Erin's presence, approached the professor's desk. She opened the drawers then, finding them empty, swiftly shut each one. Pausing for a moment, she searched the underside of the mahogany desk. Erin's pulse quickened; she needed to act before it was too late. An idea came to her upon seeing something.

As Seraphina reached for another drawer, Erin seized the opportunity. She grabbed a heavy ornate vase from a nearby table and hurled it across the room. The ceramic described a perfect arc before shattering against the opposite wall.

Alerted by the noise, Seraphina swiftly turned toward the source. Erin dashed to another hiding spot behind a luxurious chaise lounge. Seraphina pointed her empty hand, sweeping the room with it. A short, clipped whoosh sounded in the air.

Something thudded into the lounge, ripping through its frame and cloth and exiting the other side. It brushed past Erin's hair, missed her scalp by an inch, and lodged in the wall behind her. She glanced at the object. A dart! With adrenaline-fuelled instinct, Erin dodged the second dart, dropping to the floor.

The cabin turned into a battlefield. Deadly darts launched from a device strapped to Seraphina's wrist. Five embedded themselves in a line on the wall, following her in a beeline as Erin raced towards the door. Erin's mind raced, contemplating her next move. She tripped on a chair, toppling it and crunched into a dining table by the window. Her hand clawed at the curtain which billowed in the chaos.

Something silver caught her attention: a silver tray on the floor. She grabbed it, held it up as a shield. A dart hit its dead-centre, denting the metal.

Seraphina strode closer, wrist extended towards Erin. The assassin's fingers twitched. Nothing happened. She glanced in frustration at the misfired device. That was all Erin needed.

The silver tray streaked through the air like a deadly Frisbee. The agent's chin stopped it with a sharp crack, followed by the clanging as it dropped to the floor. Erin shot forward, aiming to kick the assassin, who was now shaking stars from her eyes, but she was too slow.

Seraphina blocked the kick, flicking the foot to the side. Overbalanced, Erin fell, her elbow slamming on the hard polished wood floor. Pins and needles flared through her joint, making her hand spasm. She dodged Seraphina's fist, but only just. It grazed her cheekbone. She delivered two uppercuts to the enemy's belly, winding the bitch enough to make her double over, gasping. But it was a ploy.

Seraphina's body collided forcefully with Erin's, and together, they tumbled to the floor in a tumultuous entanglement of limbs and piercing screams. As they rolled and fumbled, finally separating, both women exhibited the aftermath of the intense struggle -- dishevelled hair, torn clothing, and mutual glares akin to hissing cats.

"Your fighting technique is commendable," Seraphina huffed, blowing a strand of hair from her eyes and stumbling a few backward steps towards the desk. "For an amateur."

Erin couldn't reply. She was too out of breath, and her eyes caught a movement. But she couldn't dodge in time.

The silk handkerchief snaked towards her throat like a whip, winding around her windpipe. Seraphina flew like a wraith of doom after it. In a flash, she was behind Erin and pulling on the garrote. The silk felt harder than Erin expected as her fingers clawed at it, trying to gain room to breathe.

Her opponent pulled harder, crossing the cloth behind Erin's neck, drawing it tighter. The wire inside the silk square cut deeper into the soft part of her throat. She sputtered, feeling the hot blood trapped in her flushed face.

Desperately, she twisted, another hand flailing for the desk. Fingers stretched, hoping for anything as a weapon, but all she could do was pull the top drawer. It banged on the floor, breaking. Erin kicked backwards, hoping to knock Seraphina off her feet. It worked.

The pair dropped, Erin twisting away to ram her elbow into her opponent's stomach. Breath rushed from her enemy's mouth. Erin punched hard. Blood splattered from Seraphina's lips. With a hard twist, she rolled, reversing so that Erin was on the floor.

Pain flared through Erin's mouth. A coppery taste exploded across her tongue as blood filled from where she bit her tongue. The pain paralysed her, and the pounding persisted. The cord wrapped again about her throat like a silken snake constricting her breath. It tightened, and Erin's tortured lungs cried for release. She stretched her fingers, scrambling, grasping, until they gripped something. And she swung.

The heavy object hit home. The silk loosened from her throat again, and she drew in a deep breath. All the time, she kept bludgeoning with the tome in her hand. And even after her opponent's limbs relaxed, dropping to the side,

Erin kept dropping the weight on the defeated woman's head and face.

At last, puffing with exhaustion, her weapon dropped from her fatigued fingers. She smirked upon seeing the object that had saved her -- a Bible. "How's that for a Bible bashing, bitch?"

She rolled away, tried to stand, and couldn't. With a glance, she looked at Seraphina, her glassy eyes staring at her, a look of astonishment plastered across her death mask. The adrenaline still pumping through Erin's body mixed with her stomach, swirled about, and she hurriedly staggered towards the toilet to vomit.

The room fell into an eerie silence, broken only by the distant hum of the ship's engines, a stark contrast to the recent fracas. Erin's cry for Tony echoed into the toilet bowl.

The sound of heavy footsteps reached her ears. She listened, hope building as the door open. A shocked gasp echoed as Erin's head swam from the recent ordeal. "Seraphina!" said a man's voice, shocked, distorted, and shaking. "Who did this to you?"

A curious sliding sound, like metal on metal, came from around the corner as a man's stealthy steps on the polished wooden floor slowly approached. She lifted her head in expectation of her saviour, but the sight beholding her washed away all relief.

"What have we here?" hissed the voice of Victor as her vision turned black.

Chapter 16

**Electronic Diary of Anthony Nowlan
Titanic, English Channel
8:11pm 10th April 1912.**

"Stay away from me," she cried in a hoarse and breathless voice. Her eyelids flickered, the eyes rolling back in her sockets, then shut. "My husband is coming," she mumbled, limbs falling limp as she fought to keep her head up. It seemed she didn't even recognise me.

"Oh, shit, Erin!" I gasped, hurrying to Erin. She collapsed, her head hanging over the toilet bowl's edge. I gently lifted her, shifting to let her rest across my lap on the ensuite's tiled floor, and cradled her.

Carefully, I brushed a few strands of her sandy-blonde hair away to reveal her face. Despite her Lammermoor Beach tan, a pallor had spread across her face. If she were any paler, I would have thought her dead. Only her shallow breathing indicated life remained in her as I lifted her limp form into my arms.

Guilt washed over me as various memories flashed through my mind. I should have stood my ground, refusing to let her come along on this mission. Technically, it was too much for both of us. We weren't cut out for this James Bond crap. Anger rose within me as I thought about Gary Cutter and how he opted to stay in 2019 instead of joining us in the past. As an experienced ASIS agent, he should have been the one accompanying me -- not Erin.

My wife felt heavier in my arms than usual, heavier than when I carried her pregnant over our threshold. Another terrible thought crossed my mind as I remembered our baby son, Connor, was waiting for us at home. The last time we had seen him, soon after our six-month training for this mission, he had been sitting up. He had giggled on that day as we gave him our kisses and hugs goodbye, planning to see him again in just an hour.

Careful not to drag my feet, I carried Erin towards the professor's bed. Ever so gently, I placed my unconscious wife on the soft covers. Her eyelids flickered as I did, looking up at me with her green eyes. "Tony?" she said, her voice weak but full of spirit. "Why the hell are you crying?" I struggled for an answer, and she managed a small grin. "I'm alive, right?"

I sniffed, feeling a slight turn of joy lift me at Erin's voice. Yes, she was alive. "I'm sorry," I responded, acknowledging the consequences of my lapse in judgement at the Palm Court.

"Stop your blubbering," she replied. "You're not the one who bitch-slapped me."

I turned to inspect Seraphina's inert form on the floor. The blood oozing from her nose and mouth had at least slowed. Nothing dripped to the floor as the dead spy's eyes gazed blankly towards the window. Then my eyes spotted the heavy book near the body. Its golden cross on the cover seemed to shimmer in the overhead light. "First time I've seen the Bible as a blunt instrument of death," I murmured before realising it.

Erin chuckled, and I turned back to see her eyes closing. "That's what I said," she murmured, exhaustion in her voice. Her body trembled as though cold, and I realised what was happening.

"You're in shock." I pulled the covers up to keep her

warm. "Just a moment. I'll get you a drink. Stay awake."

"Yes, dear," she mumbled sleepily with a slight slur. Leaning forward, I tenderly kissed her forehead before hurrying off to return with a glass of water from the sink. She mumbled something about needing sleep when I lifted her head and shoulders. "Shh," I replied, lifting the glass to her lips. "Sip this."

Erin complied, then slurped a huge swallow, prompting a coughing fit. "Slowly," I chided gently.

"He'll be back soon," Erin said, reminding me we weren't in our own room. "The professor."

"Just rest," I responded with a quiet shush. I'd stay with her even while the world crumbled on our heads, but she had a point. "Did you find it?"

"No, but neither did she."

Well, that was something. Even if we didn't have it, we weren't behind in the game either. But Erin had a point. I checked the clock on the wall above a desk. Twenty-five past eight. The professor would still be having dinner in the dining room now, but was Victor with him? I shook my head. Never mind that. The mission had changed slightly; we had to adapt. But first, I had to clean up.

I contemplated Seraphina's corpse on the floor. Even in death, she remained alluring. But beauty could be deceiving, like the mystique of snakes whose bodies still needed disposal if found. How the hell was I going to dispose of hers?

My eyes roamed the room and locked on the parted curtain. Ah, the window! Seraphina could sleep with the fishes. I headed for the window, then stopped with disappointment. The windows weren't made to open.

Why? My head answered that question quicker than expected. Maritime safety designs would have dictated windows shouldn't be open to protect the hull's structural integrity and prevent water surging through the open space and possibly sinking the ship. Considering the Titanic's impending disaster, I couldn't help laughing to myself at the irony in that. But that didn't help with the question of the body.

The ship's crew or passengers would soon notice if I walked Weekend at Bernie's style with a dead body to the deck. And they would definitely notice if I tipped her over the railing for the propellers to mince up for the sharks. Perhaps if I waited until after midnight, when there were fewer people to notice? Nope, the professor would return by then.

"Damn it all," I hissed to myself, then stopped. Of course! It was a dicky idea, but it might work. Professor Stockwell and I had designed a quantum tracker device for use on the Titanic. Given we couldn't track the Titanic's movements precisely to know where we might end up if we travelled through time, this gizmo would help us avoid ending up in the ocean... or in a different room. But I had to hide it where no one else would see it and disturb it.

I slid the marker behind the en-suite's toilet. Upon activation, it glowed blue, blinking three times before the light turned off again. I carried the spy's body to the bathroom and activated my ChronoSpace. An instant later, I returned from the future empty-handed. I just didn't want to be around when it would eventually reappear.

After painstakingly reassembling the desk's wrecked drawer, I replaced it before tidying the room. Erin was sleeping fitfully, the colour returning to her face by the time I had righted the toppled furniture and disposed of the broken vase pieces. I could only imagine what had happened in that fight I heard.

I cast a final gaze over the room, my mind racing with the need to erase any traces of the recent struggle. Something caught my eye. Approaching it, I discovered a line of darts embedded in the wall. I pried one loose, noticing some liquid oozing from its flattened tip. It smelled terrible. Had Seraphina shot them at Erin? I carefully pulled them out of the wall, the tips flattened and oozing a terrible liquid. After smoothing the wallpaper the best I could, I stashed them in my pocket.

Although not perfect, I thought it would at least pass a casual glance -- if you looked at it with squinted eyes, maybe. I set the ChronoSpace for our suite and transported Erin there, tucked her into our bed, and returned to the professor's room to tidy up his bed. A sudden discovery struck me as I glanced at the sheet.

"He got chocolates on his pillow? We didn't get that."

* * *

Professor Albert Cardnell
Titanic, Atlantic Ocean
10th April 1912

At 9:15pm, Professor Cardnell returned to his cabin after a satisfying dinner. Although not his initial plan, it would have been impolite to leave his well-wishers after Mr Devereaux's mysterious appearance and winning the chess game for him. Who knew that so many shared his love for the game?

A prickling sensation raised the hairs on his neck. He quietly shut the door behind him, letting the steward return to his post with the master key, and scanned the room. His eyes narrowed, having noticed the curtains. He had shut them earlier before leaving Veranda Café, a nighttime habit he'd followed since childhood. At least, he thought he had.

Striding across the room, he adjusted the drapes, avoiding a glance through the crack at the dark outside. As a child, he had dreamed about a monstrous female demon standing outside, leering at him through a fanged smile. Some dream-based fears never fade, even in adulthood. He turned and viewed the suite from a different angle, wondering what else he might detect. There it was.

His gaze fixed on an irregularity in the wallpaper's pattern, glaring at him from the side wall. Intrigued, he stepped closer, discerning a linear pattern in the spacing of the holes. Each mark was roughly 6--10 inches apart, as if following a deliberate path. Placing his fingers on them, he gasped in surprise upon discovering they were actual holes. His probing digit revealed a depth of a half inch for each one. Closer inspection revealed that someone had attempted to obscure them by smoothing the surface. A weighty foreboding settled on his shoulders like an ethereal creature lying, waiting.

The idea drove a shocked gasp from him. He stood, scratching his trimmed beard as he contemplated the findings. Someone had been here while he was out. But why would they move the curtains or hammer holes into a wall? Curiosity collared him as he created a theory in his head.

Housekeeping staff might enter a room, but that didn't fit his theory because they had no reason. However, he wasn't like other guests. He carried a secret for delivery to the

United States. Someone could have seen through his cover and investigated while he was away. They would have reason to believe he had hidden documents in the room, he reasoned, so they would first search the most likely place: his desk.

He pulled open the top right desk drawer, the most likely place to search first. It caught at first, as though the wood had swelled. He yanked it, and almost fell backwards when it finally gave way. Its sides clattered away to the wooden floor, a heavy Bible dropping too. Then he spotted it, a stain across the golden embossed cross on its cover. Rubbing a fingertip across it revealed a crimson smear that stuck to his fingers. Blood! His heart jumped at the sight as he quickly retrieved a handkerchief to wipe it off.

There had been more than one person here. They had been here together, unless one had a nosebleed. The large indentations in the book's cover indicated something had pressed it or been beaten by it.

A wave of dizziness swept over him, and he grasped the edge of the desk to steady himself. His heart raced, pounding in his chest like a runaway carriage. The innocent voices of young children walking in the hallway outside his door increased his anxiety as he contemplated the situation. He took three deep breaths and fought to steady his trembling hands. His gaze fixated on the hidden package, still nestled where he left it. The realisation struck him like a blow, and for a moment, the weight of danger bore down on him. He had to collect his thoughts, piece together a plan.

He flopped onto the couch, reclining with closed eyes. His heart raced faster with the shock of everything. He had been warned that others would hunt him, and the choice of the Titanic as his mode of transport had been deliberate. Despite its publicity, it seemed the safest option under the circumstances, given its speed compared to alternatives like the Olympia or the Carpathia. The military had opted not to assign him a bodyguard to avoid drawing attention to a single man.

He opened his eyes, gazing upward at the ceiling. Something new caught his focus. He placed his finger on the mark on the couch, then gasped as it absorbed his finger. His eyebrows raised as he sat up to examine it further. Through the hole, he spied the curtains, which he had just fixed. Intuition and logic combined. He sprang from the couch to trace a line of trajectory through the couch, noting the missile's exit through the back. Whipping aside the curtains, he found it. Another dart. Lodged fast in the interior wall, its impact had crushed its tip against the ship's exterior steel hull.

"I say," he uttered to himself as he examined the metallic projectile.

His analytical mind raced through the events of the past 24 hours. Heady from the gravity of his mission and its inherent danger, he felt a wave of dizziness wash over him, causing his knees to buckle. With a surprising suddenness, he found himself seated on the floor, the warning from his military contact echoing in his thoughts. It was true. People were coming after him and his discovery.

A familiar fragrance wafted by, stirring memories of the Veranda Café. Why? Then he remembered the Devereaux couple. The woman had worn it, but why was it in here? Only one conclusion came to mind. Both Seraphina and the Devereaux woman were here. She had been missing from Palm Court during the chess game, and so had

Seraphina. The mystery deepened as he pondered the significance of the darts.

His thoughts turned to Victor, the lovely attractive man with a mind like iron. Yet his will proved useless against the refined steel of Tony Devereaux's mental faculties. Reflection on his reaction to Tony's intervention, which had saved him from defeat at Victor's hands, spoke volumes. He had allowed primal instincts to overcome his better judgement. Pieces of the puzzle fell into place, forming a vivid image in his mind. The clandestine struggle, the distressed condition of the desk drawer, the embedded dart, and the cryptic markings on the wall -- all began to make sense. He had placed his trust in the wrong people.

* * *

Victor Sinclair
Titanic, Atlantic Ocean
9:20pm, 10th April 1912

Victor entered his suite, shutting the door behind him. He cursed under his breath, listening to the steward's departing footsteps.

If not for the watchful steward, he could have used his own skeleton key to enter the professor's room. Instead, the polite attendant cleared his throat and offered an "Excuse me, Mr Hartwell. I believe your room is this way." Under different circumstances, he would have dispatched the steward. All he could do, without jeopardising the mission and his cover, was to follow the steward. Perhaps Seraphina had escaped in time; if not, she would catch up to him there.

But she wasn't in the room. Just a hollow emptiness, the

scent of her femininity like a haunting shade, and the ticking of the clock on the wall. He sat on the bed, dimly aware he could have been making love to her there tonight. Not that they could reveal that knowledge without blowing their pretended guise of brother and sister for the sake of seducing the professor.

The thought occurred that perhaps that was Seraphina's plan. If the professor returned sooner, before dinner, and found her there. She might take that path. The pillow talk could result in revealing the secrets they sought.

He hated the thought. The idea of the bookish man, probably inexperienced with the needs of a woman, with Seraphina, boiled his blood in his veins. There was no worry the man would harm her. The femme fatale was an assassin, a trained killer who could match him in unarmed combat. That's what made them the perfect team.

Victor lay back on the bed, nestling his head on the pillow as he watched the clock's pendulum swing to and fro. Its minute hand traced its way from the 1 to the 6, his eyes barely glancing from it. He sighed. No word. She must still be there.

He shook his head, clearing it, and thought back to the evening. Her words before the chess game came to mind. *Has it occurred to you that we may have competitors in our cat-and-mouse game?* The question had surprised him. Yes, he had considered it. There were the Austrians who would be interested in this man's project. Not just the Germans. And there are the Americans too, but he knew they would be no problem.

The images of Seraphina bedding the professor changed. Now in his mind, she was giving him pillow talk, suggesting they leave the ship together. He could work for her employer, she would say, thinking to keep the bounty for herself. It was too late to disembark at Cherbourg, but they were headed to Queenstown. She has contacts there. They could disappear quickly, leaving Victor alone and with a failed reputation in his employer's eyes.

He blinked. Paranoid thinking would get him nowhere.

No, if there were any competitors, it could as likely be that Devereaux chap. The way he introduced himself, pressed himself into the chess game to defeat Victor with so few moves. How had he not seen that happening? Impossible! Then to follow up with the Knights Tour and trounce him again. It was unthinkable.

Victor's jaw set, his teeth grinding. Now there was an opponent, but was he really a competitor? And if so, could he have been working with Seraphina? It would prove the perfect misdirection. While Victor had been distracted by the foppish Tony Devereaux, Seraphina could have found the formula and left to join with him later. Then they would have to escape at Queenstown before the Titanic takes to the open sea.

Victor released a long breath. It was best he rested for now. If Seraphina turns up tonight with the formula, or even tomorrow, then he would worry less. For now, he could only wait until morning.

Chapter 17

Professor Albert Cardnell
Titanic, Atlantic Ocean
7:45am 11th April 1912

The professor's red-rimmed eyes peered through his spectacles across the ocean, his gaze fixed on the tips of Cornwall's cliffs in the growing distance. He blinked against the glints of sunlight catching from the water's surface and stifled a yawn.

"Your breakfast, sir," stated a waiter, presenting a plate with scrambled eggs in white-gloved hands.

He thanked the server, who acknowledged him with a nod and a smile before leaving him to eat.

Strangely, he felt no compulsion to eat. There was no hunger, not even a slight twinge in his stomach. The same troubling thoughts that had furrowed his brow the previous night persisted into the morning. Out of habit, he loaded his fork with food, but his mind remained elsewhere as he watched the distant shores of his homeland vanish from view. He attempted to recall more innocent days spent in the town of his youth, Tintagel, but found the memories elusive. Instead, the memory of the dart embedded in the wall consumed his thoughts---a stark reminder of the danger lurking on the ship and the urgency of his mission. Nearby, a violinist played 'Autumn' by Edvard Grieg, the melancholic strains evoking a sense of quiet contemplation amidst the uncertainty of his future.

"Good morning, Mr. Thornton," a familiar voice chimed in from beside him. At first, he didn't register that the name was his alias and assumed they were addressing someone else. When the man cleared his throat, the professor looked up in surprise.

"Oh, Mr Devereaux!" he exclaimed with a hint of uncertainty in his chest. "I beg your pardon. I was far away, a hundred miles or more. Good morning to you, too."

Tony Devereaux's eyes appeared weary as he gazed into the distance. England was a fading shadow on the horizon. Then he turned back to the professor. "Is this your first time away?"

"Indeed," the professor replied, finding himself warming again to this man with the Australian accent, almost similar to the New Zealand lilt of his colleague Rutherford. The man's wife beside him looked lovely, so young, with minimal makeup. She smiled at him. "And how are you enjoying the voyage?" he asked them both.

The couple shifted, brief glances exchanged with each other. Although they tried to cover it with pleasantries, their discomfort with something was palpable. Something drew Cardnell's attention to Mrs Devereaux. She offered him a quick smile, but without revealing her teeth. A second later, she diverted her gaze towards the ocean, focusing on a rowdy seagull that floated above the deck.

"Seasickness," Tony explained, his gaze catching the professor's look, "but we're hoping the worst of it has passed."

The professor nodded in understanding, his mind whirring as he processed the additional information. The woman's difficulty in maintaining eye contact with him struck him as odd, especially when he noticed the faint discoloration beneath her facial makeup. Was the port wine-coloured shape a bruise? He hadn't noticed it earlier. While he could assume marital discord, the type where the husband inflicts harm upon his wife, something told him otherwise. The genuine attention the man bestowed upon his wife, and the ease with which she stood by his side, suggested a natural and unforced dynamic.

"Please, where are my manners?" he uttered, standing and pulling out a chair for the fair lady. "Have a seat. Would you like to order anything?" he asked as she accepted his offer and sat.

Both men took their seats around the breakfast table, and a waiter brought them a menu. They briefly perused the menu, ordered fruit for the morning meal, and returned their attention to the professor.

The professor cleared his throat to speak. "I confess I haven't slept last night myself," he said, observing his companions. After a pause, he added: "Despite the comfort of the suite, it's larger than my room in London. I couldn't help feeling as if someone were in the room with me."

Did the woman's eyes flicker with guilt? Granted, she was uncomfortable, but it didn't look like seasickness to him. Not if she ordered the fruit, anyway.

"It must be," Mrs Devereaux replied, her voice steady and firm. A strength existed in her, a steady confidence unlike anything he had seen in a woman before. She looked back at him, her blue eyes steady as they gazed into his. "But it's as much the voices of people passing in the hall outside. The sound carries."

"Speaking of sound," Cardnell said, allowing a smile as he gestured towards Mr Devereaux. "You missed a daring demonstration of chess from your husband last night, Mrs Devereaux. Did he tell you about it?"

She smiled, her hand reaching for her husband's. "He is a man of many surprises," she admitted. "I didn't even know he played."

"Indeed?" The professor's eyebrows rose at that. He turned to Tony Devereaux with a benevolent expression. "I didn't get a chance to thank you. The way you saved my skin on the game was astounding. Where did you learn?"

"Online," the man replied, then paused, his eyes shifting towards his wife. Was that a flush of red in his cheeks? He stumbled for words for a moment, then answered, "I mean, from books and tutorials. I've always had a fascination with the game and spent a long time studying various strategies and tactics from chess literature." He took a deep breath and let it go.

"What did you mean by online?" the professor asked and watched as the man hesitated in his answer.

"I have a condition," Tony answered at last, taking his time to speak. "Sometimes nonsensical words blurt from my mouth. It's a kind of tic, especially when I am tired."

"I see," Cardnell replied, taking a moment to digest the information. He had read about the work of a French neurologist named Dr Georges Gilles de la Tourette in 1885. "My apologies for inquiring. However, I appreciate your assistance. Your demonstration of the Knight's Tour impressed me, not only in following your own while blindfolded, and tracing Mr Hartwell's journey, too. Truly astounding."

Tony nodded, then stopped, his eyes narrowing at something near the door. The woman followed his gaze, making the professor turn to see the subject of their conversation.

Victor Hartwell emerged from around the corner. His dark eyes scanned the deck as he strode past, giving them a mere glance. Passing along the deck's railing, he afforded another look as though gazing past them, but something told the professor otherwise. Then he continued his journey back towards the bow along the port side.

"Seraphina's not with him," the professor noted, "and he doesn't look happy."

At the mention of the woman's name, Mrs Devereaux's grip on her glass of water tightened enough to spill it. A surprised cry came from her lips as she tried to mop the small splash from the table cloth. The professor offered her a smile. "Never mind. It's just a drop."

Tony leaned forward towards him, his eyes fixed directly on him. "We have to talk, Professor."

Cardnell flinched at the title, his stomach tightening as his instincts cried at the discovery. He tried to cover, stammering. "Professor? I'm definitely not that."

But his breakfast companions only smiled. This time, Mrs Devereaux leaned closer, close enough for him to recognise the scent that had lingered in his room. Yes, of course. She had been there. This was the moment of truth. "Professor Cardnell, isn't it? Don't bother denying it. We know who you are. We mean you no harm, but we must talk. Let's talk in private, yeah?"

* * *

Professor Albert Cardnell
Titanic, Atlantic Ocean
8:20am 11th April 1912

The news filled Professor Albert Cardnell's head. It felt like it might explode with the shocks. His capacity to endure was uncertain. He almost wished he hadn't come back to their cabin to listen. He never expected to hear such an incredible story or witness the peculiar inventions.

"By Jove," he stammered, wiping his brow with a handkerchief from his jacket. "You're spies from the future?"

Tony Devereaux's admission, corroborated by his wife Erin, astounded him. While he had expected spies to follow him onboard the Titanic, vying for his secrets, he had not appreciated it until now. The cat and mouse games had become real.

"We're not exactly spies," Tony replied, his voice tinged with uncertainty as if he were searching for the right words. "We're from the future, tasked with protecting your formula from falling into the wrong hands. In 2019, evidence of your creation came to light. Our government is concerned about the potential consequences if it were to be misused. We know you went missing on the Titanic. Our mission is to ensure your formula remains safe."

"From the future," Cardnell echoed, his voice sounding lost in a dream. "This is reminiscent of an H.G. Wells novel."

"I've met him," the other man blurted out. "An intelligent man, although surprised when I appeared in front of him near the Thames."

The professor's mouth dropped open. "You have met the author? When?"

Tony shrugged, thinking, his gaze lost. "1888, I think. Not sure now. I'd have to check my records."

"Twenty-four years ago?" The professor's voice carried more than surprise. It held disbelief. "That's impossible. You appear young, not a day over thirty."

"Actually, it was last year for me," Tony replied with a boyish grin. "That's the thing about time-travel. Life is not entirely linear, jumping around from point to point."

Mrs Devereaux clapped her hands and gained their attention, her gaze unwavering. "Stay on point, boys," she interjected, then directed her gaze to Cardnell. "Here's the thing. Victor Hartwell's companion was in your room last night. So was I, but solely to protect your formula from her. We fought, she died; I barely lived to tell you. Victor's still onboard, likely looking for Seraphina. He may believe her to be dead and is undoubtedly seeking your formula, too. He works for the Germans. Your life is in danger."

"Can I be certain you're not collaborating with them and deceiving me?" Cardnell wanted to know.

Tony calmly responded, "Because we haven't killed you," leaving the professor speechless as he recognised the undeniable truth and sensed no hostility in Tony's statement.

"Yes," he stammered, a foolish grin forming, "I am grateful for that."

"But it gets worse." Tony replied, fiddling with his left sleeve as he spoke, covering the peculiar-looking device he called an iBioPad. It had flashed glowing images of archive photos to him earlier. "The ship will have others onboard soon. I've met them, and they're as dangerous... if not worse. At least two come from the future. One is from the second world war."

"Second world war?" the professor echoed. "Good God! How many will there be?"

"The first war is in three years' time. The War To End All Wars," Erin chimed in, her voice fading as she noted the irony.

Professor Cardnell nodded thoughtfully, attempting to process the information. "I understand. We can't allow my formula to fall into the wrong hands." His heart quickened with the implications of such a scenario. Then a realisation struck him. "When you mentioned my disappearance, what would be the reason behind it?"

"Because you are likely to die," Tony replied, empathy in his voice as the Professor felt dizzy at the revelation. "Records don't indicate exact details, but my guess is Victor or the others find you. We can't let that happen."

"Will they kill me?"

"Or you die when the Titanic sinks," Erin replied, a touch of impatience and pragmatism in her voice.

Chapter 18

Victor Sinclair
Titanic, Atlantic Ocean
8:40am 11th April 1912

The morning's earlier events consumed his thoughts as he idly gazed at the dolphins' graceful swimming below. He had arrived before the passengers disembarked at Queenstown. Only seven had left the ship. None of them were Seraphina. Familiar with her disguises, he was certain she hadn't double-crossed him that way. No betrayal, no early departure with the formula. It was still onboard, and so was she, unless.

He sensed rather than heard the approaching footsteps only when someone coughed.

"Good afternoon," a man's voice chimed from beside him.

Turning, he faced three unfamiliar passengers: a woman and two men. Their demeanour was serious, almost aloof, their eyes gleaming with intent. But was it trust or treachery? "Good afternoon," he replied with a nod, turning his attention back to the ocean to avoid talking. Unnecessary talk would distract him from his important dilemma.

"We know who you are, Mr. Sinclair," the tallest of the three spoke, his voice low and steady. "And we know why you're here. We are on the same side."

Victor's mind raced. How could they know his true identity? He kept his expression neutral, hiding the turmoil within. Trust or treachery? He needed answers.

He turned back to them, taking in their appearance. The

tallest man caught his attention first. With a blend of light-brown hair peppered with vibrant orange flecks, he bore a striking resemblance to the Devereaux man, yet there was an air of authority in his demeanour that set him apart. Victor narrowed his eyes at him. "Do we know each other?" he asked.

His chess rival's lookalike shook his head. "This is our first meeting. I am Heinrich Schneider." Indicating his companions, he introduced the woman as Isabella D'Aubigny, a fair beauty with mesmerising green eyes that sparkled with intelligence. For a moment, Victor equated her with Seraphina, despite her French accent. The other man, bald and an inch shorter than Heinrich, appeared massive, his suit barely concealing his colossal frame. Introduced as Hans Hoffmann, he had piercing, bright eyes that Victor interpreted as burning with a sadistic light.

"The rain in Spain falls mainly on the plain," Victor said, quoting the first call-phrase as an identification. It was crucial to gauge their reaction and determine their allegiance.

Heinrich's gaze flickered, lips twitching before he replied, "Except when the west wind blows." Amusement touched his voice, but his eyes remained guarded. "Satisfied? Such a cliché."

Victor noted the slight shift, sensing a hidden game. He glanced around, ensuring no one else paid them any mind. The stakes were too high for mistakes.

"Seraphina is missing," Victor stated bluntly.

"She is of no concern," Heinrich responded. "What about Professor Cardnell?"

"He's here, posing as Albert Thornton, an architect."

"Follow us," Isabella said, her French accent mesmerising like a perfume against her high-cheeked beauty. "We have much to discuss."

She turned and led the way. The men hung back a second, their attention turned to Victor, who decided he would follow. He had not seen such independence in a woman since Seraphina.

As a group, they passed the other passengers, who were enjoying the sun's relief against the cold winds on the deck. Once onboard, they made a beeline for the opulent first-class area, where a steward promptly escorted them to Isabella's suite.

As they approached, Victor noticed a commotion down the hall. From the cabin emerged Professor Cardnell, accompanied by two more passengers who trailed closely behind. Victor subtly tapped Heinrich on the shoulder, silently directing his attention.

The couple that followed the professor caught Victor's eye, and his heart skipped a beat as he recognised them: the Devereauxes. In a fleeting moment, their eyes met, conveying unspoken tension and rivalry. A slight flinch from Mr. Devereaux caught his eye as he focused on him. This brief exchange confirmed Victor's suspicions: the Devereaux couple were indeed his rivals and were already in pursuit of the same target.

Victor glanced at Heinrich. His new ally appeared composed and unperturbed by the encounter. Without hesitation, Heinrich led the way into Isabella's room, followed closely by Hans.

Meanwhile, Victor could sense the Devereauxes heading further down the hallway towards the Professor's cabin.

With a sense of urgency, he hurried inside, closing the door behind him.

"Who are the man and woman with Professor Cardnell?" Heinrich asked, sitting at the table in the suite with one foot crossed over the other's knee.

"The man calls himself Anthony Devereaux. He may prove an impediment." Victor took a seat opposite Heinrich, noting that the room's features closely matched his own in appearance. He refocused attention on his host. "I suggest we take the documents now. They're likely to have moved already towards the cabin they left."

"All in good time, Mr Sinclair," Heinrich responded, his accent almost matching that of a New Zealander. "We happen to know that a reasonable distraction will happen, engineered by Fate. We can take advantage then, taking the professor and the documents, and kill anyone who tries to stop us."

* * *

Electronic Diary of Anthony Nowlan
Titanic, Atlantic Ocean
12:55pm 12th April 1912.

My heart skipped a beat upon recognising Stan. The man whose visit had sparked this whole thing. Until now, everything had seemed dangerous enough.

We locked eyes for a brief moment. He undoubtedly took notice of the professor with us, but no visible signs of recognition registered on his face.

"That's him, isn't it?" Erin said in a low voice that I doubt she wanted him to hear. The uncertainty in her words reminded me she hadn't seen him for maybe ten months by her time. But his memory sat fresh in my mind.

Meanwhile, the professor had caught sight of his own nemesis, Victor, with Stan and their entourage. He audibly gulped.

"Come on," I said to them both, my mind racing as I realised why Stan hadn't reacted to seeing us. In his relative timeline, he hadn't yet met us. This was one of the first times he had seen me. "Stay calm and follow me," I added, taking each by the arm and turning in the other direction down the hallway.

"But my formula." The professor pulled back on me, but I held my grip.

"It's safe for now," I replied confidently.

"How do you know?" Erin asked, and I sighed to myself.

"Because they'll still be looking for it on the night of the 14th April." I checked no one was about before I added. "That's what happened when I first came back. They were checking the professor's room then and discussing the Difference Machine."

"Difference Machine?" Surprise crossed the professor's face. "What's that?"

"You mean you don't know?" I asked. Surprised, I glanced at Erin, then at him again. A lady with three noisy children passed us in the hall, and we waited until they were beyond earshot. Cardnell shook his head, and I explained: "I assumed that's the name of your invention. They said it when I listened to them..."

The professor looked around us. Seeing no one within earshot, he replied, "No! My invention has no name yet, but it dilates gravity and time, and manipulates it like an elastic thread. It can stretch or it can compress."

The explanation overwhelmed me as I tried to fathom its meaning until a lightbulb flickered in my mind. "You're describing gravitational time dilation," I said, excitement building inside me. "But that won't be confirmed until 1959 by the Pound-Rebka experiment."

Both Cardnell and Erin gave me curious looks before my wife said, "Can we not talk in the hallway?" Her stomach grumbled. "I'm hungry, and if everything is still safe in our rooms, let's get something to eat."

As we walked, the corridor gave way to the opulent surroundings of the First Class dining saloon on D-Deck. Opulently decorated with wooden panelling, painted white, and blue linoleum tiles with an elaborate red and yellow pattern, it reminded me of an old CWA hall my grandmother frequented to play Bingo when I was a kid.

We chose a table that seemed safe from other ears. Although that proved difficult, Erin said the chatter of the other diners would more than cover our conversation. I accepted the idea with some hesitation. Our time-travelling counterparts could have espionage tools to help filter out sounds if they listened, but maybe I was overthinking it. With proper equipment, they could breach our walls, making nowhere safe.

"I've thought about it," the professor started after the waiter had taken our orders and departed. "You can take my formula, but only on one condition."

Erin and I exchanged glances. "What's that?" she said.

"If you can truly travel time," he replied, pausing as a lady pressed past us to reach her chair at an adjacent table. "Take me with you."

I hesitated. I wanted to do it, and I know someone who'd

appreciate the man's intelligence like me. But it couldn't work. "I'm sorry, we can't."

A look of resignation crossed his face. He nodded. The poor guy. If he didn't die when the ship sank, the enemies onboard could capture or kill him. "It could change future history, maybe for the worst," I added as an explanation.

"Wait a minute," Erin interjected, prompting us to look at her. "It's okay, professor. We can take you."

"Erin!" I exclaimed, then dropped my voice. "If we do..."

"History can change; we might end up being ruled by lizards," she responded, cutting me off. "Are you listening to yourself and actually thinking?"

Aware of the professor's gaze on me, I nodded. "Yes, of course. It could even affect what happens in Australia's history."

"Think again," she said. "We don't know what happens to Albert. There are no records of his fate. Nothing definite at least."

"But..."

"No," my wife insisted in a voice that told me I would soon learn I was wrong. "Remember where or when I came from? And what about my mother? Or *your* migration?"

The penny dropped as I saw Erin's point. She was referring to her origins in the 1600s before I brought her forward in time. I had done the same for her mother, saving her from a witch trial. It hadn't changed history because it had already happened. Then there was my case to prove her right.

"You're saying we wouldn't be changing history?" I asked.

"See?" she said with an angelic smile, fluttering her eyelids. "Now you're thinking."

Albert's eyes lit up. He began to speak, then stopped as if afraid to ask.

"Yes," I said, amused, as hope returned to his face. "You're coming with us."

"Damned straight, he is," my wife replied.

At that moment, I recognised the moment in my wife's image. It was the instant captured in the photo Cutter showed me before the mission. I tapped my glasses to preserve the image on its camera. She looked so beautiful. I did it for our future selves, when we are old and wrinkled.

I offered a hand for the professor to shake. "After lunch, let's pack your things and blow this Popsicle stand."

A confused expression crossed his face. "Popsicle stand?"

"You're coming to 2019 with us," I confirmed. "One way or the other. I suggest we make this our last meal before the journey."

Chapter 19

Victor Sinclair
Titanic, Atlantic Ocean
1:40pm 11th April 1912

He didn't care what Heinrich had suggested. That formula was his mission. Perhaps they did know about him, his real name, and his purpose on the ship. But he wasn't unknown in his circles. They may have been looking for him, intending to distract him from his goal or stealing it for themselves. While the story of the Titanic's upcoming sinking might be true, they could have been revealing their own plans for the ship. Their story was too wild for him to believe.

Under the guise of returning to his suite, Victor had slipped away from the trio and headed to the professor's cabin. He had glimpsed Cardnell, disguised as Thornton, leaving the Devereauxes' suite, but his intuition told him to investigate the target's cabin. Answers would surely be there.

And there were more than he could have known. Holes in the wallpaper stood out to him like makeup on a burlesque dancer's face. They imprinted the wall deeply, puncturing the panelling. He identified them. Dart holes from Seraphina's wrist shooter. Capable of firing with compressed air, they were a silent method of killing someone; efficient too. He deduced by the line that she had been shooting at a fast target. He had found another hole in the sofa but couldn't find any of the darts. Someone had already removed them, but was it his partner? Something told him otherwise.

His eyes narrowed, studying the carpet, and stopped. There was something. A stain. While faint and dried, he recognised it. Blood. But to whom did it belong? He took a breath, calming his mind as he took in the evidence, building a picture of what had happened.

If Seraphina hadn't left the ship, she must still be onboard, either alive or dead. Considering the circumstances, Victor suspected Mrs. Devereaux's involvement in her disappearance. Her absence from the events in the Oasis Room seemed suspicious, especially since seasickness didn't seem plausible while in port at Cherbourg. He knew he needed to adjust his plans, disregarding Heinrich's and the others' intentions. As he pondered, a click at the door caught his attention.

With a racing heart, he dashed for the first hiding place he could find: the nearby ensuite. There he stepped behind the bath curtain and hunched in the bathtub.

Voices floated through the bathroom to him. At first, he didn't recognise them for the other sounds in the hallway. The door shut, muffling outside voices and ship sounds, and he recognised Mr Devereaux's voice.

"Okay, get the formula and your things, Professor," Mr Devereaux said. "We have to leave as soon as we can."

The professor's footsteps came closer, suppressed by the carpet, then louder on the bathroom tiles. Victor held his breath, staring straight at the plughole. For some strange reason, looking away from a target can stop them from perceiving you as easily, even when sneaking up on them. The professor fumbled at some things in the bathroom cabinet. Probably a toothbrush. "I can't believe this is happening," Cardnell said. He was close, close enough that

Victor could have reached through the curtain and broken his neck with a quick grasp.

"Where is the formula?" Devereaux asked from outside in the lounge and study. "In the safe?"

"That would be the first place they would look, I imagine." The professor's voice faded as he quit the bathroom, then amplified a notch from the other room. "But to be safe, it's in two places. I would never have guessed Seraphina to be a spy, however."

"Oh, she was," Mrs Devereaux's voice responded, and Victor detected an undertone that confirmed his suspicions. The two women had battled each other. "But no more. She was here to look, and I suspect she would have next seduced you too if she couldn't find it the first time."

Victor nodded to himself. That was the plan. His eyes widened as the woman continued.

"But too bad. She couldn't have been more wrong about you, right?" she said with a hint of irony.

"Whatever do you mean?" Cardnell responded.

"Oh, come on," Mr Devereaux said with a knowing chuckle. "We can tell a mile off. You're a homosexual."

Victor's eyes widened at the revelation. He had suspected it, but hadn't considered the idea plausible. Their research hadn't revealed that information. Then he shuddered at the thought of the alternative plan. He would have preferred shooting Cardnell than lying in the same bed with him. It had been hard enough knowing Seraphina would do the deed.

"A Uranian," Cardnell said in a correcting tone. "But how could you tell?"

"Where and when we come from, it's common and open for gay people to be out," Mr Devereaux replied. "You'll see."

"Gay?" Cardnell asked. Victor realised he had silently worded the same thing in unison. "What has being happy got to do with my secret lifestyle?"

At this, Erin Devereaux laughed. "That's right. Gay means happy in this era, but in the future it means... Uranian or homosexual." Victor's eyebrows raised at the way she said it. What did she mean by *this era*?

"Are you sure Seraphina would have tried to seduce me?" Cardnell asked, his voice drifting back toward the hallway door.

"She'd do anything to escape her brother," Mrs. Devereaux sneered with disgust as they exited the room, closing the door behind them.

Victor waited until he was certain they had left before emerging from the bathtub. Emotions churned inside him as he processed the revelations. Seraphina had indeed been here, and she hadn't betrayed him. Relief warred with sadness and anger over her death. What had they done with her body? How had they disposed of it?

As he left the ensuite, Victor's mission was clear: locate the formula, eliminate the professor and the Devereauxes, and then navigate the voyage without his adversaries. A sound caught his attention.

His gaze flicked to the desk. What had he heard? Ah, there it was again---the faint sound of something shifting.

Approaching the large desk, Victor noticed a drawer that had been hastily repaired. But the noise had come from elsewhere. He glanced behind the desk and a smile curved his lips. How intriguing.

***

Electronic Diary of Anthony Nowlan
Titanic, Atlantic Ocean
1:45pm 12th April 1912.

Professor Cardnell groaned as I swung open the door to our cabin, his frustration palpable. "I forgot the envelope," he said under his breath, shaking his head in annoyance. "Silly me, it sometimes happens when something distracts me."

Erin and I exchanged exasperated looks. I could guess what else Erin was thinking as she shook her head. It was the same expression she showed whenever I forget to take out the wheely bins on collection night. "Well, I guess we can use the exercise after that luncheon," she replied as we followed Cardnell back to his suite.

"I appreciate your positive outlook, Mrs Devereaux," he said with a sheepish smile. "And your patience."

Instinct surged within me upon seeing Victor with Stan. I recognised the woman and the monstrous man from my earlier encounter on the Titanic. They must have arrived through time travel. Their connection with Victor was troubling; I pondered how long they had been collaborating.

"Make it quick. The sooner we can leave, the better," I pressed when we reached Cardnell's suite. "Victor has friends, and we are outnumbered."

"Of course," Cardnell replied as I unlocked his door with my skeleton key.

He entered first, Erin following close behind, and I shut

the door. The professor strode straight to the desk.

"We've already searched there," I said, stopping when I noticed the heavy piece of furniture pulled away from the wall.

A triumphant smile on his face, he retrieved a manilla envelope from behind it and waved it high. "Got it!"

I was about to speak, but things changed fast.

Victor emerged from behind the curtains, his expression one of hard-core determination and wrath. Before the professor could react, Victor threw Cardnell aside like a rag doll, sending him flying across the room to land hard against the wall with a resounding thud. As Cardnell fell to the floor, Victor launched an attack on Erin with a punch, but she countered with a block. Her fist connected with Victor's nose, causing blood to splatter, but he shook it off and continued his assault. However, none of his blows found their mark.

I brought him to the ground with a tackle. We rolled in a mass of twisting limbs as the basic combat training came back to me. Although my wife could have handled him, having received the same training with me, I couldn't let him take her. His fist connected with my chin. Stars danced in my vision as his weight held me to the ground. The next thing I knew, he was off me. Erin had stepped in and pulled him off me.

Now they were sparring, trading blows and thrusts. Thanks to our friend from Hong Kong, Erin's training stood well. Victor attacked like a savage tiger, his muscles seeming to bulge against the sleeves of his shirt and jacket as he advanced with a rapid combination. His breath exploded from his nose with each hook and uppercut.

With an economy of movement, Erin parried his practised punches. But his energy was powerful and focused. He had experience on his side.

I spied the chair from the writing desk, where it had toppled to the floor. Kicking, I broke off the two legs and grabbed one in each hand. The first I swung at his head. It grazed his temple as he dodged, drawing blood. His attack slowed, giving my wife a chance to step back. As he turned his focus back to me, I noticed him retrieving something from the bed - his cane. With a swift motion, he transformed it into a sword, aiming a lethal blow at my throat. I barely blocked in time.

The blade sliced the chair leg as if it were a carrot. He laughed, parried my stab at him, and nonchalantly struck at me. I screamed, thinking I was dead, but my pants dropped to the ground. They caught my feet, impeding my footwork. I tripped, falling, and plopped on the polished floor. He advanced, ready to impale me with his weapon, when something flashed in my peripheral vision.

Victor stopped, the red fury fading from his face as he turned pale. He turned his widened eyes to his shoulder. His shaking fingers dropped the cane as he reached for the thing sticking out of his flesh. "Seraphina..." His voice came as a whisper, eyes rolling back in their sockets, before he dropped to the floor.

Standing above him, the professor watched in muted horror, staring at the metallic object in Victor's shoulder. "I'm sorry. I didn't know what else to do. Is he dead?" he asked in a shaky voice. Puzzled, I crawled the brief space to inspect it and found it was a dart. "I found it yesterday behind the curtain. It was in my pocket."

"He is," I replied as I extracted the dart, smiling at the residue of the yellow fluid that dripped from its point. "Poison dart," I answered, showing it to Erin. "I reckon it hit the mark."

She exhaled sharply, her breath hot against my neck as she wrapped her arms around me and kissed me. "I'll let that pun slide." Her words came as a whisper in my ear. "I want to go home." We clung to each other, our bodies trembling.

"Yes, let's leave this place," I agreed, then turned to the professor. "Get your shit together. We're leaving."

Cardnell, still pale from the shock of having killed Victor with Seraphina's dart, rushed to retrieve the folder from the floor. He returned to us, clutching his Gladstone bag, his hands trembling with adrenaline and remorse. "I'm ready."

"Tony, we need to go," Erin said, her voice weary. My legs were shaking from the adrenaline rush. "We have all our stuff."

The urgency in her voice matched my feelings. With a nod, I held her hand. "Come here, Professor. Bring your bag and the formula." As Cardnell joined us, Erin reached out to take his hand. "We're going home," I said, then we jumped time.

Chapter 20

Electronic Diary of Anthony Nowlan
Apricot Corporation, Yeppoon, Queensland.
Australia.
10am 21st October 2019

The sharp scent of disinfectant filled the air, mingling with the faint hum of computers and the soft rustle of papers blown by the ceiling fan's breeze. Overhead, fluorescent lights buzzed, casting a sterile glow over the conference room. I had timed our return precisely, aiming to minimise the effects of time travel on our bodies after Tenner's warning about its toll. Our trusted teammates awaited us: Tenner, our favourite hacker, and Sam Stockwell, whose concerned expression mirrored Tenner's.

Sam's eyes widened at the sight of our bruised forms. "What the heck happened to you?" His voice rose with concern as he dashed to Erin's side to guide her to a chair. Meanwhile, Tenner caught Albert Cardnell in time as he drooped. He was looking green around the gills, his face pale from the trip. Maybe I should have warned him.

"I feel queasy," he admitted, his voice strained and face pale. I grabbed a plastic bucket from the corner that was filled with brooms. Just in time. He vomited the ox tongue and salad he had eaten at the luncheon on the ship. The smell told me it didn't taste the same the second time.

Tenner shot me a frustrated look as she dodged the splashes. "Who's the new friend?" she asked, handing Albert a paper towel to wipe his mouth and beard.

"This is Professor Albert Cardnell," I replied, holding down my lunch too as I hurried to serve glasses of water to him and Erin. "Just sip the water," I added. "Same thing happened to me the first time."

He thanked me, then sipped some, swishing it in his mouth before swallowing. "Where are we?"

"Apricot Corporation," I answered, swallowing some water. "Our workplace."

"Professor Albert Cardnell?" Sam asked aloud, his recognition clear. "Not the assistant professor to Charles Rutherford?"

At the mention of his old colleague, Albert looked up in surprise. "You have heard of me?"

"I'm a fan," Sam replied, taking Albert's hand to shake it. Their grip lasted longer than I expected as they regarded each other. "I read about you in textbooks while studying in university," he admitted. "Not much there, but enough to tell me you did more than they wrote about you."

Albert smiled graciously at the compliment. "Thank you."

Before the two could lose themselves in conversation, I intervened, eager to get started. "Let's see the documents."

"Give us time to fart before we get into that," Erin chided me, then turned to Tenner. "Where's Susan?"

Tenner told her about the week while we were away. She had been helping Susan with babysitting Connor and "Boss Baby," as she nicknamed my infant self. While my son distracted them, I turned back to Albert and repeated what I had said about the documents.

With trembling fingers, he removed the folder from his Gladstone bag and flipped it open. Scanning the sheets inside, he nodded at them. "Yes, yes, this is the one," he muttered, his voice hesitant as he checked his handiwork.

"But don't worry about the last one. It's something else I've worked on, my impossible equation. It's a good thing no one got that one, too."

He handed me the papers. In the background, I overheard Erin talking on the phone to Susan. "Ah, well, I'm glad he's behaved himself for you," she said, then paused. "Oh, another call. It's okay. It's just Jenny calling on the other line. She can wait."

Confident I could work undisturbed by Erin, I spread the documents on the table for closer inspection. They bore similarities to the mathematics underpinning my ChronoSpace, focusing on time dilation within a defined area. What intrigued me most was the way he used gravity manipulation to achieve this effect---a testament to Albert's brilliance. Despite history's oversight and the tragedy of his disappearance from the Titanic, I felt proud to know him and to have rescued him from a watery grave, or worse. There was hope yet for him.

For safe-keeping, I lifted my iPhone from a nearby stand and activated its camera. It flashed at each shot, removing any chance of shadows affecting the picture quality.

A curious expression appeared on Albert's face. He reached a hand for my iPhone, his eyes shining with curiosity as he examined it. "What is this?"

"We call it an iPhone," Sam explained to him in his usual calm tone.

"A phone?" Albert enthused, removing the glasses from his face as he looked closer. "Incredible. It takes photographs too?"

"That and more," I replied, musing over the formula for time dilation, swapping pages from top to bottom as I did.

"Such as?" Albert asked, hesitating as he touched the screen as though afraid of breaking it.

"It plays music, you can play games on it, read the news, or watch it," I replied, my eyes scanning across the second equation, the one he called the Impossible Equation. From what I could tell, it looked incredible, too. It appeared to deviate from Einstein's Theory of Special Relativity, akin to my own ChronoSpace, but different. It appeared to be about two portals, but there was something weird about it.

The two professors, representing centuries of scientific thought, were deep in discussion about the iPhone. Then, something in their conversation caught my attention.

"Incredible!" Albert said, placing it down on the table. "So many things miniaturised into one contraption. Do you know something? The device's flare reminds me of the most curious thing. On the night before I boarded the Titanic, I chanced to see flashes of lightning from the study. Yet there was no thunder, just the strangest sound like a thump, as if something displaced a pocket of air."

"What?" I asked, glancing up from the Impossible Equation, a horrible feeling gnawing at my gut. "What do you mean?"

"Seven flashes of light," Albert answered, unaware of my growing concern.

"Seven? And no thunder?" My voice wavered with a shade of dread. An eerie familiarity wrapped around me as I considered the details: the flashes, the absent thunder, and the peculiar thud. The pattern was too uncanny to dismiss as coincidence.

He shook his head. "No. No thunder," he replied, stroking his beard as he recalled the details. "Rather strange. It had been a lovely clear sky in Southampton that night; I could see all the constellations despite the street lights. Not even a shadow of a cloud."

"And you heard a thump?" Professor Stockwell asked aloud, the tone in his voice signalling he shared my growing concern.

"Why, yes, that's correct," Albert Cardnell replied, his sharp eyes catching us exchange worried glances. "What do you make of that?"

My mind churned, struggling to grasp the implications, while a primal instinct screamed to reject the unsettling truth. Could it be true?

Chapter 21

Electronic Diary of Anthony Nowlan
ASIS base, Northern Territory, Australia.
2pm, 21st October 2019.

After so much time-travelling, I'd say I was finally acclimatising to it. I hardly felt any dizziness at all when I appeared at the ASIS base in the Northern Territory. Maybe it already spun from what I had just learned.

Cutter's office's features melted into solid form around me. He was sitting at his desk, face buried in some documents, his look intense. I cleared my throat. He remained fixed on his task. "Let me guess. You failed to get them."

I held up the folder. "No, here they are."

"Interesting," he said, reminding me of a cartoon character my grandfather used to imitate. His tone made my spine shudder.

I stole a sneaky glance at the document on his desk to see what I could learn. Not enough depth, but enough to make me suspect Cutter knew more than I did about the Titanic. "What do your archives say?"

"That the past hasn't changed," said Cutter, pragmatic as usual.

The absurdity of it all hit me hard. After travelling back to the Titanic, saving the documents, then taking Albert Cardnell from sharing the ship's fate, how could it not have changed a thing? Then came the charge of anxiety as I realised my discovery might be true. Cutter already knew.

"You may have brought the documents to me, but the

Germans have them too," Cutter added, gazing as if into my brain.

"And I think I know how," I replied with a sigh, sitting down. I considered my next words. Although we were working together, I remembered Cutter will try killing my younger self in 2042. Government workers, you can't trust them.

Cutter leaned closer. With his elbows on the desk, he waited with an expectant expression. "Continue."

"When I found Professor Cardnell, he noticed the flash from my phone's camera," I began, thinking on the fly as I spoke. "He said it reminded him of lightning he had seen the night before he boarded the Titanic."

The ASIS agent's eyebrows furrowed, his gaze raising to the side as he listened. I trod carefully with my next words. "The thing is, there had been no lightning, no storm. Clear night," I said, waiting as he thought.

"I shouldn't be surprised," Cutter replied at last. "Tony, we are dealing with other time travellers. If I failed my mission---"

"You'd travel to before the Titanic and steal them," I said.

He shook his head. "That would change history. Stealing the documents before the event would mean you never get them. It could change things in time for whatever future they came from. They'd photograph them."

"The flash looked like lightning reflecting off the walls." Cutter nodded in agreement and smiled at my conclusion. "They still have the documents. Took them to Germany."

"History didn't change," Cutter remarked, his tone heavy with resignation.

"I'll go back," I announced, fired up to fix what I'd missed. Cutter's disapproving shake stopped me. "What?"

Without a word, Cutter slid a photocopied document across the desk. Its cryptic message, written in German, puzzled me. Though I recognised the language, its meaning eluded me. "German cipher the Russians intercepted before Operation Barbarossa," Cutter explained. "The Nazis had plans for a new weapon: a difference machine." He observed the flicker of recognition in my eyes. "Do you know what that is, the difference machine?"

"I heard something on the Titanic between the people with the Nazi officer," I replied, deciding to reveal this nugget to Cutter. "Since our meeting in my office, I thought it was to increase productivity."

He asked me for the documents, thrusting a hand out for the folder. Taking it brusquely, almost snatching it, he flipped it open on the desk. Flicking through the pages, he stopped near the end. His eyes hardened, showing not a hint of confusion. I knew he had come across the second formula. Professor Cardnell had called it his Impossible Equation.

"Know what this second one does?" Cutter asked, his tone rhetorical. His eyes bored into me as I hesitated to answer. I opened my mouth, but he interrupted.

"This is related to your time travel, although I'm unsure how. The difference is it uses a sender and receiver, kind of like using a computer to send an image to another through email or file transfer." An ironic smile crossed his lips upon seeing my jaw drop at his knowledge of the formula and diagrams. "Relax, Brainiac," he said, using my old nickname for his first time. "I'm guessing. The look in your eyes tells me I'm right. Here, I want you to tell me what happens when you put them together."

I took the documents, and after clearing a space on the desk, I laid them out on the surface to take everything in. At first, it seemed out of place. Yes, I understood in theory the first formula, the reason for my trip back to the Titanic. The second was just like he said, a method of sending a solid object from one place to another. Teleportation in its base form.

"This is amazing," I said to myself, loud enough for Cutter to hear and nod. The Caltech guys were working on something similar, or would be in 2032, a version from an old movie. Their method copied the object, recreating it on the other side, and destroyed the original. I wouldn't use it because of potential errors. Cardnell's version was different. It didn't copy; it sent the object directly.

"Your lips are moving, but what are you thinking?" Cutter interrupted me.

I shook my head in amazement at the process. Then I turned to the next part of Cutter's question. What would happen if someone used them together?

"The first formula creates a time dilation, making things happen quicker or slower. The second can transport an object from one place to the other," I replied, giving a shrug, my mind still searching for what Cutter meant.

"Yes," he said. "You can weaponise it. Imagine creating tanks and planes and planes quicker than any assembly line. Now, picture shipping instantly. A military group can place armies at will anywhere in a blink."

"It's like reshaping the chessboard to suit your strategy," I remarked, my jaw dropping in shock.

"Scary, right?" His tone softened. "The Russians knew about a weapon, but not everything. There's more. The Russian archives mention you were there too, Buck Nowlan."

He pointed to another file, and I saw the name: Тони Новлан. So that's what it looks like in Russian. Clipped to it was a blurred photo, but I knew it was me. And other photos peeked from behind mine. I shifted them and groaned with disappointment upon recognising their subjects: Stan Nowlan and Isabella D'Aubigny. My spirits dropped further. Still tired from the recent leg of the mission, I knew what was coming.

"My name's there, too," Cutter added. "We have to help find the secret laboratory and de-"

A blast of heat, debris, and thunder filled the air. The shock flung me across the desk. Papers flew around, obscuring my vision. As the pressure faded, a faint ringing filled the silent void. I realised it had been a small bomb.

Disoriented, I fell. Hands grabbed and pulled me down. My eyelids opened to see Cutter diving between me and two small flashes. His shoulder exploded. Something warm splashed my face. Cutter's weight pinned me down. My limbs refused to move.

The intruder, face hidden behind a helmet visor, aimed at me like a child's pretend pistol. He mimicked a shot, then vanished as alarms blared. Agent Sofia Nguyen rushed in.

"Gary!" she shouted. "Man down! Man down!"

I turned my head. Cutter's mouth moved. I struggled; placed my ear to his lips.

"T-th... Thirtieth... Nov... Twenty... Seventee..."

His eyes rolled back. Eyelids closed. His body went limp.

Chapter 22

Erin Deering-Nowlan
Lammermoor Beach, Yeppoon, QLD, Australia
Evening, 29th October 2019

Erin looked up from feeding Connor as she listened to Tony talking on the phone. Although a week had passed since she and her husband had arrived back in 2019 from the past, her body still ached from the fights. She had hoped it would be over. The unresolved situation was a bad sign for her.

Connor squawked from his baby seat at the table. He opened his mouth wide like an expectant chick in the nest. Like the mother bird, Erin shoved another teaspoon of mashed food past his waiting lips. She loaded another while listening.

"Yes." Tony's voice carried a heavy undertone of resignation. A momentary pause followed as presumably Sofia responded from the other side. The agent witnessed the aftermath of the incident that caused Cutter's hospitalisation. He had sustained critical injuries, but the doctors had thankfully stopped the internal bleeding. Now, it was simply a matter of time and luck for him. "We're ready," he answered, but she knew he wasn't. Neither was she. The mission was still on.

Tony ended the call, promising to meet Sofia and Gary Cutter soon. Erin's heart sank at the idea of another trip back in time. Why did she go the first time? She wondered, her mind drifting to the unsettling events of their previous escapades.

Caught in her thoughts, Erin mechanically wiped a wet

face washer across Connor's soupy lips. Tony's arrival in the kitchen interrupted her reverie, his expression a blend of emotions she couldn't decipher. "Well?" she said. "How's Gary doing?"

"Sofia says he's out of his induced coma. Security's been ramped to the hilt there since the attempt." Tony pulled a chair from the table to sit. His gaze diverted towards their baby son, who was now banging the highchair's table with the plastic teaspoon.

Erin pushed the empty plate across the dining table, her voice firm. "Tony, I'm going to sit out on this mission." She braced for his response, aware that he might say something since photographic evidence showed she had travelled back in time with him to World War Two. He wouldn't want the chance of that possible deviation.

To her surprise, Tony released a relieved sigh. "Good idea," he said, his smile genuine. "After what happened on the Titanic between you and the spy, I want you as far away from that as possible."

Noting her husband's tired expression, Erin reached out and placed her hand on his. It was warm and still felt soft. He hadn't been born to be a spy, cavorting through time and space. But destiny had somehow thrust him into this role. If he hadn't created the ChronoSpace, the device that had ultimately set everything in motion, none of this would have happened. But then they'd never have met. He wouldn't have returned to see his parents, the family he had never known. And she wouldn't have had the chance to meet and marry him, creating their young family. 'Everything happens for a reason. It must serve,' or so Tony's friend from the future, Claire Hilyer, had said.

He returned her squeeze, his smile softening for her. "I don't know what I'd do if I lost you or Connor," he added. "Although I know I have to go through with this, to keep things in balance, I---"

"But you don't," Erin replied, realising that she was wrong. Of course he did. He wouldn't be Tony if he hid from what he had created, even inadvertently. That's what she loved about him.

"I do," he answered, echoing her thoughts. "But I would like us to do something when it's done."

"What's that?" she asked, hope building in her chest.

"I want us to get away, to find a place, anywhere, any time, where we can create our own future."

As the words left his lips, Erin realised he had been planning something. But what? "Whatever it is, we're going to do it together. Just remember, if I'm stuck somewhere like a deserted island, you'd better be there too."

Tony chuckled at that. His mannerisms and nostalgic expression conveyed a lot to her. Not on an island, but in the same metaphorical boat.

He stood and lifted Connor from his seat. "Come on, kiddo," he said to his son, whose eyes lit up at Dad's voice. "Let's have a bath, so Mum can relax, eh?" Father and son then headed towards the bathroom.

The evening progressed. Erin cleared the table and filled the dishwasher, an amused smile on her face as she overheard Tony bantering with Connor during his bath. Their son's giggles filled the house as he splashed in the water. After Tony, now soaked from the bath, took their freshly cleaned son to his room for bed, Erin finally found her moment of respite. She drew a warm bath, dropping a fragrant foaming ball into the water.

She sank into the soothing water, let out a content sigh, and allowed the tension to melt away. Its warm embrace enveloped her, easing the aches in her muscles and calming her restless mind.

Tony poked his head around the door, ogling her with a cheeky grin. He gave a low growl. His eyebrows waggled, evoking a laugh from her, as he knelt by the tub. Their eyes locked together, embracing each other in their gazes, as he reached to brush a stray strand from her forehead. Erin stirred at his touch.

"G'day," he murmured, his voice filled with longing.

Erin couldn't help but smile as she held his hand. "G'day yourself."

For what seemed an eternity, they simply sat in silence, basking in each other's presence. The world's weight lifted off her shoulders. It was just them, together, as he joined her and they washed each other, caressing, manipulating responses with the touch of their fingers.

Later, laying together in their bed, the room washed in the silvery moon's glow through the bedroom window, they held each other close. Strength and comfort conjured from the warmth of their embrace as the night deepened around them. Then, as one, they surrendered to the quiet rhythm of their bodies, their hearts beating faster, until it ended before sleep finally came.

* * *

Electronic Diary of Anthony Nowlan
Lammermoor Beach, Yeppoon, Queensland, Australia.
2am, 30th October 2019.

It wasn't easy leaving my wife behind in our bed, especially in the wake of our lovemaking. Something inside me said that each trip I took in time would bring me closer to the final journey. One day I may never return, according to one of the pictures Cutter had shown me of a mummified corpse with my ChronoSpace.

But I had to do it. To ensure there could be more moments like this, Stan and his mob had to be stopped.

Dressed in my jumpsuit, ChronoSpace secured to my belt buckle, and my iBioPad strapped to my wrist, I checked my equipment a final time. Two tasks remained.

I followed the dark hallway towards Connor's bedroom. There my son lay, a light blanket kicked aside through the night as he slumbered. I reached in the cot and drew it back over his form. "Sleep well, mate," I whispered, committing his image to my memory. If this was my last time seeing him, I wanted to remember it until the end. At least he would have video to remember me by as he grew, hopefully to know me better. My fingers drifted from his tiny hand as I retraced my steps to Erin.

Too beautiful for a memory. She is everything I wanted in a partner. I leaned forward, gently placed my lips on her forehead, careful not to wake her. My body yearned for her again. Something deeper within me echoed the wish. And my heart broke as I stood, taking one last look at her with a silent promise. "Bye, beautiful," I mouthed.

Turning only briefly to check my ChronoSpace's

destination, my gaze remained fixed on Erin. With a deep breath, I pressed the button and jumped. Destination: 2017, after a quick visit to pick up Sofia.

Chapter 23

Electronic Diary of Anthony Nowlan
ASIS, Pine Gap, Northern Territory, Australia.
10am, 30th November 2017.

Sofia gasped as we reappeared in Cutter's office. At first, I thought it was the disorientation that comes with it. Then I noticed the room's layout interested her more. She glanced towards the overhead flickering fluorescent lights, then at the wooden desk.

"I forgot how the bulb flickered all the time," Sofia muttered to herself. A large-backed chair behind the desk swivelled to face us, revealing a familiar face. Sofia stared at the younger version of Cutter, who appraised us with equal surprise.

Top points to him, though. He retained his deadpan voice as he lifted a heavy pistol, pointing it at us. "Mr Nowlan, I presume."

In that instant, my heart jumped. This younger version was the man I had thwarted by taking Professor Stockwell away from him that year, believing he worked for the Russian Mafia, like in 2042, before my initial time-jump. Thinking about the timeline and what had happened since, I replied, "Looks like you got out of jail with no issues." He'd know I meant how the police had detained him for questioning around Erin's disappearance, which had occurred three months prior. He didn't yet know it was a time travel accident on her part.

"Thanks to Erin returning." He remained relaxed, keeping his weapon on me. It brought back memories, something horrid, which I couldn't reveal to him. "Imagine my surprise upon my release to receive a message signed by you," he continued, retrieving a slip of brittle paper. "Dated 1945, too. Is this a joke?"

Sofia moved to step forward. Cutter diverted the pistol towards her, and she stopped. She raised her hands, palms outwards. "Gary, it's me."

"Is it? You should be in Yeppoon surveilling Mr Nowlan here."

"She is," I said, as Sofia echoed the sentiment. She shot me a dirty look, so I took the hint and shut up.

"At this moment, I am. My younger self, that is," my companion responded, her voice easy and calm.

Cutter pondered that for a second, then turned back to me. "I presume you time-travelled here, surprising as it is. Can I trust you?"

I reached towards the shoulder strap of my backpack. The pistol's barrel flicked to me with the speed of a taipan. "Relax," I replied, my voice tense as I knew his shooting accuracy. "I'm just about to take something from my backpack for you, okay?"

Cutter's fingers tightened around his pistol's grip. He stood from the chair, allowing him a better range of movement. "Proceed, Mr Nowlan. Keep your hands steady and visible. If I see a weapon, I will shoot you."

I gently removed the backpack and lowered it to the floor. "I'm unzipping it," I answered, feeling stupid for narrating something so obvious, but I knew I had to gain his trust. In time, this would help him gain mine, which is why I had prepared for this moment. "Years from now," I stated, opening the backpack wide open to allow visibility for him, "you told me that I gave this to you. Apparently, you will need it to gain my trust again, and I can vouch for that."

"Action, not words," he answered, gesturing with his pistol. "No sudden moves."

As my fingertips passed against the familiar smoothness of the poly-carbon surface, I stared back into the Colt M11's barrel. Another part of me cringed. Should I give this item over to him? There had to be a better way to communicate my trust to this man who felt obvious distaste or something towards me. His whole demeanour reminded me of a bad policeman; the kind who gaslights a witness, judging them as guilty before examining the facts.

Cutter cleared his throat, motioning with one hand to hurry up. His pistol never wavered.

Then I remembered what Cutter, the older Cutter, had told me at our first meeting in April. I had given this to him to prove he could trust me. In turn, I was giving this to him so he could trust me. It was another bootstrap's paradox, a time loop without a beginning or an end. My part in it insisted I keep turning that wheel. I removed the old object and held it out for him to take.

He hesitated. The weapon in his hand shifted as he took it. Sophia moved like a whip and disarmed him, taking the pistol before he could fire a shot.

"Gary, you can trust us," the female agent said, releasing the magazine and releasing the cartridge from the breech.

I collapsed to the ground with a sigh. Cutter gave a derisive snort, smoothly holstering his weapon, then extended a hand to help me up. "This note and package arrived by special courier from MI6. I dismissed it as a mundane jest."

"When did you get it?" I asked, realising I had more work

ahead of me to keep time flowing right. Was it this hard for that TV guy in the blue box?

"After my release from police headquarters when you gave my name as a suspect for Erin Deering's missing status," he responded, presenting me with an old postage time-date stamp dated months ago in March 2017, well before my initial visit. "Photographs and a note inscribed by your hand, it appears. Inconsequential, yet kept for reasons undisclosed. I was tasked with surveillance in Queensland, overseeing Professor Stockwell before your initial arrival, as you know."

"Why trust me now?" I asked, not believing this gift alone could sway him.

"Because I learned your allegiance does not lie with the Russians," he retorted with a dismissive gesture. "Nor do Stockwell's. You executed the instructions verbatim. Precisely as dictated."

Something didn't ring right for me. Too many loose ends. I turned to Sofia, half-expecting her to give a nod of something to confirm. But no clues came from her, not even a shrug.

"Enlighten me on the purpose of your presence," Cutter demanded, smoothly pulling out another chair as Sofia seated herself. "You haven't come to deliver the news of my demise, have you?"

I shook my head and took a seat. "No, thankfully not," I said, then recounted how he met me, sent me on a mission, and why. It took half an hour, with Sofia filling in gaps, both of us careful not to reveal too much about the future. Sofia and I had agreed to keep some details scarce. If Cutter knew the full story, he might change events, like arresting Agent Liam Park before his attempt to kidnap Connor, altering the future and undoing our work.

The only part we chose not to hide was that something had happened to Gary in our time. We came to this date based on what his older self gave: today's date. The Gary Cutter of this time would tell us yet another date to visit, one that only he knows.

"So, Agent Gary Cutter," I said, looking straight into his blue eyes. "You are going to tell us the date to which we will travel."

For a moment, he pondered our words. He pressed his elbows on the desk's surface, steepling his fingers, over which he gazed first at me, then back to Sofia. His eyes measured us as the cogs and wheels of the decision turned behind them. At last, he gave a sigh and referred to the old letter from 1945.

"I have checked the writing on this letter. Your fingerprints match from the glass in the Pandanus Restaurant from Yeppoon." He said with a hint of a smile as he noticed my surprised expression. "Your handwriting matches the letter, which we have authenticated as eighty years old. I'm convinced that you are real, given that I have also found photos of you in the archives from different points of the twentieth century. We should visit Poland in June 1944, Mr Nowlan."

Chapter 24

Electronic Diary of Tony Nowlan
Biala Podlaska, Poland.
4am, 31st May 1941.

Two weeks have crept by since our arrival in this war-torn city. Death lurks around every corner. The echo of Nazi boots serves as a grim reminder of the dangers that surround us. Despite this ominous atmosphere, we have pressed forward, mindful that we are both hunters and prey. Yet the Reaper's shadow looms ever closer, gripping my mind with the realisation that my time may be running out.

Sometimes, gunshots pierced the night, their thunder a flag of terror. No injuries yet apart from my pride when I slipped on a dog turd and landed on my bum.

The three of us navigated the treacherous lanes and alleys with caution. Sofia's presence is a beacon here. Her Vietnamese heritage contrasts with the pale faces of the locals. It draws attention, unwanted scrutiny, from the enemy.

A patrol stumbled upon us last night, their suspicion palpable as they checked our forged papers. One barked something I couldn't understand. Only Cutter and Nguyen caught the words, although the tone spoke volumes. Sofia's efficiency and deadly precision saved us with unchecked ferocity, dispatching them with ease. But one slipped through our grasp to alert his comrades.

Now, marked for death, we were on the run from the Master Race's relentless hellhounds. Our only solace rested in information gleaned from someone we had identified through historical records. We were on our way to meet him at this specific time.

Moonlight reflected from the cobblestones, slick from recent rain, illuminating a thin veneer of steam. Ahead of us, we spotted a flicker of flame. It came to life, revealing a brief sliver of a person's face before it extinguished. A pinprick of red floated from its spot, blazing brighter for a second before disappearing. The smoker had hidden the cigarette behind his back to hide it.

My heart pounded hard in my chest as we neared it. Cutter's hand settled on my shoulder for a moment, calming. No spoken words came. But I knew the meaning: relax, we will handle this.

We reached the end of the alleyway, a dead-end. In an instant, my brain overloaded with panic. I suppressed it, breathing deeply as Cutter approached the man and spoke in Polish. Although I know neither language, the difference is plain. Polish carries more nasal vowels and a rich cluster of consonants. Listening to it was a curious composition of staccato and melody. In contrast, the speech of the Germans was more even in rhythm and distinctly guttural.

Suspicion glinted in the Pole's eyes as Cutter spoke to him. He assessed me, then Sofia, as he replied, his tone cautious and guarded. Cutter must have sensed the same thing and kept his voice steady. Meanwhile, in the glow of a waxing crescent beyond our gloomy location, the tramping of boots on the streets floated on the air to our ears. At last, the Pole gave a nod. Clicks of gun hammers came from different angles. Realisation that they had surrounded us prompted a squirming sensation through my guts.

The Polish man lifted a hand and uttered another word I didn't understand. Then he fixed an eye on me, surprising me with his next words.

"You are safe. Zese are my men. Now, come. I take you."

* * *

Electronic Diary of Anthony Nowlan
Biala Podlaska, Poland.
4:45am, 31st May 1941.

The Polish agent's name turned out to be Piotor Nowak, a member of the Polish Home Army. After a brief stopover in a seedy backroom to receive stolen German uniforms, we were on our way. The streets and alleyways served as grim reminders of the ravages of war. Desolation and despair met us at every turn. Buildings lay in ruin, their heaps a reminder of what once was before the bombing raids. Piles of rubble littered the streets, obstructing pathways. At least three times, we had to double back to take a different track.

The air, thick with the acrid scent of smoke and ash, was choking, reminding me of Ancient Pompeii. And the sound of trucks filled with harbingers of chaos and mad thugs echoed from the broken brick walls. Through the near-pitch blackness, an occasional square of light shows people still live here. Families, couples young and old. But non-Jewish people. What atrocities existed in the Jewish quarters? Did people still live there, or had they left, herded like cattle in trains to their fates?

Yet not all had suffered destruction. Some neighbourhoods bore fewer scars. Some of the swastika flags hung from buildings, torn or spattered with paint. Defiance lives in their hearts. Still, peppered lines of bullet trails score the brick walls. The people's enemy had retaliated n turn with a Draconian iron fist. I wondered if Piotor or his comrades knew those who had died for their defiant displays.

For a second, the idea occurred to me. What if I used the ChronoSpace to travel time, to meet Hitler, then kill him? Would it prevent the destruction and save millions of lives or lose something worse? Is any of this worth it?

At the moment these thoughts presented themselves, another vision revealed itself before us. Beside a crumbling monument, a colourful display stood. A finger of sunlight touched upon a small patch of vegetation. The vibrant hues of beautiful wildflowers blossomed, petals opening towards the light. It contrasted with the obvious grey atmosphere of the city.

Sofia noticed them as well. A fleeting expression of admiration crossed her features with an awestruck gasp. To me, it hinted at a glimmer of hope. Maybe my purpose here would find success, even though I lacked a clear understanding of why I was present. Events since before Connor's birth unfolded rapidly, tossing me like debris on a raging sea. Would this tumult ever cease, and how would I recognise its end?

A tap on my shoulder brought me back to the present. I turned to see Cutter. His grim expression reflected his mind caught on the mission. "Stay awake, Brainiac," he said, motioning me towards the street ahead.

Nazi guards waited at what I took to be the road leading out of Biala Podlaska. They hadn't seen us, but the dawn's growing glow would soon blow our cover.

Cutter described the plan. Reach the German facility, plant

21st century plastic explosives in it, then run like hell. "If we succeed," he said, "then history will continue as intended."

A simple plan, but we are acting against someone who wants to divert time from its course. I didn't believe Cutter understood that. When I said this, he shrugged it off, saying we would deal with that when it came. "I take it you're not soft on your descendant?" he asked me, hinting what it would take. I shook my head in response, although it didn't sit well that I may have to kill my flesh and blood to save my own family.

"Let's work out how to pass those krauts without waking the whole town," he said, readying his pistol.

"We do that," Piotor replied, and I caught sight of a large bow in his hand. A plume of smoke trailed him as he stalked forward towards one of his comrades. After a brief discussion and waving of hands, they split in opposite directions.

Sofia, Cutter and I huddled behind a stone monument fifty metres from the exit. We watched and waited for what would come. The six Nazi sentries stood in a loose formation, their rifles slung heavy but poised ready. The dim light glinted from the sharp bayonets on them. A stray breeze bore their sounds: a muttered comment followed by a gruff laugh from another. Then a bolt of black slashed through the air, ending with a thump. Its end protruded from the head of the man who laughed.

"Vas ist das?" I heard one respond. He soon met a similar fate when another arrow ripped through his throat. Blood sprayed the brickwork behind him as he dropped to the ground. No one else had time to cry out. All six fell. No sound alerted nearby patrols, and none came running as the soldiers lay crumpled on the stones.

"Come on!" Cutter's voice hissed in my ear as he lifted me from my crouched position and urged me forward.

We sprinted across the space towards the gate, careful to avoid slipping in the crimson pools that haloed the dead men. It took a hard run, carrying the stolen uniforms on our backs, and my legs cried by the time we crossed the small field beyond the gate into the nearby forest. Only Piotor and his friend Aleksander remained to guide us through the dense woods to our possible target.

* * *

Electronic Diary of Anthony Nowlan
West of Biala Podlaska, Poland.
5:58am, 31st May 1941.

After an hour of navigating through dense foliage, we finally reached the forest's edge. Piotor, our guide, signalled to stop. A lit cigarette still protruded from his mouth. Its long ash refused to drop from the main cancer stick. Each time he moved, I expected it to drop, but it remained like the last autumn leaf to its branch.

"We are in proximity to the Belarus border," Cutter whispered to Sofia, who nodded in response.

Piotor stepped to Cutter and spoke in his unique dialect. My companion nodded, answered in a similar vein, and moved his hand. After a brief exchange, Cutter replied with a nod. Our Polish guide roughly shook my hand, then Sofia's, before turning and heading back the way we had come.

"This is the end of the line for us," Cutter explained,

waving off Piotor and Aleksander. The pair disappeared like wraiths through the tendrils of fog amongst the ferns. "Piotor mentioned the existence of an ingress point to a German installation. They had observed the ingress of trucks carrying individuals, distinct from detainees or military personnel."

"Probably scientists," I surmised aloud. Cutter responded with a nod, then pointed north. "We're heading that way about 100 metres, but we change into the Nazi uniforms first."

We unpacked the uniforms, each finding one that fit, and changed into them. Fifteen minutes later, we had repacked our equipment ready and were heading northward. It didn't take long before we reached the edges of a barbed wire perimeter. A gap of about fifty metres separated our hiding space from the perimeter and guard towers. Although dressed in the clothing of Nazi officers, not mere soldiers, we dared not leave our cover yet. If someone stopped us, what excuse did we have for our whereabouts?

With the upcoming attack by the Germans on the Russians, patrols roamed this area more frequently. It didn't take long before one passed our way. As they approached, we stepped out from cover, feigning to refasten the buttons on our trousers as we did. Sofia muttered something about it, and I took a casual step between her and the Germans' eyes. It was enough to hide her gender without obscuring the sign of her uniform's rank.

Cutter stepped forward, barking at them in a harsh guttural tone, "Achtung!"

The nearest trooper shouted a hasty "Jaworl" as he hastened to attention. His comrades followed suit, heels clicking. With a set jaw, Cutter stalked behind them, finding whatever small thing he could find wrong with their appearance. Each gave a disappointed look as he pointed out either a piece of grass on their shoe, a smudge on one's face, a wrinkle that looked too crumpled. It was gutsy, and my companion acted his part well. If not for the tiny bead of sweat clinging to his brow, I would have believed him myself.

He uttered another order with equal conviction and the four guards marched forward, leading us towards the gate's entrance. The two sentries attending snapped to attention as we passed, saluting with their hands outstretched. I looked forward, avoiding eye contact for fear of blowing our covers.

As we parted ways with the guards, I couldn't help imagining their relief at our departure. On one side of the compound lay a horror I had only seen in photos, old movies, and documentaries. It was the foreboding sight of a concentration camp. Timber barracks formed in a line served, I believe, as the housing for those fated to die a terrible death, a small mercy for a horrific life's ending. Even Cutter found himself drawn to the appalling site of terrors. Only Sofia pulled our attention to what lay in a different direction: a compound of concrete built into a mountainside.

"Is this the place?" I asked Cutter, careful not to be heard by a passing soldier.

"Remain composed and self-assured," he replied, taking a step forward. "Emulate my demeanour and refrain from direct eye contact."

We followed him into the cavernous space, our eyes searching and taking in all details around us. Mine sought the Difference Machine and anything else that looked out of place.

Everywhere I looked revealed something related to a scientific experiment or research at this end of the gaping cathedral of horrors. In one quarter, I spotted what looked like diagrams and twisted wires and metal for a vintage V2 rocket. But this wasn't vintage; it was here and now in 1941. Still, it wasn't just the V2 rocket that caught my attention. It was an entire section filled with completed missiles.

My gaze traced the corridors lined with assembled V2 rockets, each mounted on a Meillerwagen, primed for towing. The sheer scale of the operation hinted at meticulous planning and extensive time for assembly, likely aided by the use of nearby concentration camps for slave labour. While the Germans had previously deployed these rockets in their assaults upon Britain, the sheer volume before me far exceeded any previous efforts. There was only one conceivable explanation for this alarming accumulation...

Cutter's voice interrupted my thoughts. "I am of the opinion that we have arrived at our destination," he declared in his typical deadpan manner.

I turned to see him and Sofia standing awestruck at something else beyond the corridors of V2s. Looming there in the darkness, it waited. Lights flickering like blinking eyes from the gloom.

"Holy crap," I whispered, quickening my pace alongside the arsenal of potential destruction. As we neared the cavern's end, the air thickened, smelling of machinery and damp concrete. My heart raced at the corridor's terminus as I beheld the sight.

The Time Dilation and Difference Machines both loomed before us, their portals emitting pulsating blue and red light. The energy surrounding it crackled with intensity, causing distortions in the surrounding space-time, like ripples on a pond.

"That's it," I whispered, not daring to believe our luck.

Sofia and Cutter exchanged glances, their expressions mirroring my mixture of apprehension and determination. With measured steps, we edged closer to the machine, the sound of our footsteps muffled by the vast expanse of the compound.

The air grew thick with the smell of machinery and dusty concrete. Every step echoed in the cavernous space, amplifying the dread creeping over me. The dim lighting cast long, ominous shadows that seemed to reach for us from the walls.

"Stop right there!"

I spun around to see a group of soldiers emerging from the shadows, their rifles trained on us with chilling precision. My heart sank as I recognised the familiar figure leading them---Stan Nowlan, flanked by Hans and Isabella.

"Stan," I exclaimed, the word heavy with disbelief and betrayal.

His eyes bore into mine with a mixture of contempt and triumph, a cruel smirk playing at the corners of his lips. "Well, well, well, look what the cat dragged in," he sneered. "Tony Nowlan, the man who started everything we have achieved."

That stung. Conflicting thoughts and guilt battled in my head. Yes, I invented the time-travel technology, but I wasn't responsible for this madness. Without my invention, no one would have misused its secrets. Stan wouldn't have been born.

"Don't pout, great-great-great-something-granddaddy," Stan chided, signalling for a Nazi goon to approach and disarm me.

I swallowed hard, struggling to maintain my composure in the face of his taunts. Beside me, Sofia and Cutter tensed, their hands inching towards their concealed weapons, but I knew that resistance would be futile against the overwhelming force before us.

"Stan, what are you--I mean, why are you doing this?" I demanded, my voice strained but defiant.

He chuckled darkly, gesturing towards The Difference Machine with a sweep of his hand. "Oh, this?" he mused. "Let's just say it's the key to our glorious victory. And you've delivered it straight to us."

My blood ran cold in contrast to the heated anger within. We had walked straight into a trap, but who could I blame for it?

Chapter 25

Electronic Diary of Anthony Nowlan
West of Biala Podlaska, Poland.
5:58am, 31st May 1941.

"Frisk them," Stan ordered Hans, his tone carrying a subtle disdain as he glanced briefly at the towering figure beside him. Hans stood with a confused look, his head cocked to the side in an attempt to comprehend the command. For a moment, the 7½-foot tall giant hesitated until Stan added, "Search them for weapons."

As Hans began to pat me down, I couldn't help but notice his puzzled expression. It reminded me of encounters I had in the future. Back in 2042, I once met a perceptive boy on a bus who claimed he could recognise time-travellers by the way they "shone." The memory sparked a thought: Did Stan's peculiar condition draw Hans' attention to him similarly?

Hans removed my iBioPad, his face full of awe as he checked out its design. Then, as his large sausage-shaped fingers undid the ChronoSpace from my belt, recognition crossed his features. His eyes turned to my face as he studied me. "Hey, I know you!" he exclaimed. "You're the man we tied up on the Titanic."

Stan rolled his eyes. "Hurry up, oaf!" he snapped, stabbing a finger in Cutter's and Sofia's direction. "Search them for guns or anything else they have as weapons."

Hans' bottom lip drooped. "Okay," said the gentle giant with the deadly hands. A nervous giggle escaped his lips as he patted down Sofia, his hands lingering around her chest and hips. Fourteen weapons he found on her. Each discovery met with a childlike chuckle. Dropping them on a nearby table, he glanced back at her with a mix of awe and excitement. Before long, he came to Cutter. This time he checked quicker, but still as effective in his search.

Keeping a watchful eye on us, Stan picked up my ChronoSpace and turned it over in his hands. "Interesting," he noted. "This is a different case to the one you had when I met you and your wife."

I said nothing but dropped my gaze towards the device on his own belt. So too, I noted the one on Isabella's belt beneath her German overcoat. Yet none could be seen on Hans' self. That information found a special place in my head as Stan issued a command to the German soldiers whose machine guns pointed at our bellies.

"You know, I know that I'm not your son," I said to our captor with a hint of defiance.

Stan's laughter reverberated from the walls of the cavernous space. "No shit, Gungadin," he replied, his voice dripping with sarcasm. "But you have to admit the family resemblance is strong, right?"

"You talk too much," Cutter interjected. That drew Stan's attention. He fell silent, a confident look on his face as he lifted his iBioPad to my companion's face. A thin green beam from the device scanned Cutter's facial features before a holographic image appeared.

"Gary Cutter, I see. The real one too, not the one I..." Stan paused as he read the glowing blue writing that floated before his eyes. The text scrolled upward, then stopped as he pointed at a section, opening his fingers to zoom in. "Well, that's interesting," he muttered, then turned to compare what I realised was a photo of the older Gary

Cutter, not the younger one with me. "It seems my mission here may actually succeed, since there is no way I am letting you escape."

"Yak, yak, yak," I said. "Hasn't anyone told you you talk too much?"

"Maybe my mother," he replied, closing in on me until his face was inches from mine. "But my daddy did... before I killed him." Something strange and unsettling glinted in his eyes, making me shut my own mouth as he revealed shiny white teeth in a wide vicious grin. His hot breath on my skin made me flinch. Despite this, he remained close, watching me with eyes as cunning as a shithouse rat. "He wasn't so easy to kill, but it proved satisfying in the end. The man always pops up, though, like a case of herpes."

"Spoken from experience?" I enquired, trying not to laugh, though I overheard Isabella suppress a snort. So did Stan. Too late, I realised that making a woman laugh at him was a mistake.

His fist smashed into my face. Dazed, I dropped to the ground, where he continued to kick me. I heard the soldiers bark at Cutter and Sofia to remain still, while more blows battered me until I felt dizzy. The coppery taste of blood lapped across my tongue. Hans lifted me by the collar until my bruised face was level with Stan's angry eyes.

"You won't laugh at me when I tell you my plan," Stan hissed, spittle flying from his lips. "When I am firmly in control of Germany and lead them to victory, no one will laugh at me."

As blood filled my mouth, I pondered what to do. I couldn't swallow it, nor could I spit it back at Stan for fear of a reprisal. We needed to know his plan, so said nothing. My bleeding dribbled from my mouth, splashing onto the stone floor. I hung my heavy head to mask it, but he grabbed my hair and held me up still to give me a leer. "Take them to the cells."

I managed to keep on my feet as the guards urged us forward with the machine guns in our back. My left eye was swelling. It hurt to blink and I couldn't open my eyes properly. Through my other, I noticed Cutter's sideways glance at me. He offered me a brief smile, which I took as encouragement.

Although he said nothing, I could sense the wheels turning as they herded us from the cavernous space down a corridor carved from the rock. Wires had been connected along its ceiling as a string of bulbs that emanated a dim glow.

"Mind if I guess your plan, Stan?" I asked, spitting the last bit of blood to the side. He offered a silent nod in response. "It's audacious, but here's my stab. You plan to alter the course of World War II in favour of the Nazis. Changing their destiny at Operation Barbarossa seems your likely best bet right now. You're going to use time dilation to boost productivity of the V2 rockets, maybe even warplanes and Panzer tanks too. Power of numbers, yeah?"

Stan stopped and turned towards the soldiers, giving them an order in German. They stopped urging us forward and waited for further orders. Their weapons remained trained on us. My descendant gave a slow clap of the hands with a mocking smile. "Not bad. The apple hasn't rolled far from the tree." He stopped himself there as if measuring his words, then continued: "Germany needs the lands in the

USSR to further its cause, for farming and industry. Dilating time will optimise our selective breeding program, to create perfect humans in every way possible. No sickness, no ailments, no undesirable elements. A better life."

I cast a sideways glance towards Hans when I noticed his weight shift. An idea came to mind.

"And what of Hitler, your Führer?" Cutter asked in his characteristic deadpan manner.

"Hitler? His problem the first time was that he lost the war. I will win it myself." The words came with such cool, confident conviction that it shocked me. "I have other plans for him."

Beside me, Hans grunted. I turned to him. "Hans," I said, making eye contact. "How do you feel about this? Creating a race of perfection? Killing those Stan or Hitler see as undesirable? Too skinny, too large, too slow to think, too different?"

Hans' expression turned to shock. His eyes shifted and a tiny muscle in his jaw bulged for a brief moment. I held my breath when his gargantuan fingers balled into a fist. He was about to hit me, I was certain, so I shut my eyes. But the blow didn't come from him.

A rifle butt crashed into my guts. Another into my back. A pain in my head. Darkness took me.

* * *

Electronic Diary of Anthony Nowlan
West of Biala Podlaska, Poland.
8:58am, 31st May 1941.

As I gradually woke in the darkness, a throbbing headache

pounded in my skull. Confusion clouded my mind as I tried to piece together how I had ended up in this unfamiliar place. Only a moment earlier, I could have sworn that I was with Erin and her birth mother. Although I couldn't remember the conversation we had around that kitchen table, the taste of the tea still lingered in my mouth.

A greater shock hit me when I realised my head was bald, completely shaven. I gasped to discover it was almost as smooth as my baby son's backside. Well, not quite that smooth. Tufts of hair still stood out.

Cutter's voice floated through the blackness to me. "Are you awake, Brainiac?"

Darkness brightened a little, and I realised why I had trouble seeing. My eyelids were swollen, obscuring my vision. Sharp pain shot through my nose when I touched it, probably broken.

"Your cousin, or whoever he is, broke your nose," Cutter explained, his face blurry but recognisable through my inflamed eyelids. "I set it back the best I could."

Sitting up slowly increased the dizziness, and I dropped back onto what must have passed as a pillow of sorts. As I glanced down, I realised that my clothes were missing, replaced by a set of coarse, grey flannel pyjamas that seemed straight out of a bygone era. The fabric felt rough against my skin, and the loose fit only added to my discomfort.

A thin-sounding chuckle pealed from across the room. Looking in its direction revealed an old man in similar garb. Only the wrinkles and lines carved in his face hinted at his age, reminding me of Patrick Stewart in one of his final films. In a sober voice, he uttered something in Polish. "What did he say?" I asked, my voice strained.

"He says they'll take your clothes soon," Cutter translated with a tinge of resignation in his voice.

My jaw dropped at the unspoken meaning. "Why did he laugh?"

"Because when your back's to the wall, and all seems lost, it's the best thing to do," my companion replied with an uncharacteristic wink. Cutter's jaw tightened, his eyes betraying a flicker of concern beneath his usual stoicism. It dawned on me then that even the unflappable Cutter's spirits were low, worn down by our dire circumstances. He had been awake longer than I, therefore his spirit had suffered, unlike mine, while I had been unconscious.

"Could be worse," I muttered, trying to sound more confident than I felt. But deep down, I couldn't shake the sinking feeling that our situation was far from ideal.

Cutter's eyes flared in anger. He pressed me against the wooden wall with a clenched fist. I snaked my hands up to guard. "Hey, settle, Gretel," I said. "Laughter is all we have, right?"

The ferocity in his face dimmed back as he released his grip on my collar. "Yes," he said, his deadpan tone returning. "You said before we came here that we had already done this."

"Remember the letter you received before my arrival?" I asked him, and he nodded, wheels turning in his head. "It was dated 1945 in my handwriting. I haven't been there or then yet."

It took him a moment to consider that, with eyes not focusing on anything as he did. At last, he gave a nod.

"Then I will trust in that," he conceded. "Good is yet to come."

"At least they haven't given us tatts," I offered in weak jest, hoping to lighten his spirits.

At that moment, the sound of boots reached our ears. They marched closer until they stopped, muffled somewhat by a barrier I couldn't quite detect in the gloom. A key clunked in a lock, and a door squeaked open, scraping against the cell's floor. Dim light filtered through the doorway, silhouetting the Nazi guards who entered, kicking us to our feet and ushering us out with harsh words. A surge of fear gripped my chest as I stumbled out the door and down the hall and into the blinding sunshine.

Blinded temporarily, I tripped and staggered as the rough treatment continued. They led us towards a solitary building, distinct from any other I had seen. Adrenaline flooded my stomach, curdling my intestines and their contents, as I noticed the absence of witnesses. I anticipated the worst was imminent.

But they led us past the building towards a waiting van. There, they forced us to undress. If someone was slow, they ripped the thin clothing from us. My fingers trembled as I disrobed, feeling exposed and vulnerable in the harsh sunlight and under their gaze. I exchanged a worried glance with Cutter.

A guard barked an order at us. When we hesitated, the old man from before received a vicious blow to the shoulders. He shouted in pain, slowly raising his arms. Catching onto the foreign command, I lifted mine to the sky too. "Why are we doing this?" I asked Cutter. "Why are we raising our arms?"

Guards ushered us into the open rear doors of the vehicle, pressing us in tight.

"It is to pack us in tighter," Cutter explained, gasping as our flesh pressed together. This would have been uncomfortable in normal circumstances, the contact between two or more males. This situation was noticeably hellish. For then, I realised the practicality of overcrowding us with our arms raised. It reduced the amount of air in the tight space. When they start the gas, it would kill us quicker. I cursed the Nazis for their efficiency.

"If you know how we'll get out of this," Cutter complained as the doors slammed on us, "do it now."

Before I could respond, the ominous rumble of the van's engine roared to life, drowning out any hope of escape. The stifling air thickened, grew hotter still. A wave of panic gripped all of us. I heard my screams joining their fearful chorus, a few minutes away from death's door.

Chapter 26

Electronic Diary of Anthony Nowlan
West of Biala Podlaska, Poland.
8:58am, 31st May 1941.

Panic erupted in the back of the gaswagen amongst us. With roughly 20-30 of us in that airtight compartment, we knew time was short. It wasn't just the oppressive heat of our bodies together. A wave of dizziness washed over me. At one point, knowing my fate, I tried to hold my breath. But it was no use. The chaotic terror, the jostling of naked figures, and the deafening screams overwhelmed me sooner. The next lungful affected me worse than the first. Dizziness dropped on me like a heavy cloud as the odourless gas lulled me into a suffocating slumber. Through it, I sensed a man's weight increase as the strength left his legs. Our crammed positions held him up, but as more succumbed, their bodies dragged us down.

Only one thing could do this in a van, I thought to myself. Exhaust fumes. I hadn't even known such things existed. Did this barbaric invention inspire the suicide method employed in my grandfather's time? Or did war imitate life in a sick way?

Next to me, Cutter staggered, his eyes glazed with fear and confusion. I would have reached out for him if my state had allowed. The airtight cabin's darkness grew blacker still as I felt consciousness leaving me. Sensations soon left my awareness. Even the throbbing of the van's engine faded into obscurity as I felt myself tip for a last time.

Suddenly sunlight streamed into the van as the doors burst open. A sudden rush of cool air filled the chamber. A few bodies tipped and rolled out the door. Through blurred vision, I saw a monstrous creature catch and extract them from our chamber. With great effort, I lifted my head to see better, squinting against the harsh light. But his features eluded me.

With amazing strength, the male figure hoisted Cutter and me from the gaswagen. Fresh, clean air flowed through my nose. Already my senses sharpened upon realising that I was in the open. Cutter coughed, so did I, and we greedily sucked in more refreshing air.

"Who is that?" Cutter asked, coughing up something before spitting it on the ground. Though his voice was weak, his spirit remained strong.

"It's Hans Hoffmann," I croaked in disbelief.

In the meantime, our saviour hurried, helping the remaining prisoners from the van. Once finished, he turned his attention to those who had brought us here: the guards and drivers. Their bodies lay strewn about the place. I watched in awe as the man single-handedly picked them from the ground, muscles bulging through his shirt's material. Two at a time, he flung them eight feet away in a perfect arc to land with a thud in a deep trench I hadn't seen.

"That could have been us," I muttered loud enough for Cutter to hear and nod.

Once finished, Hans turned towards us. "We must move fast," he said, his voice low and urgent. "Time is short."

Cutter and I exchanged wary glances, avoiding lower gazes, then I said, "Hans, we need clothes."

The gentle giant slapped a pan-sized hand to his face with an exasperated groan. "Dumbkopf, dumbkopf!" he uttered aloud, slapping himself repeatedly each time. He would have continued if I hadn't stopped him with a hand on the shoulder. "I am sorry," he said in a pathetic tone. "I didn't mean... I am idiot." He was about to resume when I stopped him.

"Hans, it's okay," I replied, seeing again something of the kid from my past. "Thank you for saving us. You did good."

He removed a hand from his face, revealing large wet eyes like a Manga cartoon character's. "Really? I did?"

"You were magnificent," Cutter responded, having regained his deadpan voice again.

"You just had a lot going on, right?" I offered him a grin, putting my hand out to shake his. With a moment's hesitation, Hans regarded my hand before accepting it, careful not to squeeze too hard. As we shook hands, a smile spread across his face, reflecting his excitement.

"Ja! I had much happening." Hans giggled, pumping my hand harder until the shoulder hurt. When he saw me wince, he started to apologise again, but I stopped him with another reassurance.

"Seriously, though," I said, looking him in the eye, which was hard as he towered over me like a certain big, green bulky hero from the comics. "Do you think we can get some clothes from those bad men?"

"Mean men," he said. "They would kill me for being different."

Just as I realised how my half-baked desperate plan had worked, the sound of branches breaking and undergrowth stirring amidst footsteps reached us. We turned, ready to fight in the raw, when a group of armed men and women emerged from the vegetation. The leader bore a strong familiarity to us. Piotor!

He greeted us with a smile. Cutter approached, and the two exchanged pleasantries and conversation. A few other men stepped forward, offering longer jackets to a couple of the prisoners. Two young women, probably in their late teens, giggled amongst themselves while stealing glances in my direction. I tried to appear nonchalant, attributing it to the chilly morning, and covered myself with one hand, opting for two to be sure. The older of the two, a brunette, approached and offered me her jacket. I reached for it, but she deliberately dropped it before I could grasp it, prompting me to bend down to pick it up. A playful slap on my arse resonated through the trees, followed by laughter from some of the other resistance fighters. She winked at me as I tied the jacket around my waist to conceal things.

"Sorry, spoken for," I announced, catching Cutter's smirk as he glanced over. "But thanks anyway."

Piotor stepped forward, including me in the conversation with Cutter. "Come. We disconnect ze exhaust from ze van so you can ride in back. We take you to safe place."

* * *

Electronic Diary of Anthony Nowlan
West of Biala Podlaska, Poland.
12:58pm, 31st May 1941.

The resistance members took us back through the forest in the vans. After a lot of bouncing around, we stopped and stepped out. Sunlight filtered through the branches, casting a dappled pattern on the ground below. Tree trunks were adorned with patches of light green moss. If not for the atmosphere of war and the urgency in our mission, I would have wanted to hang around longer.

Our rescuers soon separated the rescued Jews into groups. The first for those willing to stay and fight with the resistance. This included those whose family had died and had no one else to live for. Piotor made sure they understood, explaining the risks. Close to half nominated for the role. Those who wished to reunite with family, who had evaded the Nazi claws, split off in a different direction. It included those who wished to leave the country, which is as risky.

Cutter and I joined the first group and trudged through the forest, our bare feet making the journey more challenging. Piotor was good enough to be patient, sending some fighters ahead as scouts. Twice we hid when a patrol came, our hearts racing as we waited for them to pass. Otherwise, we had no incidents.

At last, we reached the forest's edge and ventured upon a lush green countryside dotted with fields of wheat, corn, and sunflowers. Rolling hills nestled a meandering river beside which stood a tiny village overlooked by a church with a tall spire that loomed above the roofs.

"Come!" Piotor said, leading us through a nearby wheat field.

At last, we arrived at the village's outskirts, feeling tired and sore. The resistance divided us into three groups and escorted us to houses deemed safe by Piotor. He prided himself on having weeded out the collaborators and Nazi sympathisers early. "We still have some who claim they support the Germans," he confided to Cutter and me. "But they are there for show. Smoke and mirrors to defy

Hitler and provide him inaccurate information."

He led Cutter and me, along with Hans, towards a rustic farmhouse of wood with a thatched roof and shutters with faded paint. I guessed it had once been vibrant upon sight. Wartime would have changed all that. Smoke followed him like from a train as he walked to the front door. He pushed it open and nodded, his eyes friendly as he invited us in. "Welcome to my home," he uttered in a deep voice, ushering us inside to the main room.

There we found a large wooden table at the centre, surrounded by mismatched chairs. A single oil lamp hung overhead from the ceiling, casting a warm glow that illuminated the room. Faded photographs of scenes from rural life and, presumably, family adorned the walls. From the side wafted the smell of fresh baking. And sitting at the table was a familiar face.

"Sofia!" Cutter exclaimed, somehow still keeping his deadpan voice. She stood up and came over to shake our hands.

"I see you missed visiting the hairdresser," I said, grinning as I noticed her with a grin as she gripped my hand.

"Hans helped," she explained, looking past me towards the front door where the gentle giant was stooping to fit inside. At the mention of his name, he gave her a shy grin, his face a gentle crimson.

"Nice lady looks different too," he said in his broken English. "Hitler wants to kill people who are different. I had to save her."

"Glad you didn't shower," Sofia added, taking in our changed appearance. "Otherwise I couldn't return this." She produced my ChronoSpace and iBioPad, along with a couple of other things for the mission.

With a sigh of relief, I thanked her, taking them in hand and strapped on my iBioPad. She turned and spoke with Cutter while I checked my device's security logs. Built in 2042, its security and biometric measures are better than the smartphones of 2017. I was worried that Stan or his friends might have accessed it after taking it from me. The logs turned out fine, showing no access. But I did see someone tried 8 times before it locked further attempts by pass-code. My Electronic Journal is already being updated, extracting my memories via electrodes in contact with my skin.

Once satisfied that all was well, I checked the ChronoSpace and found no tampering. Hooking it up to my iBioPad, I further verified its firmware and operating system. Its checksum passed inspection. Further inspection on the other tech equipment I had also showed up all clear. At least we aren't trapped in time.

Cutter noticed my satisfied grin as I returned to the table. "Is everything in order?" he asked as I sat, and I gave him a nod. "Excellent. We are just discussing our updated plan."

"A new plan?"

Cutter took a deep breath as he considered everything before speaking. "By now, they would have detected our escape. According to my estimation, they would be aware of the absence of the vans. Your gadgets have vanished, Sofia as well, and the absence of Hans won't go unnoticed. Your grandson, or whatever he is, despite his arrogance, isn't a simpleton. They will anticipate our next move. Security would have undoubtedly escalated by this point, perhaps even doubled or tripled. Continuing would be tantamount to suicide."

My brow crinkled as he laid it all out for me. "You call that discussing a plan?" I asked in disbelief. "It sounds like you're giving up."

Sofia interrupted, her voice placid and precise as she spoke. "No! There is a way."

"Please illuminate," Cutter said, his expression thoughtful as he watched his fellow ASIS agent.

"Comrades," Piotor interrupted, his tone a mix of benevolence and something that reminded me of a fatherly manner. Considering his age, about mid-fifties, he may well have been old enough. He gestured towards us with a sweep of the arm as he continued. "We've all had a big day. You're excited, but ya gotta eat and rest. My eldest daughter, Ewa, she's been preparing her late mother's recipe for pierogi. Please, it would honour us if ya enjoy the meal first."

Each of us paused to consider his words. My stomach growled, reminding me I had not eaten since lunchtime yesterday. Cutter's eyes were swollen from fatigue, unlike mine, which still hurt. That was enough to make me feel tired, too. Even Sofia nodded at the idea.

Cutter released a sigh, which I took as tiredness. He hesitated, wanting to keep going, like a child who refuses to sleep. With a resigned voice, he replied, "That is prudent. Let us dine and repose. We can deliberate later tonight, but we shall depart tomorrow morning."

Chapter 27

Electronic Diary of Anthony Nowlan
West of Biala Podlaska, Poland.
7:58pm, 31s May 1941.

Last night, Cutter was all for taking another trip into the Nazi base to blow it to Kingdom Come. Piotor shook his head at the idea; he said their guards would have increased, expecting a return. But wasn't quite what Cutter had in mind.

"If only we could be there before we initially arrived," he said. I caught onto his meaning and why he said it that way. He didn't want to give away our secret weapon of time travel to the Resistance. "We could plant charges on the Time Dilator and the Difference Machine and finish before we start."

I shook my head and explained the issue with that. It would create a paradox. If the base blew up before we arrived, we could create a paradox. Cutter raised an eyebrow at that, so I made it clear. "We could damage the fabric of time and space, or cease to exist."

"What is zis Time Dilate and Difference you speak of?" Piotor wanted to know, cocking an eyebrow, a fresh cigarette propped in his lips.

"The Nazis's secret weapon," Cutter explained, earning him a dirty look from me. "Relax. He needs to know about that," he rebuked, then sat back, steepling his fingers close to his lips. "And we need to know more about their layout."

"I can help with that," Sofia answered, drawing our attention to her. "Or at least, Hans can."

Upon hearing his name, Hans glanced from the hearth where he was playing with Piotor's granddaughter. She had arranged daisies in his hair. The flowers seemed comical on this man, whose history as a killer I had read, a man who could crush a skull with one hand. "Ja?"

"We need you to tell us about the base," Sofia said in a friendly voice. We had heard how he had rescued her from the cell and taken her away to safety. Their camaraderie was clear in her tone, and I suspect he held a crush for her.

"Okay," he replied, coming over to us and kneeling at the table. Chairs couldn't support his weight, and on his knees, he still towered above us. "What do you want to know?"

Cutter drew a rough map on a sheet of paper, including the mountain, the forest, and the Jewish prison camp. "Tell us what you know."

Hans cast a quick glance over everything before shaking his head and flipping the paper over, revealing it to be a poster for Nazi propaganda. His gaze hardened at the sight of Hitler's likeness printed with a message I couldn't decipher. With a snort, he turned the sheet to its blank side. The sound of the pencil scratching filled the room as we observed him sketching a map of the area. Cutter's eyes widened, and he exchanged glances with us as the rough outline transformed into a detailed map and illustration of the area around the base. Once he finished, Hans leaned back with a smile, watching Sofia like a dog seeking approval.

"This is wonderful work," she said, sensing his need. "Thank you, Hans."

The gentle giant had captured the layout of the facility nestled within mountainous terrain. A simple gate depicted the entrance, surrounded by rough lines representing the barbed wire fences and guard towers. Underground tunnels and chambers formed the hub, with sections cut away to reveal the layout within the mountain. In each of three areas, a copy of the Time Dilation machine stood. That made sense to me; they didn't have a system yet to operate everything from a central control.

The first section showed the breeding program facilities as a hospital ward, a classroom, and a nursery. While we hadn't seen it, we noted it was in an area next to where we had found the V2 rockets stored. If we had progressed further, we would have found them and the food production area closer to the other side of the mountain. Stick-figures and crude outlines of guards and fences showed the prison camp's position.

Cutter made a low whistle as he examined everything, his keen eyes flicking back and forth. "Three Dilation Machines," he uttered in a thoughtful tone as his finger traced passageways. "We were only expecting one."

"What powers them, Hans?" I asked the gentle giant, who had since taken to drawing a perfect likeness of Sofia. At first, he didn't answer, but looked up with a questioning expression when I prodded him again. "How do they get the electricity for it all?"

He slapped his forehead with a hammy hand. "Oh! I forgot," he said, and took a pencil to the diagram, adding a building. "They use the star people to run the power station. They shovel coal."

"Jewish labour," Cutter muttered. "This gives me an idea. We blow up the power station and the three chambers. Timers for the power station as a distraction while we blast the rest."

"But the children!" I retorted.

"Nazi bred," Cutter confirmed with a nod. "Best to kill them before they grow up."

"No!" I replied, thinking about the babies in the hospital rooms and the nurseries there. Yes, there were propaganda and facilities to train those children to be killers, but... "Children are children."

"You can't kill the little babies," Hans said, his voice escalating. "They can't help it."

Sofia and I both nodded, and Cutter looked at us all. He took a breath, the wheels working behind his eyes again. For a moment, I wondered how this murderous streak originated in him, then I remembered his pragmatism. Shaking his head, Cutter gave a sigh. "Okay, we'll play it your way, but it's still war."

* * *

Electronic Diary of Anthony Nowlan
West of Biala Podlaska, Poland.
11:58am, 1st June 1941.

We enjoyed a lengthy rest in a concealed chamber beneath a hidden trapdoor in Piotor's barn. The sun was already up when we woke, alerted by the mooing cows at milking time. Our host knocked twice on the trapdoor, our signal that it was safe, and we emerged from below. We worked chores to repay his hospitality, then did a workout before tucking in to a hearty breakfast.

Later, we revised the plan, making certain that we would keep Hans in view. Despite his actions saving Sofia, Cutter still harboured suspicions about him. I hope he's wrong.

The lovable juggernaut reminds me of Frankenstein's monster, from the movies. To me, he seems a simple man who sometimes mixes with the wrong people, who soon exploit him. They made him do terrible things in exchange for feeding his desire for inclusion. Now he's realised it's worse than he thought.

Tonight, after dark, we are taking a truck into the forest. From there, we will visit the Nazi base. I'm nervous about it and hope this is my last time-trip for some time, that it will succeed. Being away from my family is murder. I'm about to sleep now, recharge myself before we go.

Electronic Diary of Anthony Nowlan
West of Biala Podlaska, Poland.
9:58pm, 1st June 1941.

The mission started well. Piotor's son-in-law took us in the truck to the forest's edge. The moon, now a night away from its first quarter, cast curious shadows from the overhead trees. The dappled shapes seemed to ripple like a disturbed pond as we trekked through the forest.

We took a different path this time towards an alternative entrance. This brought us closer to the section for selective breeding. Only two guards stood by it. While one lit a cigarette for the other, it was a simple matter for Cutter to apply a choke hold on one. Sofia took care of the other, but something was different.

"Did you break their necks?" I asked Cutter as we headed inside.

"Was there a loud crack?" he responded. When I shook my head, he shrugged. "That's good enough for me."

Then I caught Hans' eye, and he nodded a yes. I gulped. So, movies always make it a dramatic crack, not the dull snap I heard. How boring. Meanwhile, Cutter and Sofia moved deeper down a corridor lit by dim lights. That left us to complete our part.

"This way," Hans said, his voice a whisper, and led me down a side corridor that followed the mountain's contour.

The lighting surged as we pressed forward, casting a stark brightness over our surroundings. The concrete walls took on an antiseptic sheen reminiscent of a hospital's sterile confines, chillingly out of place in this grim setting. As we reached a corner, Hans's grip on my shoulder tightened, a silent warning to remain silent. I froze, my senses on high alert, awaiting his next move. "Wait here." His voice was a whisper, filled with a dangerous edge. "I will handle them."

I was about to poke my head around the corner when he stopped me. "No!" he mouthed, his whisper exploding like a pop of gas in marshlands. Once certain I would do as instructed, he loped down the corridor. A harsh guttural word of "Halt!" reached my ears.

Figuring he was far enough away not to notice, I poked a mini-camera around the corner. I watched on my iBioPad's screen as Hans stood above two Nazi sentries. They seemed to know him as they conversed. While I couldn't tell what they said, I understood when Hans' hands struck like twin snakes for each guard's throats. With great ease, he lifted them each into the air, dodging the wild kicks from their feet as they tried to scream. But no screams came. Only a gurgling from each as their windpipes relented to the pressure from their attacker's grip. A moment later, each red-faced man's head fell forward in a faint. Hans held on, looking into their eyes, a disgusted expression on his face before dropping them.

They landed in a crumpled heap against the wall.

Shocked, I darted back behind the corner, hiding the mini-camera in my pocket. My heart beat a furious tattoo inside my chest as I realised what I had seen. A second later, he emerged from behind the corner, a calm look on his face. For a second, he regarded me with an impassive look before saying, "I did a bad thing. But I did it to bad people. That is good?"

I glanced at his large hands, realising the power in those deadly fingers. No way was I going to argue with him about that, so I nodded. "Yeah, mate. All for a good cause," I replied, forcing myself to deliver a calm smile.

The expression in Hans' eyes shifted to one of relief and comprehension. He nodded and pushed open the doors leading into the breeding program's section. Recognising my lack of a weapon, I retrieved a Luger PO8 pistol and its holster from a deceased guard. I left the submachine gun behind.

As we passed through the main doors, a sight of sheer horror greeted us, causing my jaw to drop in mute shock. The air was heavy with antiseptic, underscored by an unmistakable aura of malevolence. Rows of pristine white beds stretched out before us, each occupied by a pregnant woman. Some appeared well-rested, embracing their role for the Fatherland and the Master Race. Others seemed less at ease, but resigned to their fate. For a moment, I couldn't help but imagine the possibility of one of these women being my wife. The mere thought sent a shiver down my spine. What if this were to happen in 2017 or 2042? I recoiled at the idea, thankful that it wasn't the case.

Nearby, nurses clad in crisp uniforms bustled with an

automatic efficiency, attending to the needs of newborns in the nursery. The sound of a baby's cry echoed off the sterile walls, reminding me of lost innocence through manipulation and exploitation. My stomach churned at this grotesqueness, exacerbated by something else.

They were all moving faster. The women's bellies swelled like balloons, weeks passing in minutes. When they neared term, a nurse and orderlies hustled them away to another room. Soon after, they emerged, carrying newborns. The babies grew into toddlers, then children who attended private tutoring lessons that cycled rapidly. Finally, guards took the young men and women to another area.

I should have been ready for it, the horror of what one might call God's work being manipulated for evil. This had to stop. I knew what I had to do.

Casting my eyes over the expansive area, my gaze landed on the Time Dilation machine for the selective breeding project. Closer inspection revealed a dial. I realised turning it clockwise would speed up the process, anti-clockwise would decelerate it. Hans and I were standing outside the demarcated range, marked by yellow lines on the floor. My mind raced with possibilities. Outright destroying risked early unwanted attention, yet adjusting the dial might raise suspicions or someone could revert it to its original setting. And I couldn't use a bomb in case I destroyed the innocent lives of the children. Then inspiration struck.

A blinking set of lights caught my gaze. Somehow that made me think about looking behind the machine at its power lead. That brought me to the next idea: covert sabotage. Catching sight of the vacuum tubes inside it, I gingerly reached for one. I'd never seen one before, but it looked like the old fluorescent tubes I grew up with in granddad's place. I twisted the tube one way until it popped out.

"They have slowed down!" Hans said with surprise. Panic hit me as I realised someone else might notice, maybe not from within the time dilation zone but from outside. So I moved faster, bending the pins on the tube's end and placing it back as best I could without it being obvious. The other two tubes received the same treatment. Casual observation would not reveal the sabotage at first inspection. To cast further misdirection, I turned the dial anti-clockwise to make it appear a simple deceleration occurred.

"Has anyone else noticed?" I asked Hans. "Any other guards?"

He shook his head. "They are in bed, or outside dead."

"Hans!" I said with a laugh. "You're a poet, and you didn't even know it." His eyebrow rose in confusion until he caught my meaning and laughed.

We hurried out the door before anyone noticed and headed back to the main corridor. There was still no sign of Cutter or Sofia. Thinking we had been quicker, I decided we should split. I suggested Hans stay here out of sight in case the others returned. In the meantime, I would head towards the V2 rockets' area. "But the angry man said stay here," Hans said.

"I'll be right back," I promised as I hustled into the dim passages.

Five minutes later, the reason for the commotion became apparent. Nazi guards had caught Cutter in a deadly crossfire, and I arrived just in time.

The chamber reverberated with crackling bursts of gunfire,

signalling that the weapons production sector warranted far stricter security measures than the selective breeding program. Panic surged through me as I took in the chaotic scene. Where was Sofia? Had she become a casualty in the hail of bullets?

My hand trembled as it sought the reassuring weight of the Luger holstered at my hip. Though I detested firearms, I saw no alternative but to engage in the armed conflict. Without hesitation, I released the gun's safety mechanism and sought cover nearby, positioning myself to gain a tactical advantage.

I aimed, my finger tightening on the trigger, and the shot rang out. The bullet tore into the Nazi's leg, eliciting a piercing scream as blood sprayed the area, and he collapsed to the ground. His machine gun clattered and skittered across the floor, coming to a stop near me. With wild eyes, he turned his gaze towards me, his face contorted with rage. But before he could react, a blur swept past my peripheral vision.

A moment later, a massive hand gripped him by the helmet, lifting him off the ground as his legs flailed. With a sickening crunch of metal, his helmet and skull collapsed under the force of Hans' powerful grasp. Hans flashed me a grin before moving on to engage another pair of soldiers.

A sudden loud whistle pierced the air, followed by the crackle of a PA system. A familiar voice, that of Stan Nowlan, barked orders in English. "Cease fire!"

An instant calm fell over the area, providing respite for my still ringing ears. I cast an eye around, looking for my nemesis. From my vantage point, I spotted Cutter reloading his weapon. He spotted me too and gestured to my right. Unsure what he meant, I shrugged.

"Tony Nowlan!" Stan's voice barked. "Come out now. But drop your weapon first. You too, Agent Cutter."

"Not by the hair of my chinny chin chin," I retorted, glancing at Cutter, who was now covering his face and shaking his head.

From behind a dozen crates, a confident figure in Nazi officer uniform strode. Beside him was a female officer, Isabella, guiding three prisoners at gunpoint towards the centre of the chamber. Two of the prisoners looked alike, with only twenty years difference. My heart jumped to my throat as I realised who they were: Erin with Connor in her arms, and her mother Jenny. Fear had etched itself into their features, save for my son's face, which was contorted as he started bawling. Erin bounced him, whispering in his ear, then turned his mouth to her chest to quieten him.

From behind a cluster of crates emerged a confident figure clad in a Nazi officer uniform. Beside him, in the officer's clothing, Isabella directed three prisoners at gunpoint toward the centre of the chamber. Two of the captives bore a striking resemblance, despite their twenty-year age gap. My heart leapt into my throat as I recognised them: Erin, clutching Connor in her arms, and her mother Jenny. Fear etched itself into their features, though Connor's face contorted as he cried. Erin bounced him, whispering in his ear before pressing his mouth to her chest to soothe him.

"Tony, Cutter," Stan's voice boomed, dripping with malice. "Come out from your hiding spots, or these three will meet a swift end."

Despite my sinking spirits, my mind raced to find a solution. Across the clearing, I saw Cutter shaking his head, his gaze unwavering as he weighed the options. Adrenaline coursed through my veins as I exchanged a silent nod with him. At once, we emerged from our cover, hands raised in surrender.

"What do you want, Stan Nowlan?" Cutter's voice rang out, a mixture of defiance and desperation.

Stan's lips curled into a sinister smile, his grip tightening on the gun. "Oh, just a little chat, Cutter. And perhaps to demonstrate the consequences of crossing me."

Chapter 28

Electronic Diary of Anthony Nowlan
West of Biala Podlaska, Poland.
11:58am, 1st June 1941.

"Quit wasting time," Stan shouted, his voice booming through the PA speakers, sparking off more cries from Connor. He turned towards Erin, his voice caught by the microphone but fainter as he spoke. "Shut the damn kid up before I put a bullet in his head."

My wife made no retort. If circumstances were different, she may have done, though. She focused her attention on Connor, settling him, doing her best to console our son.

"Okay," I called across the empty space, nearing the centre by now. "But don't shoot my son. You could end up not existing yourself."

Stan was about ten feet away by now and stopped. He cast an eye over me and Cutter, assessing us before ordering a Nazi soldier to take our guns. As the German left with them, Stan blinked in surprise. "Your ChronoSpace," he said, his eyebrows lifted. "Where is it?"

I shrugged in response and exchanged a glance with Cutter, who did the same with nonchalance. "Somewhere safe." The truth was, I still had it on me, strapped around my midsection beneath my clothes. My shirt concealed it. Even with my jacket open, it was almost undetectable against the cloth. "I didn't want to risk you taking it again."

With that, my descendant chuckled at my forethought. "We must stop meeting like this, I agree," he said, his voice booming again. He handed the PA microphone to a soldier and glanced at the Time Dilation zone. There,

Jewish slaves were assembling V2 rockets, flitting about their tasks, the V2 rocket assembling in mere minutes. It reminded me of a time-lapse video. "What should I do with you?" he asked, almost as if he were pondering a huge dilemma. Then his eyes lit up with inspiration, the sight sinking my hopes. "Ah, I know!"

He pointed his pistol at us. "Eeny meany miney mo," he chanted, alternating the pistol between Cutter and me on each word. "Catch a nigger by the toe."

"Stanley Joseph Nowlan," Jenny interrupted him, her hands on his hips. Her Scottish accent had returned to the full strength of our first meeting, losing her acquired Australian voice. "Watch your language!"

He froze at the mention of his name. My jaw dropped too at her words. "How do you know him?" I asked.

Jenny ignored the maniacal grin on her captor's face as she addressed me across the gap. "I'm terribly sorry, Tony," she began in a sincere tone. "He has had a tough life growing up without his Da'."

"Your husband died early?" I asked, feeling a giant butterfly hatch in my stomach. Stan was now giggling at the expression on my face, turning to Isabella, who joined in the laughter.

"It's a long story... Dad!" Stan cut in before Jenny could reply. "But I have trouble calling you that. Maybe it's because you seem so much younger than me." A gargoyle's grin stretched his lips as he continued his Eeny Meany Miney Mo. The gun ended on me. "You're first. Cross the yellow line."

I froze, realising his plan. Another part of me reeled with shock at the revelation. Stan had claimed to be my father in the distant future, a paradoxical descendant of mine. Now I faced something worse. He is my son by a terrible mistake with Jenny? The conflict between trying to process everything rendered my head useless. "Pardon?" I stammered.

"Cross the line and stand there before me," Stan said, urging me forward with a wave of the pistol. Still shocked, I hesitated, but Cutter's firm voice snapped me back to reality.

"I'll go," he asserted, placing a hand on my chest to stop me. His eyes locked with mine, a look exchanging with me an unspoken message. Although I wondered what he wanted me to understand, I gave a vague nod. "Don't give in to him," he added.

Stan turned his attention to Cutter and shrugged. "Okay, a delaying tactic," he sneered. "Do it, Agent Cutter."

My enemy-turned-friend took a look at me, offered me a wink, then turned to my wife. Tears streamed from their eyes as she exchanged a glance with him, her head shaking in denial at the events. For a moment, I remembered that she and Cutter had dated months before I met her. Although she no longer held those feelings for him, I could tell his gesture for me was also for her. I just didn't know what I was going to do to help him, to repay his sacrifice.

My comrade remained outwardly calm. He strolled towards the yellow line that marked the border between his present and his impending end. My eyes turned red as I realised I was about to learn the answer to another riddle. For a second, he hesitated. Then, with a step over the line, he turned to face us.

"Keep going!" Stan urged him. Cutter tilted his head, a confused expression on his face. "Damn! He doesn't understand because time is moving faster there. It's distorting my voice."

I almost laughed at that, wondering how time might have distorted Stan's voice for Cutter. When my wayward son waved the pistol again, Cutter caught his meaning and stepped back a few more paces.

At first, I noticed nothing. Half a minute passed before I saw the first lines etching onto his face. A streak of grey bloomed in his hair. Two gunshots reverberated. Cutter's legs erupted in a geyser of blood, and he crumpled to the ground, shouting, his voice distorted by the shift in time. He writhed in agony, blood staining the ground within seconds. The sight ignited a blaze of defiance within me as I realised I was next. I had no intention of letting him triumph or harm those I love.

"He has twenty-five minutes to live before old age kills him." Stan's voice was like ice. He aimed his pistol at me. "Now, Daddy-oh, it's your turn."

I gulped. Time had run out, and I had no backup plan. Mind racing, I glanced at my wife. Her lips moved, mouthing, "I love you", as I took my first step. I pursed my lips in a kiss for her to see. Jenny's face tightened, her expression unreadable.

"Move!" Stan demanded. "Or I'll shoot you now before I shove you in."

I took another step. Jenny shouted something that I missed. His gun blasted at me, but something blurred. At first, I didn't realise what happened. Jenny fell at my feet, a bullet hole spewing blood from her back. Erin screamed. I dropped to my knees at the sight as Stan bellowed in rage. "Look at what you made me do, you interfering bitch!"

* * *

Electronic Diary of Anthony Nowlan
West of Biala Podlaska, Poland.
12:48pm, 1st June 1941.

Erin's scream filled my ears. Stan's jibes and insults to his mother were worse. A pool of blood spread beneath her, but she still moved. Anger creased her face so that she looked like the tough and crabby old Scotswoman I'd expect. She rolled onto her opposite side to glare at him.

Despite what she had done to me, tricking me into impregnating her, I didn't think about the twisted karma of it all. I actually felt disgust towards Stan. Yes, he is (by Jenny's admission) my son by the said deceit, but that fact hadn't yet processed in my mind. It was that a man could shoot his mother without remorse that made me so angry. My eyes flicked towards Erin and my legitimate son, Connor, those who truly mean everything to me. A knowing glance passed between me and my wife. She knew what she had to do.

"Ya fookin' lil arsehole," Jenny screamed like a banshee, catching all our attentions. "I should'a drowned you in the tub when I had the chance."

The Nazi soldier's eyes widened in disbelief at the gruesome scene unfolding before him. Whether it was because he harboured doubts about the Nazi ideology or because Stan's act of shooting his own mother had rattled him, I couldn't tell. His grip on the trigger guard of his machine gun slackened as he became transfixed by the horrific sight. Oblivious to his surroundings, his attention was momentarily diverted by the unfolding tragedy, allowing Erin to slip away with Connor and seek refuge behind a pile of crates. I silently approved of their escape, grateful for the opportunity it afforded them to evade further danger.

I lunged at the guard, wresting the submachine gun from his grasp and belting his face with the weapon's butt. As he fell, I aimed the MP40 squarely at Isabella. But she was quick on the draw, her pistol trained on me with deadly precision. Adrenaline surged through my veins as I braced myself for the impending exchange of gunfire. Bullets whizzed past me as I dove to the side. One graced my cheek with a stinging sensation. I rolled, stopping behind a nearby stack of crates. Every nerve jangled as I prepared for further shots.

Puffing hard with adrenaline, I waited, straining to hear any sound. A scrape of a boot to the side alerted me to Stan's presence as he rounded the crates from the other side, closing in on me. Trapped with nowhere to escape, I braced myself. Then, from behind, came the sound of a drawn breath. Instinctively, I sidestepped away from the crates just in time.

A hand flashed down past me, adorned with a glinting ring in the dim light. Something sharp protruded from the ring: a poison needle. Acting on reflex, I swung the submachine gun's butt hard, connecting with Isabella's hand. Her hideous scream reverberated off the walls as Stan lunged around the crate at me, his Luger ready. I fired a short burst from the gun, forcing him to retreat.

Instinctively, I rammed the gun's butt into Isabella's stomach. She doubled over, winded. A swift kick broke her nose against a crate, and she crumpled to the floor.

Blinded by pain, she lifted a hand to her bleeding face. I kicked her hand into her face. The poisoned ring pierced her skin, and horror filled her wide-open eyes. Within seconds, she succumbed to the poison, staring hopelessly into space.

Darkness fell over the room, and all went quiet. I hadn't realised how noisy the machinery had been until then. Exhausted, I leaned against a crate, a smile stealing across my face. Sofia had accomplished her goal, killing the main power source at the station. More than likely, she had used explosives to do it. Time for a situation check.

"Erin!" I called, listening still for Stan as I hoped my wife and child were still alive. "I'm okay here. Say nothing in case..." Then I heard it. A quickly drawn breath.

I ducked just in time. The whooshing sound above my head ended with a clang. I pivoted, swinging the gun with all my might. It connected, and a man screamed in pained fury. A fleeting thought told me it was Stan. I had unknowingly belted the shit out of his testicles. Gleefully, I swung again to ensure he wouldn't sire me any undesirable grandchildren. He screamed again, then something crashed into my leg, felling me.

Footsteps hurried away. Then, the sound of fumbling reached my ears, followed by a distinct click. Suddenly, lights blazed in the room as a generator whirred to life. I should have known he'd have a backup plan.

But it wasn't the Time Dilation machine that turned on. A set of frames containing three rings of metal that began to glow with a dull reddish tinge. Before long, the red rings' glowing intensified, humming. An undulating aura of blue emanated from within them, bending the surrounding light. Shocked, I realised this was the Difference Machine turned to life.

The rings were portals, designed to transport objects from one place to another. But I knew they could do more if used the wrong way. The question stood. Did Stan know too?

A pained cry echoed from Cutter's direction, catching my attention. I turned, but saw nothing. A heavy blow landed on the back of my head, sending me sprawling to the ground. The world spun as I struggled to regain my bearings. Stan's fist rammed across my jaw, sending me spinning.

With maniacal fervour blazing in his eyes, he seized me by the collar and yanked me to my feet. "You thought you could outsmart me, Daddy-oh?" he sneered, venom dripping from his voice. "You and your friends are no match for the Third Reich."

I gritted my teeth against the pain, defiance burning in my veins. "You don't know what you're playing with, Stan," I growled, tasting blood in my mouth. "These portals are dange--"

He interrupted me by clamping his hand over my mouth, forcing me close enough to see the blackheads on his nose. His laughter rang loud, mocking. "Oh, you haven't given me enough credit. Here, let's test the portal for ourselves."

With a brutal tug, Stan dragged me towards one of the glowing portals. Its blue shimmering aura now forming a swirling vortex like water in a drain. Terror surged through me as I fought his tight grip, but I was still dizzy from the blow to the head. Inch by inch, he dragged me closer to the pulsating ring.

The portal seemed to hold its own intelligence, a malevolent force that recognised me as its meal. A hot sensation flushed across my face from its energy, reaching for me, drawing me closer. I clawed at the ground with my feet, searching for anything to resist its pull. Stan's maniacal laughter echoed in my head as he forced me closer. Inches away from it, I was close to its inexorable grip when the unmistakable report of a shot rang out.

Stan's grip loosened. He cried in shock as he dropped me. I caught myself from the fall and looked up in time to see blood oozing from the exit wound in his right shoulder. Another gunshot ripped through his leg. Scrabbling out of harm's way, I turned to see Cutter had escaped the Time Dilation area and found a weapon. A dull pop sounded beside me. I looked in time to see Stan vanish with his ChronoSpace.

I switched off the Time Dilation device and the Difference Machine, then approached Cutter. The sight that greeted me as he emerged from the shadows was shocking. The once young Gary Cutter I knew from 2017 had transformed. Though he still stood strong and tall, he had aged twenty years in a mere fifteen minutes. Words failed me as he offered a relieved smile. "You fought better than I expected," he said. "The bullets had passed through both legs, and it healed fast."

"The Time Dilation field," I surmised, puffing still from the fight. Then I remembered something. "I need to check on Erin and Connor." I turned, called for my wife, and felt the breath catch in my throat.

There stood Stan Nowlan, his grey Nazi officer's uniform replaced by a tight suit of a design I hadn't seen before. The wounds on his body had healed. His leering grin stood prominent as he indicated he had my wife and son in his grasp.

In the instant it took to know how he did it, it was too late. Stan vanished with my wife and son before our eyes. Into what period or location, only he knew.

Chapter 29

Electronic Diary of Anthony Nowlan
West of Biala Podlaska, Poland.
1:18pm, 1st June 1941.

"No," I shouted, dashing to the spot where my wife had been an instant ago. My fingers clawed in vain at the empty air.

Thoughts about my failings as a husband, a father, and a protector filled my head, making it ache. By not involving Erin in this mission, I thought I had kept her out of harm's way. And now Stan had her and my son. Worst, I had no idea where or when they were.

Cutter called out something from behind, but I missed what he said. A movement from the corner of my eye caught my attention. Pivoting towards it, I spotted two familiar figures: Sofia and Hans. The former lifted a hand in greeting, oblivious to the admiring looks the gentle giant sneaked from behind her. She approached us while Hans diverted towards the Difference Machine and the Time Dilator.

"Jenny's still alive," Cutter yelled again from the side. "She needs medical attention fast."

I raced back to my mother-in-law's side, painfully by her close resemblance to Erin. As much pain as she had caused, including indirectly, I couldn't let her suffer without helping. Most would be happy to see their mother-in-law on the side of milk carton, but not me. Her mouth hung open, the jaw slack, and her skin paler than I remember.

"The bullet lodged in her lower back." Cutter rolled Jenny

onto her side, and pointed to the area. "I don't think it's hit her spine, but she's lost a lot of blood."

"I can take her to a hospital in the future," I offered, my mind flashing back to when I had done the same thing already for her months ago, or over 400 years ago. Time travel makes things difficult to relate sometimes.

"We'll take her to ASIS, to just after you met me in 2017," Cutter replied fast, then addressed Sofia. "Is our objective completed here?"

"Check." Sofia flicked the hair from her face and nodded. "Power plant is gone. So are the machines in the food production area and the breeding area. Disabling them wasn't enough." She cast me a look, which I figured could have been her judging me for being too merciful to the children. "A hammer and some battery acid I found helped that," she added.

At that moment, a cacophonous rending of metal crunching and crushing distracted us. We whirled to see that Hans had just ripped the Time Dilator apart with his bare hands. Gripping a huge piece of its frame, he swung hard, smashing into the Difference Machine's controls. Sparks flew from the severed circuitry with sharp hisses and spits. Five more solid kicks reduced the rest to fist-sized pieces of debris. He watched its sparks and flames for a moment before giving a satisfied nod.

"Good work, Hans!" Cutter yelled to the gentle giant. "We're leaving now. Do you want to come with us?"

The giant's face dropped in disappointment, his eyes drooping as he looked towards Sofia. "Going?" he said, masking a sniffle.

"We have to take this lady to hospital," Sofia explained.

"But we have to be quick. Are you coming?"

He shook his head sadly, but puffed his chest in a show of strength. "I will stay and fight the Führer and protect the poor children," he announced.

"You're a good man," Cutter replied, shaking the juggernaut's hand. "We may see you again."

I shook Hans' hand too, amazed with how gentle he was when he took mine, before Sofia pulled him down to her height and kissed his cheek. "You're an amazing man, Hans," she said, her eyes catching the blush and mushy expression on his face. "I know you will save many."

"Go, save the lady," he urged, turning away and heading towards the corridors.

We huddled together, and I hit the ChronoSpace's Home button.

Electronic Diary of Anthony Nowlan
ASIS Headquarters, Northern Territory, Australia.
10:18am, 1st December 2017.

As soon as we arrived in Cutter's office, he picked up the phone while I sat on the floor, cradling Jenny's body. "Medical emergency," he barked. "Send paramedics. Gunshot wound to civilian."

Five minutes later, they arrived along with another two agents. One of them took a shocked second glance at Agent Cutter and his severely aged appearance. Sofia intervened when he reached for his weapon, explaining we had just returned from a mission. It took some more quick thinking as no one else knew about the time travel.

Meanwhile, the paramedics took Jenny to an operating theatre in the complex as I discussed things with Sofia.

"I have to save my wife and son," I explained, speaking fast. Time-travel allows the luxury to pop into any time and location. But it's hard to tell the brain that it's okay, to slow down, to rest and recuperate. Sofia and Cutter seemed to have grasped that concept well. They can think under pressure, thanks to training. It seems Stan can do it too.

"She will be okay," Cutter answered and showed me the same photos he would (or had) shown me in 2019. Pictures of Erin on the Titanic and another in what appeared to be in an English pub, and even that had not yet happened for me. "It's destined," he explained.

"But how do I know that time won't change? How do I know that I won't make a slightly different choice or action, step on the wrong piece of grass, and set off a different timeline?" The possibilities seemed endless, each worse than the other to me.

"Have faith," Sofia replied and placed a hand on my shoulder. It calmed me. She offered me a smile and urged me to breathe.

Cutter gave me a playful punch on the arm, not something he would normally do. "You can do it. I'll hold the fort here."

I took his hand, shaking it. "See you in March 2019," I answered, giving him a smile. "And I promise I'll find a cure for you if there is one."

He ran a hand through his grey hair, glancing at his reflection in the screen of a nearby computer. "Or I'll get used to it. Now, go. I'll let you know when you can collect your mother-in-law."

With a nod, I took Sofia's hand. The ChronoSpace took us

away...

* * *

Electronic Diary of Anthony Nowlan
Lammermoor Beach, Yeppoon, Queensland, Australia.
10:18am, 1st November 2019.

We arrived in my study at home. As soon as we did, I held my finger up to my mouth for silence. Pressing my desktop's computer keyboard, I brought up the security camera footage and scanned the different rooms. No one was home. The house was empty except for my study, its camera showing a clear black-and-white image of Sofia and me. The outside camera showed my Jag was still home, and Jenny's car parked out the front.

"The cars are here, but they aren't," I confirmed to Sofia. "He's been here."

"Rewind the video," she suggested. "They might have gone out for a walk or something."

So I did. The tracks warped and squizzled backward until I caught a movement on the screen. Stopping the rewind, I noted the date: 31st October 2019. Yesterday's date! I pressed play.

The video displayed Erin feeding Connor his breakfast in his highchair at the table. Something caught her attention. She looked up towards the front door and headed into the living room to answer it. It was her mother, Jenny, who kissed Erin on the cheek and offered a huge grin for Connor. He raised his arms towards her in that familiar gesture, and she obliged, lifting him up. Soon, they were all inside the living room, with Connor surrounded by his stuffed animals while his grandmother watched, a loving smile on her face as she interacted with him. Meanwhile, Erin was in the kitchen making cups of tea.

Suddenly, our nemesis appeared in the kitchen behind my wife, a gun in his hand. She turned, likely alerted by the thud sound of his appearance, and started at the sight. He ushered her towards the living room. At gunpoint, he ordered his mother to pick up Connor. Erin took him in her arms a few seconds before Stan moved in, and they all disappeared.

Then, another movement on a different monitor caught my attention. I focused on it, saw that it was me, holding a small gun aimed at where they stood.

I knew what I had to do. So did Sofia.

"Go, come back once you've done it," she said, her eyebrow arched.

Electronic Diary of Anthony Nowlan
Lammermoor Beach, Yeppoon, Queensland,
Australia.
11:08am, 31st October 2019.

The dizziness hardly affected me on this leg. My study was the same as it would be tomorrow. And why wouldn't it? I thought to myself as I listened through the closed door.

Connor was yapping in his enthusiastic voice. Thanks to the video footage, I knew he was talking to his stuffed gorilla. "Kong, Kong!" he shouted at it, using the name I had given the toy.

"Monkey," Jenny said, trying to correct him. She was obviously unfamiliar with the movie character. And Erin replied, "It's named after the giant gorilla from the movie." After a pause, she added, "Oh, that's right. You probably haven't seen it."

The kettle was boiling viciously now, reaching its climactic point, and I heard the noise I had been waiting for. The faint thud.

"I have seen it," Jenny answered. "About ten years ago at the cinema. Just because I was born centuries ago doesn't mean I'm not up-to-date with pop culture."

"Yes," sneered the intruder's voice. "She and I saw it together."

Erin cried out in surprise, echoed by Jenny at the sound of the voice. I visualised the scene in my head just as it had played out on the screen. Waiting for Stan's command to Erin to move into the living room, I held back, listening intently. When his voice finally emanated from there, signalling me to act, I cautiously opened the study door, mindful of any squeaking. Moving swiftly, I tiptoed to the kitchen and positioned myself just around the corner, out of sight. Though the gun in my hand seemed to urge me to fire it immediately, I resisted, biding my time, poised for the opportune moment.

"Get the kid," Stan said harshly.

"Where are you taking us?" Erin demanded to know. It was good to hear the protectiveness in her voice. Although trained to fight before we went to 1912 together, she knew how to pick her battles. This wasn't one right now.

"I'm taking you and your family to talk some sense into your arsehole husband," he replied.

The moment of truth arrived. I swung around the corner, aimed and fired. If it were a bullet, it would have killed him instantly. But it wasn't, it didn't. The last thing I saw was Erin's face light up with hope at spotting me, a second before she faded away.

**Electronic Diary of Anthony Nowlan
Lammermoor Beach, Yeppoon, Queensland,
Australia.
10:38am, 1st November 2019.**

I reappeared in the study, surprising Sofia, who was lounging on the bed in my study. She sat up in a heartbeat, "Did you stop him?"

"No," I replied and shook my head. A second later, I was at my computer and logging into the Apricot Corporation mainframe.

"What are you doing?" she asked with curiosity.

"Tracking the tag on him," I explained as the remote access accessed the VPN. The screen turned blue and green, a map of the world. Figures and coordinates scrolled by on the right-hand column and I read them to myself.

"Why don't you just get to 1941 and take him out there before he escapes?"

"Remember when Cutter shot him?" I answered impatiently, concentrating on the coordinates and readouts. She replied in the affirmative, her tone open for learning. "Well," I said, clicking my fingers as the quantum mainframe at Apricot fed information to my desktop. "He disappeared, presumably healed, somewhere sometime, before returning with Erin and Connor and her mother. I'm hoping to catch him at whatever home base he has. My guess is that's where he's taken them."

"It could be a trap," she said, catching my meaning and stroking her chin.

A smile crossed my lips as the screen displayed a destination. "Got him."

"Where?"

"In the future," I replied. "Germany, 2023."

Chapter 30

Electronic Diary of Anthony Nowlan
Northwest of Mayen, Germany
6:00am, 13th September 2023

Thin clouds softened the pre-dawn sun's rays into a rich array of golden hues as we made our way through the woodlands of Rhineland-Palatinate. Dense foliage obscured our path, wrapping us in a cocoon of fallen leaves. The air carried scents of damp earth and fresh fragrances, reminiscent of rainy days in Binna Burra's rainforests.

"Stay away from the leaves if you can," Sofia whispered, her breath forming clouds in the morning air as she pulled me out of a pile. I nodded, remembering what she had told me earlier about European asps and vipers. Although not as venomous as Australian snakes, they presented a real danger to the unwary.

We continued our journey until the woodlands cleared to reveal a bitumen road. It forked along a rutted dirt road, flanked by a closed wooden gate that beckoned us into the shadowy gloom. "That's the path to Schloss Brynhild," I confirmed, checking my map. My heart beat harder at the prospect of seeing my family again, but I would have to rescue them first.

Sofia consulted her watch. "We'll split directions at that gate," she explained. "Twelve minutes to reach our positions, then we rendezvous in its inner yard." A moment later, she disappeared into the undergrowth, heading northwest.

Yesterday's reconnaissance, combining aerial surveillance

with a drone and ground observations by Sofia, revealed the castle's defences: cameras, guards and dogs. The medieval structure had once been a museum open to the public. That is until someone bought it in 2019 and closed it to the public, the reclusive owner stating he planned to reopen parts to the public. From what we could tell, that had not yet happened. According to Sofia, that fit our purpose well, as we knew whoever we would see to be an enemy.

After six minutes through the woodland, I reached the eastern wall, dawn aiding visibility. Yesterday's hacked footage concealed our movements as we passed the perimeter's surveillance cameras. No dogs disturbed the silence, no scent gave us away. Sofia's voice crackled. "At the target," she said. I signalled readiness to climb.

Although I could scale the castle's rough exterior, urgency demanded speed. I removed a CO2-powered grappling hook from my belt, a gadget I had gained from ASIS for the mission. It shot skyward, lodging in the stone. Testing its grip, I ascended, assisted by a tiny, quiet motor to the top of the wall. "At the top," her voice whispered in my ear, followed soon by, "Clear."

I peered over the edge of the wall into the castle's interior. It was nothing like I expected, perhaps influenced by too many old films. Parts resembled remnants of an old German village, with bright green doors adorned with intricate woodcarvings around the frames. Flowerbeds boasted wildflowers in full bloom, one even featuring tulips.

"Careful," my companion's voice hissed in my ear. "The motion sensors will wake soon. Take the corner to your left. Plenty of hand holds there."

I noted the sensors pointed in my direction. Although I was moving in front of them, and in their range, they hadn't lit yet. But time was running out as Sofia said, so I scooted towards the section advised and climbed down. My rock climbing with Erin had found a practical application. A tight-lipped smile crossed my face as I refocused my descent over the wall and into the courtyard.

My boots softly met the cobblestone pavement. The serene courtyard glowed in the morning light. Beside colourful flowerbeds, a fountain bubbled near a wall. Sofia waved from a shadowy doorway across the yard. I swiftly and silently traced the walls to reach her.

Intricate carvings adorned the doorway, which I recognised as scenes from biblical tales and ancient legends. David standing in defiance before a taller Goliath, who reminded me of Hans Hoffmann, his slingshot ready to strike. A nativity scene of Mary and Joseph kneeling beside the Son of God's manger, bathed in the soft glow from a shining star. Interestingly, another panel included something that baffled me.

A powerful-looking warrior clad in armour and wielding a mighty sword. He stood tall and resolute, his gaze fixed on the horizon. Beside him, a warrior princess contrasted, radiating strength and beauty, her flowing hair cascading like a waterfall around her shoulders. He was reaching out to her, offering his hand in friendship and alliance, while the flames of passion and destiny flickered behind them. The artist, long dead, had interwoven runes or pagan symbols. Whatever their meaning, they were lost on me.

Sofia pushed open the door, signalling me to stay behind as she checked inside. A moment later, the gloom swallowed her, and I followed, keeping close to the wall.

My iBioPad scanned for motion detectors and heat sensors. Finding none, I released a sigh of relief.

Ancient tapestries, illuminated by flickering torches, adorned the walls. The thick scent of incense added to the atmosphere of mystery and intrigue, its slight vapour reminding me of my grandfather joking about Catholic priests waving it in ceremonies on the television news. "The mosquitoes must be bad here," I mumbled, waving it out of my face. Sofia's eyes pierced me through the half-light, her expression annoyed. With a sheepish grin, I nodded, and we headed towards the altar at the front of the chapel.

"Where now?" she asked.

I paused, recollecting what I had found in my research on the castle. Some rumours had passed on different internet sites that an ancient order of warrior monks, similar to the Templar Knights, had first built the castle. They had blended ancient Germanic traditions with Christianity apparently, but little else existed apart from the mention of Schloss Brynhild as a main hub. The chapel seemed the obvious place, a Christian front for casual visitors. The altar seemed the obvious place to look.

A single candle burned on it, almost reaching the end of its wick as the wax had melted into a white mass. Hewn from granite, it exuded ancient reverence and history. Carved with intricate symbols and runes of forgotten origins, the altar's surface bore the marks of centuries past. They seemed to move with a life of their own in the dancing candlelight. Most eye-catching were the naked figures on either side of the altar. One, a woman, stood proud with her back against the altar as though leaning against it, her bare breasts proud and firm. The other male, equally bare-chested, sported genitals of an aroused state. Between them, on the front of the altar, an angel with a beautiful face and magnificent wings faced where the congregation would sit.

"Any idea on how to find the chamber?" Sofia asked.

I shook my head. "Only the altar," I replied, eyes searching for some mechanism. Nothing stood out on the back, so I circled the structure, checking the woman first. For a second, I thought of something in a movie and considered trying what the archaeologist did.

Sofia snorted. "You think grabbing her breasts? Typical man." When I paused, embarrassed to try, she nonchalantly cupped the stone mammary glands and pushed hard. Nothing happened. So I tried the nose and eyes of the stone angel, noticing its cloven feet poking beneath its robes. Then Sofia gave a soft whistle, admiring the proud phallic figure of the stone man's penis. The hint of a smile crossed her face as she grabbed its shaft and pulled downward. I expected it to snap, as that of a real man might, but it didn't. A heavy rumbling of sliding stone emanated from the wall behind the altar as the penis pointed downwards.

"Who knew this could be so hands on?" I asked. With a subtle smile on her face, she pressed past me to examine the rear wall.

Sofia shoved aside the hanging tapestry to reveal an open doorway in the stone. "This is the place," she said, slipping through the gap. I hung back a few moments to place four spherical devices on the floor, activating each with the press of a button before following the ASIS agent.

We made our way through the shadowy doorway, which

slid shut behind us with a groan, leaving us in darkness. I fumbled for my torch and turned it on to reveal a rough-walled stone corridor. These Germans sure loved long passages, I told myself as we followed it for what seemed forever. The air grew colder with each step, sending shivers through my arms.

The corridor twisted and turned like the forgotten labyrinth of a forgotten age. Torchlight danced across ancient stones, casting eerie shadows that flickered and danced with a life of their own.

At last, the passage opened into a larger hall. My torch beam fell upon two frightened faces familiar to me: my wife Erin and our son Connor. Relief flooded through me, but before I could react, heavy hands fell on my shoulders. Sofia reacted with surprise too, but the strange men's efficiency overpowered her.

Overhead lights flickered on, flooding the room. Two more figures emerged: Stan Nowlan and Isabella D'Aubigny. Her presence surprised me. With a grim smile, she barked orders to our captors.

"Take them to the Truth Chamber."

Chapter 31

Electronic Diary of Anthony Nowlan
Northwest of Mayen, Germany
7:10am, 13th September 2023

We were pushed through another door into the labyrinthine chamber. The heavy door swung shut behind us, wrapping us in an ominous darkness. Through the gloom, I could barely make out the outlines of Erin and Connor huddled in a corner. Beside them stood Stan, and I could sense the gloating look on his face as I realised this was yet another trap he had orchestrated for me.

"We have much to discuss... Dad," his voice echoed off the stone wall, dripping with venom as he slowly paced back and forth across the room.

"You have no right to call me that," I replied, shuddering inside as regret blended with anger.

"You're right." Stan stopped pacing to look me square in the eye. "But blood is thicker than water. It's the only reason you are alive, including my sister Erin." The lights brightened, revealing his leering gaze at Erin. A flash of disdain coloured my wife's features. Despite the tension, she remained silent, offering only a small but brave smile in my direction.

"I am still sorry I wasn't there," I offered, sensing what was to come depended on me saying something. With that, he nodded, pacing again as his lips pursed, considering his next words. "For what it's worth, I'm sorry I killed you."

The news made me flinch. A flashback came from my meeting with Gary Cutter in my office, how he revealed he knew about my time travel. The photo of the mummified man wearing my clothes and my ChronoSpace appeared in my mind. A strange foreboding came over me and worsened when Erin gasped at the words. "Tony?" she said. "You know you're going to die?"

I shook my head in shocked disbelief, turning away to think, to process the pieces falling into place.

"Yes, he knows, Erin," Isabella answered, her voice colder than a mother-in-law's kiss as it echoed from the walls. "When Gary Cutter and Sofia Nguyen met him in Apricot Corporation."

I turned to look at Stan, staring him in the eyes. "So you have captured me to tell me you're going to kill me? Why don't you just get it over and kill me now? It'd be quicker."

His resemblance to me was uncanny in this light. It was like looking at an evil reflection of myself. He kicked a chair across the room to me, and an armed guard pushed me down on it. Zip-ties fastened my wrists behind my back to the frame with a hiss. "I learned it doesn't work that way, Tony. Do you mind if I call you that? Dad is difficult to say since I already knew another."

I gave a non-committal shrug at that, preferring to say nothing yet, and he continued. "Mum brought me up well. I can't fault her for what she did. She taught me bush-craft, which she said she had learned from the Aboriginal people in northern Queensland. And she also taught me what she knew of other ancient lore, what you might call witchcraft. She always said I looked like you, my father, and I grew up wanting to meet you, to know you, but you never showed up. I never knew why, always blaming myself."

"Perhaps I should have turned up and belted your bum," I

replied, putting on a fatherly voice for him, the same my grandfather sometimes used on me. Although a loving guardian, he was never afraid to deliver discipline, teaching me that bad behaviour carries consequences. "You needed it." Whatever reaction I expected from the man, I received no satisfaction. He ignored it, only allowing a few more seconds of silence before he continued.

"The man I called father soon came into my life. He was a man who worked with mother. He did well by me and taught me about his country of birth: Germany. It turns out this castle is my birthright through a strange organisation he taught me of, the Order of Erebos."

I raised a quizzical eyebrow at this unfamiliar name and shrugged at him.

"You will die soon, anyway." His voice carried a matter-of-factual tone, the kind a doctor might use when advising you have five weeks left. He watched me as he said it, smiling at whatever reaction he saw. "Erebos has been around a long time. When people talk about the Illuminati or whatever they call the conspiratorial organisation behind world events, they mean Erebos, although it's much bigger than they think, and not so bad."

Something tickled at my fingertips. I knew what was coming, but I couldn't let Stan know.

"When he learned about my heritage, he took great interest in it. So, you have Mother to blame for a part of it. It seems she talks in her sleep sometimes, and talked about you and the future and the past. I didn't, and she told me not to, in case people thought us mad. But Franz didn't. He knew things, he said, had heard them. And I was to be the key to making the world better, to curb world population growth, to save the environment. He was a brilliant thinker, Tony. You would have liked him."

"He took us up to Black Mountain where mother liked to visit, to talk to the people who always welcomed her. They treated her with special privileges, and me, too. So I could explore the taboo place, which I did. Can you imagine my surprise when I found this ChronoSpace in the caves within it?" Stan pulled aside his jacket to reveal my original ChronoSpace on his belt. It even had the dents in its metal surface from when it had fallen into the chasm. Erin gasped from where she sat, and I realised she was putting the pieces together, just as I had.

"You worked out how to use it," I said, amazed at the accomplishment, almost proud of my genetics running through his veins. But he didn't wear an iBioPad. How did he control it?

"Impressed?" he asked me, exhibiting the pleasure a child does at praise from a grownup. I nodded, but he shrugged it off, dashing my hopes of manipulating him through the familial link. At that moment, something caught my attention. A bead of sweat formed on my hairline as I glanced at Stan Nowlan, hoping he hadn't noticed.

"One question, Stan," I stated, injecting confidence into my voice as I looked him in the eye. "I saw Isabella die in 1941 before you disappeared here with my family. Killed by her own poison. How is she alive now?"

A part of me figured related to time travel. If Isabella used her own ChronoSpace, that would tell me more about Stan's capabilities with the futuristic technology I created. Maybe this was a past version of the female assassin here now.

Both captors exchanged glances, then burst into laughter that echoed off the chamber walls. Stan wiped a mock tear from his eye as he leaned against a stone wall. "Shall I tell him, dear, or do you want to?"

Isabella gave a shrug, smirking at me with a twinkling eye. "You can."

"My dear Isabella trained with a group of assassins in India in the early 1900s. Orphaned young, she joined them and learned their fighting techniques and poisons." Stan removed a dagger from his belt and casually used its blade tip to clean beneath a fingernail. "Killing with poison means one can accidentally come into contact with it, so she built an immunity to it. That reminds me," he said, checking his nails before returning the knife to its sheath. "We've talked long enough. It's time to tie off loose ends, starting with your wife and son."

Isabella sported an evil grin as she turned her attention to Erin, a long slender needle in her hands. A drop of something glistened on the end as she lifted it to the light, ready to strike. "Wait!" I shouted, squeezing the object that had found its way to my hand, praying I wasn't too late. "You said you wouldn't harm them."

"I won't hurt them, Dad, old chap," Stan responded with an evil glint in his eye. "But I can't speak for Isabella."

At that moment, a bright flash of light erupted from the low ceiling. With a loud pop that left our ears ringing, smoke filled the room from the same location. One of the four robots I had released earlier in the chapel emitted a beep. In the hazy pea-soup, I spotted a shape strike like a wraith. Heavy thuds like dropping sacks of dirt sounded around me as Sofia threaded her way through the inhabitants.

The sensors in my contact lenses detected the changed conditions, providing me with heat signatures. Isabella's shape lunged towards the position where Erin huddled with Connor. I leaped as hard and fast towards my family as I could, pressing the button on my belt as my arm found them.

Electronic Diary of Anthony Nowlan
Rockhampton, QLD Australia
6:00am, 22nd December 2042

"I'll be right back," I said to Erin, kissing her on the forehead before disappearing again back to Brynhild.

Electronic Diary of Anthony Nowlan
Schloss Brynhild, Germany
7:40am, 13th September 2023

I reappeared in the Truth Chamber amidst the smoke, but back where my chair had been. The trouble was I couldn't recognise which person was which. Two distinct feminine shapes were battling in the swirling haze, which thus far remained thick.

The third figure was easier to recognise. A male, about my height, coughing on the acrid smoke. It had to be Stan. Adjusting my contact lenses, I noted the robots I had released in the chapel were now positioned back in the ceiling, encircling us all. Satisfied, I activated the first of two buttons on my emergency pack, then the second.

Chapter 32

Electronic Diary of Tony Nowlan
Schloss Brynhild, Germany
7:40am, 13th September 2023

The smoke soon cleared, revealing the bodies of henchman on the ground amongst their fallen weapons. I doubted that Sofia would have left any alive. Three had their necks positioned at strange angles. A few more had bleeding wounds. Another man's jaw looked like it had tried to deep-throat King Kong. But I couldn't let the scene distract me as Stan advanced towards me, his fists raised in a classic boxer's pose. Meanwhile, Sofia and Isabella faced each other, and not in the family reunion kind of way.

Stan's stance was solid. His shoulders squared, fists clenched tight. He was ready, and so was I.

I mirrored Stan's stance, a basic tenet of the wing chun I learned in my six months' training. But Stan would not go down easy. A swift jab came at my head, but I deflected it. I countered with a low kick to his knee. He sidestepped with fluid, precise movements.

Behind him, I spotted Isabella's graceful movements as she slipped through the thinning smoke, her lethal intent betrayed by her subtle actions. A sly smirk appeared on her face as she brandished the thin needle coated with deadly toxin, its glint matching the one in her eyes.

Stan powered towards me with a dazzling combination of straight punches and hooks. I ducked one that came close before delivering a series of quick strikes, aiming for his chest and abdomen. Some landed, but I may as well have punched a wall. It was like punching a brick shithouse. His punches grew fiercer, each one pushing me back.

To the side, I was aware of Sofia dodging a lunging strike of the needle point. She dodged it, stepping back and measuring her opponent.

Meanwhile, a punch caught me in the face. I spun, struggling to keep up my guard as another struck my nose. Blood spurted hot and sticky across my face. It stunned me for a second. For a second, my fighting instructor's voice echoed in memory. Keep up your hands. Defend your centre.

By instinct, I did just that, my hands moving by instinct while I regained my sight. I dodged three more hooks, feeling the breeze cool across my bloody skin. Then, as if on instinct, I saw my opening. Stan had left himself exposed. I seized the opportunity. With a swift motion, I kicked his knee. It crunched, and he screamed. I kicked again, upwards, as hard as I could. His testicles crunched from my steel capped boot. He wouldn't sire grandchildren for me after that.

The impact echoed through the chamber, and Stan doubled over. I didn't hesitate. I grabbed his collar with my left hand, pulled it hard towards the punch from my right hand. His face broke before he crashed to the ground like a heavy tree.

Puffing, I staggered back and looked up in time to see Isabella slap Sofia hard across the face. My friend staggered, her hand flying to her temple, and my heart sank as I realised. It was the same hand on which Isabella wore her poison ring!

A soft squelching noise came from Sofia's face. She stood

up, one eye appearing puffed and closed over. Isabella advanced, a gloating grin on her face that suddenly recoiled as she beheld something I didn't see. It had to be my friend's face, but since Sofia had circled, turning her back to me, I saw nothing.

Suddenly, Sofia's foot whipped in a crescent arc, connecting with Isabella's face. The enemy fell, dazed. Sofia closed the gap, seizing Isabella by the hair on the back of her head. Isabella's mouth gaped, drawing hungrily for breath. Sofia's free hand shoved something past her teeth and forced her mouth shut.

Isabella coughed, choking, her face turning red, but she couldn't escape Sofia's grip. At once, a tiny pop echoed through the chamber and the enemy's larynx exploded. She dropped to the floor, dead.

Breathing hard, Sofia turned towards me. A grim smile crossed her lips. Her left eye socket was empty, a black hole, as she dropped to the floor beside her opponent. A bleached appearance came over her features as she leaned against the wall. I hurried to her. "Are you okay?"

She shook her head. "This is where we part ways," she said, her voice weak as she coughed. Then I saw the scratch from the needle, and I knew. Isabella had killed Sofia, who returned the favour.

"How?" I asked, unsure what to say, how to say it, as I bled in front of her.

"False eyeball," she whispered, barely able to keep her eyes open. "Didn't see eye to eye with her." A final gasp escaped her lips as she expired as I knelt beside her.

A wave of sorrow washed over me, mingling with the adrenaline still coursing through my veins. Tears burned my heavy eyelids. Although glad that I still lived, I wondered about her family as I wept. Did she have a boyfriend, a husband, a lover? What about her parents? Would they be thinking of her? Was there anyone who would miss her?

Rising to my feet, I glanced at Sofia's lifeless form, unsure of what to do next. Stan scrabbling for his fallen pistol caught my attention. Furious, I stalked toward him and stomped on his hand, bones and tendons crunching under my steel-capped boot. A kick to his cheek silenced him with a scream.

His other hand felt for something at his chest, near his pocket. Grabbing it, I twisted hard, straining his carpals, and reached for what he was after. "Is this it?" I asked with a growl, glowering into his eyes. "You want to press it and escape?"

Stan grit his teeth, blood seeping between them from the beating I'd given him. He reached for the device with his busted hand, but his fingers waved like limp noodles. I slapped his busted fingers with the remote. His cry came as a blubber. "Here," I said, handing it to him. "Be my guest. Flee like the little bitch you are."

I released his hand so he could take it. With a laugh, he punched the button. Nothing worked. Crestfallen, he lifted his gaze to me, the maniacal triumph melting to a pained, questioning expression. "It's broken."

No, not exactly. One button I had pressed was an electromagnetic pulse generator. It had wiped out any electronics he carried, including his ChronoSpace, which I knew had no shielding. Of course, he doesn't need to know that. I considered it karma for what he did to my device before it sent me to the Titanic. I allowed myself a grim smile at the idea. It felt good. Too good.

"Consider yourself grounded, *son*," I growled, grabbing him by the collar and hauling him to his feet.

He coughed up blood, spitting to the side. "Where are you taking me?"

I glared at him in silence, staring into his eyes with a fiery hatred. Words were too cheap. Actions meant more. I pressed my iBioPad, which I had concealed, and we jumped time.

Electronic Journal of Tony Nowlan
2nd May 1688, 6am
Near Dornoch, Scotland

We appeared in a setting familiar to me, one I never expected to revisit. Perhaps destiny. meant to be. Maybe it was his weakened condition that made Stan throw up. I screwed up my face at the stench of bile and kicked him along the road. He limped towards the village that waited ahead.

The same thin grey haze of the fires hung above the little town's skyline. Even the putrid aroma of something like hell on earth lingered. Stan stared in curiosity at the dead cats hanging from the nooses in the trees. I already knew what they were, the remnants of harmful superstition. The Catholic Church had perpetuated the myth that cats causes pestilence as servants of the devil. The ignorant peasants of this time believed it, killed them by the thousands. As a result, they worsened the plague besetting them since nothing remained to kill the rats that carried it.

But I didn't need to tell Stan that. I wasn't here to give my wayward son a history lesson. Not that kind, anyway.

I used zip ties from his henchmen to bind Stan's wrists and ankles. He could only stare into the town square.

"What's that?" he asked, horrified at the charred stake's remains.

"It's where your mother nearly died," I replied. "Your father saved her, and everyone saw."

He didn't understand.

"Why am I here?" he whimpered as I emptied a bottle of stimulant pills, grabbed his head, and slammed his face into the metal grille. Blood flowed from his nose and mouth into the bottle. Once enough had collected, I pocketed it.

"We will meet again," Stan spat. "I have killed you before, and I will again. Erin, Connor, anyone you love... Dad."

I froze, hating how he called me Dad. His defiance was clear, but something in his tone gave me pause. Time travel is a crazy thing, and I needed time to process. Not while he was mouthing off. I took a slow breath, then slammed his face into the portcullis again. "Knock knock!" I said aloud, then whispered in his ear, "You'd better be careful if there's a next time."

He groaned from the pain, loud enough to draw attention. Voices spoke from the other side, one half-asleep. I turned and began my lonely walk down the dirt path away from the village entrance.

Behind me, the watch-guards gasped at the sight of Stan. "It's th' witch wha' saved th' ither witch!" one shouted, mistaking the family resemblance.

With an amused snort, I realised my gamble had paid off. For the villagers, yesterday was when they witnessed demons and another witch rescue Jenny from that same stake. Some of their own had died in the resulting flames and carnage. Another had vanished with the male and female witches. If their imaginations played right, the man bound to their portcullis was the male witch. Knowing what happens to witches here, I didn't need to stick around to watch.

Stan's resemblance to me had worked in his favour before; now it was his undoing. Biology might make him my offspring, but his actions dissolved DNA's bond. I have no room for birds that foul their own nest.

I have my own family, and I must do what I can for them.

Chapter 33

Electronic Diary of Anthony Nowlan
Rockhampton, QLD Australia
6:01am, 22nd December 2042

From Erin's perspective, I returned beside her just five seconds after leaving. Her first startled reaction changed to relief as she collapsed against me with Connor sandwiched between us. "Da-da-da," he babbled with glee upon seeing me. I looked above the fuzz of blonde hair on his head and into Erin's face. Despite the tired but relieved lines on her face, she was still beautiful to me.

"Did you...?" she asked, squeezing my arm, and I gave her a comforting nod. "What about my mother?"

"Took her to the hospital at ASIS," I explained. "She's waiting there... six years ago. That was before I came for you and Connor in Germany. I suppose I should collect her soon."

"You and Sofia came for us in the castle," she stated, lines of concentration appearing on her forehead. She glanced at our surroundings, searching. "Where is she?" When I didn't answer, sadness appeared in her eyes. "That sucks. And Stan and his bitch?"

I explained how Sofia and Isabella had killed each other and how I dealt with Jenny's son. Although she knew Stan was her half-brother, Erin showed no disappointment at his fate when I told her he was likely barbeque on a stick now. As she pointed out, what little she knew about him was all bad.

Something caught her attention. The different surroundings, unfamiliar to her, but not to me. "Where are we?"

"The future," I replied, offering her a smile. "This is my house, inherited from my grandfather. In this time-period, Claire is the only other person who knows about it. Apart from Sam's hologram intelligence at Apricot. We're a few months after I first time-travelled."

"And Stan?"

"As far as I'm aware, he doesn't know about it."

"Until he comes out of the blue and takes me or Connor or you, then..." Erin's voice trailed, allowing me to fill in the blanks. The way she looked, a void opened in my belly.

"Are you okay?" I tried to read her mannerisms, to understand how she felt about me, about us, after everything that had happened.

She pulled out a chair from the kitchen table to sit, our son on her lap. "I'm fine, but a lot of things have been on my mind. For starters, there's Connor. When Stan came by with Jenny and forced us to come with him to that factory, base, or whatever, I felt afraid, Tony. I was scared on the Titanic when that woman Seraphina tried to kill me, and again with Victor. But not as scared as when Connor's life was in danger."

I drew a breath and let it out in a slow guilty breath and sat. "I'm sorry," I said, not wanting to look into her eyes. The guilt I had suppressed until now fought to escape, but crying wasn't the answer. That would be manipulation, which is weakness. "It's my fault for travelling back to check Stan's story."

Erin shook her head at that. "No, it's not. I've thought about it. Anyone would have done what you did."

"But it led to..." I hesitated. The thought of what

happened, of how Jenny has manipulated me by deception into impregnating her. "You know."

"Yeah, I know," Erin replied. "But that's not your fault. I've read your journal, listened to it, played the vision in the VR, and thought about it too. She drugged you. I remember she even tried before that, and you stood up for yourself. I trust you. You're not the problem; Jenny is."

"I should have killed Stan at Dornoch," I replied in resignation.

Erin waved a dismissive hand at that. "That's not you. You're not a killer, and you're not your son. That apple fell far away from its tree before you even met him." She paused for a moment, biting her bottom lip as she thought, her eyes distant.

I took Connor from her lap, happy to hold my son again. No way in the world did I want this time to end. Neither did I want an interruption as he reached up to play with the stubble on my cheeks and chin. He paused, eyes full of curiosity as his pudgy fingers stretched towards my broken nose, which had been set at ASIS when I returned Sofia's dead body.

"We need a holiday, Punkinhead," she said, stifling a yawn. "Somewhere no one will find us without permission."

"Somewhere without guns or killers or trouble," I added.

"We also need somewhere safe for later," Erin added, then looked over at the kitchen sink. "Do you have a kettle or anything for a drink in your bachelor pad here?" She left her chair to search. A memory came of how Grandma had once cooked scones and sponge cakes there. For a second, I fancied I could smell them even now, bringing a smile to my face. Perhaps Grandma was still watching me.

"Probably some coffee there," I said, pointing towards a wooden shelf. "I kept it there for Claire whenever she dropped by."

Meanwhile, Erin had found her way to the fridge, casting an approving glance upon opening it and finding the electricity still connected. Then she scrunched up her face at the contents. "Junk food? Is this what you used to eat before we met? That's going to change again."

I offered a sheepish grin and shrugged, turning to Connor, who grinned back with his large blue eyes. "Mummy is..." I paused, refraining from saying it: Mummy is a food Nazi.

The word had regained its true meaning with me. Time had diminished its significance, turning it into a casual term, but its original truth should never have been forgotten. I pondered how society misrepresents words and meanings for sensationalism or to desensitise us. If only people considered a word's origins and etymology more, as they once did---or experienced it as I have. Nope. Dreaming.

"Mummy is what?" Erin asked, eyeing me as she retrieved a pack of Tim Tams from the fridge.

"A beautiful woman we are both lucky to have in our lives," I replied, hoping I didn't say it too fast.

"And don't forget it." She winked, opening the packet and letting our wide-eyed son take one with joy. "We're going to need another place to live, Tony," she added, her serious tone returning.

"Not here though, right?"

Erin shook her head. "They know us too well here, I think. Maybe not ASIS, but our friends know by now, including Tenner and Jasmine. We need something like a private island, an untouchable estate, or something up high and isolated."

"Mummy wants a bat-cave," I muttered to Connor, whose face had turned brown with melted chocolate. Then returning my attention to my wife, "Let's brainstorm it."

"After we have rested," she reminded me. "I take it you have clean sheets and a bed here for your son? We still have to check on our friends back in 2019 after we rest."

"How about a couple of days here?" I suggested, almost expecting my wife to baulk at that.

"Yeah, it sounds good," she said, fatigue in her voice as she poured the cuppa.

I smiled at that and to see Erin healing, to know we still had a future together. For now, staying in my childhood home, the one I had inherited, was our haven. "Good," I answered, then felt the cylindrical lump in my pocket. "But first, I have to drop something at the lab. I have another paternity test to do."

Erin's eyes opened wide, her mouth dropping open, then clouds billowed. "Paternity test? Who is it this time?"

I waved the bottle of blood in front of her. "Stan's blood," I explained. "Call it a hunch."

"Can it wait?" Fatigue from shock lined her eyes and face. "We're barely together, and you're off again."

I shook my head. "Has to be done. Got to do it while it's fresh."

Erin glanced at the bottle, considering my words. She probably remembered how DNA tests had caused a lot of this problem for us. "If Jenny confirmed he's her son, why are you--?" Then she stopped, a light turning on in her mind as the wheels turned. "I think I know what you're thinking. Go! But bring us back some things to eat."

Chapter 34

Electronic Diary of Tony Nowlan
Apricot Corporation, Yeppoon, Queensland.
Australia.
7pm, 1st November 2019.

As we entered the Apricot Corporation, we heard the voices of Sam Stockwell and Albert Cardnell coming from the back rooms. I couldn't help but smile at the familiarity of Sam's voice, trying to remember when I had last heard him this excited, so alive. It had been ages. Erin nudged me playfully, her eyes twinkling with curiosity.

"Sounds like they're deep in conversation," I whispered to Erin as we made our way toward the back rooms.

Inside, we found Sam and Albert huddled over a table covered in schematics and equations. Sam looked up, his face breaking into a grin at the sight of us.

"Ah, Tony! Erin! Perfect timing," Stockwell exclaimed, gesturing for us to join the discussion.

"Indeed, we could use your input," Cardnell added, his eyes sparkling with a mixture of excitement and intellectual curiosity.

As I settled in, Erin bustled to the kitchen shelf for her coffee mug and poured herself some. Sam pointed to a diagram of the schematic for his SkyShield project, glancing at me, then narrowing his eyes in observation. "You look different. Almost older. How long have you been time-hopping for Cutter?"

Preferring to keep it under wraps, because of its top secret nature, I gave a nonchalant shrug. "We had a short break afterwards to recover." Not so short. It was a month, this November, actually. We travelled back to the 1st, so we didn't lose as much contact with friends, although it would be interesting to see our own joint account transactions as our "previous selves" holidayed on the Gold Coast, Sydney, and Hobart. We found it more appealing than hanging at my childhood home.

Sam considered my words for a second. Normally, he would have clucked his tongue because we had been away from helping him with his project. But not this time. He seemed lighter somehow. He nodded with a smile. "Your tan looks good," he said, then turned back to what they had been discussing before we arrived. The SkyShield, Sam's ambitious project to protect Earth from cosmic threats.

"I've been refining the calculations for the shield's energy distribution," he explained, pointing to a series of complex equations on the table. "But I can't shake the feeling that there's something missing, some key element we haven't accounted for."

Professor Cardnell leaned in, his gaze intense. Even he seemed lighter, more relaxed, although he still wore his old-fashioned shirt and trousers from 1912. He wore his shirt's long sleeves rolled to his elbows to cater for the heat. "Perhaps we're approaching it from the wrong angle. Have you considered the potential applications of gravitational lensing in enhancing the shield's effectiveness?"

Sam's eyes lit up with the revelation. "Gravitational lensing... Of course! It could provide the precise focusing we need to reinforce the shield's integrity."

As we delved deeper into discussion, I couldn't help but notice how their eyes met, the subtle exchange of glances and smiles that spoke volumes. Clearly, their connection has been deeper than mere professional admiration. The dynamic unfolding intrigued me, making me wonder how it might develop in the future.

I glanced up to see Erin had since stepped out of the computer room with Tenner. She motioned for me to come over. Excusing myself, I approached Erin, my mind still lingering on the interaction between Sam and Albert. I couldn't resist teasing Erin about the budding romance. "Looks like we're not the only ones making breakthroughs around here," I remarked with a knowing grin.

"Oh, that." Tenner, her black hair lustrous in the kitchen light, rolled her eyes. "You're lucky you weren't here the other morning," she deadpanned. "I arrived to hear them singing a duet from Gilbert and Sullivan or something. Their costuming was minimal." She shuddered as if recalling the scene, conjuring a ludicrous mental image in my head that shocked me, too. "I hold you both responsible for it."

Erin laughed at the thought. "Love can come from strange places and times," she commented. "So, what have you got to show us?"

"Here, I'll show you." Tenner turned and beckoned us into the computer lab, shutting the door on the discussion that continued around the kitchen table. Connor was in the lab's corner, playing with old USB sticks, pretending they were toy cars.

She pulled up two chairs for us at her computer. A few quick keystrokes brought up data to the screen. "The blood from 'Stan the Man'," she explained, giving me a sideways glance to see if I noticed her using the nickname I'd created. "The DNA results are in the post, but I hacked the laboratory to get a rush result."

As an engineer and physicist by training, the medical data meant little to me. So I fast-tracked to the summary. Erin's forehead scrunched as she read it; her mouth opened in surprise. So did mine.

The words escaped my mouth in a whisper. Erin gripped my hand, its strength a mirror of my consternation. "What the hell?"

"He is neither your son nor Jenny's," Tenner said, leaning back in her chair. "Good news, yeah?"

"But the resemblances?" Erin exclaimed. "And even Mum, I mean Jenny, called him her son. He said he's my half-brother!"

Understanding and empathy softened Tenner's face as she considered Erin's words. She turned to me. "How did you know to take a test?"

I scratched my head, thinking back on everything. "He tried to shoot me, but shot Jenny instead. It was an accident. But something in his manner didn't seem right. No remorse, no guilt. I couldn't believe a son of mine, even one I hadn't raised and never seen, could be so cold-blooded."

"But he said he gave us half a chance because of the blood ties." Erin frowned, thinking for a second. "I don't get it. Maybe he's crazy or something."

"He could have been playing you," Tenner suggested from the side, swishing a Chupa Chup stick between her lips. "Playing a long game of manipulation, maybe?"

I scratched the stubble on my cheek, my thought caught on the idea. Could he? That would explain a couple of other things he said. "I left him with the witch hunters in 1688 during the Black Plague. His ChronoSpace is useless, fried by my EMP," I muttered, leaning back in my chair to gaze up at the ceiling. "Maybe I should have just killed him to put us out of our misery faster."

Erin gave Tenner a look. The hacker's gaze remained blank until my wife cleared her throat. Upon catching the meaning, Tenner excused herself from the room.

"Don't knock yourself out over this, Tony." Erin placed her hand on mine. "You didn't kill him because you're not a sadistic bastard like him. I'm glad he's not related."

"Because you don't have to give him birthday gifts?" I asked with a hint of sarcasm.

Erin smiled, recognising that I had once kidded about her being a cheapskate when she insisted on budgeting everything. I had won millions on the lottery upon travelling back to 2017 from 2042. Having the results of each draw in advance was handy. Still, she had insisted on budgeting, saving the money, reinvesting it. "No, because now you can concentrate more on your original reason for inventing time travel."

I considered her words. Yes, my original reason: family. I realised my parents were still young at this point. They knew my secret, that I am their son returned from the future. Erin knows I came back to know them as they were before their premature deaths, which are approaching. With everything going on, I haven't had the chance to focus on them. They deserve it, since they now know who I am.

We never know what life can throw our way: bills, work, dramas best ignored, even shiny pebbles disguised as pet projects. Whatever happens, we mustn't lose sight of what's important. Time is always running out.

We knew what we had to do...

Chapter 35

**Östersunds Psykiatriska
Östersund, Jamtland, Sweden
18th December 2019**

Dr. Inger Johansson sat in the dimly lit observation room, eyes fixated on the man known only as Patient X. The room was silent except for the faint hum of the fluorescent lights and the occasional rustle of paper as Patient X continued his relentless scribbling. Five years had passed since the local police had found him wandering the streets, dishevelled and muttering incoherently, without identification. No clues had been found to who he was. He hadn't spoken a word since arrival at the mental care unit. No clues came from his frantic scribbling.

"Dr. Johansson, you need to see this," Nurse Adell called urgently.

Inger turned away from the one-way mirror and followed Adell into Patient X's room, where he was hunched over a fresh sheet of paper. His hand movements were different. Instead of the chopping and changing scratches, it now moved with precision and purpose, out of place for someone in his condition. His mindless scribbles had changed to drawing.

Inger moved closer, her curiosity piqued. Patient X had drawn a face in meticulous detail. The man's eyes were sharp and piercing, his jawline strong, and his expression telling of high intelligence, yet playful. Below the portrait, in a careful, almost reverent script, were two words: "Tony Nowland."

"Who is Tony Nowland?" Nurse Adell asked, her voice a

whisper.

Inger shook her head, her mind racing. "I don't know. But we need to find out."

She reached out and gently took the drawing from Patient X. He looked up at her, his eyes empty yet somehow knowing. Inger felt a shiver run down her spine. Something about those eyes that suggested he understood far more than he let on.

Inger hurried to her office, the drawing clutched in her hand. She placed it on her desk and began a search through the hospital's database. After an hour of fruitless searching, she expanded her quest to include police records, missing persons reports, and online databases. As she sifted through the information, she couldn't shake the feeling that she was on the brink of something significant.

After two hours of searching, she leaned back in her chair with a heavy sigh. Then a headline caught her eye: "Tony Nowland, Founder of Apricot Corporation, Revolutionises Smart Devices." The article featured a photo of a man who bore an uncanny resemblance to Patient X. The same piercing eyes, the same strong jawline. The only difference was that Tony Nowland looked to be the same age as Patient X. The resemblance was too close to be a coincidence. But it couldn't be the same person. The Courier Mail article was only a day old.

Inger's heart raced as she read through the details. Tony Nowland was an Australian tech entrepreneur who had recently made headlines with his innovative new smart devices designed to rival the iPhone and iPad. Apricot Corporation was on the brink of becoming a major player in the tech industry, and Tony Nowland was at the helm.

She printed out the information and returned to Patient X's room. He was sitting quietly, staring at the wall. Inger showed him the printout, watching his reaction closely. For the first time, recognition flickered across his face. He touched the image of Tony Nowland, jaw dropping, eyes filling with tears as his mouth formed a silent whisper.

Inger knelt beside him, her voice soft. "Is this your brother?"

Patient X shook his head, the first clear communication he had offered in years. His lips moved again, repeating the same shapes over and over. Inger leaned closer, her ear by his mouth, straining to hear. An almost inaudible breath carried the sound without voice. She closed her eyes to better concentrate. Upon recognising the word, she turned to watch Patient X's mouth still forming the same shapes. She imagined the same word, timing it with his lips. There was no doubt about what she thought he said, as it matched his inaudible whisper. But it couldn't be true.

"Can you write your name?" Inger asked gently, handing him a pen and a fresh sheet of paper.

Patient X took the pen, his hand trembling. He began to write, the letters shaky but legible. When he finished, he handed the paper back to Inger. She looked down and gasped. Written in neat, deliberate letters was a name: "Joseph Nowland."

Before Inger could process the implications, the lights in the room flickered and dimmed. A low, mechanical hum filled the air, and the door to Patient X's room swung open. A man and woman in dark suits entered, their faces expressionless.

"Dr. Johansson, we need to speak with you," one of them

said, his voice cold and authoritative.

Inger stood, her heart pounding, noting the mirror finish on the man's sunglasses. Her reflection stared back at her uneasily. "Who are you?"

The man flashed a badge, the official-looking emblem unknown to her. But she missed seeing which government agency they represented. "We have reason to believe that Mr Nowland holds information of extreme national importance. We need to take him into custody immediately."

Inger's mind raced. She couldn't let them take him, not without understanding what had happened. She stepped between Joseph and the men, her voice firm. "He's my patient, and I need more information before I can release him."

The agent's expression hardened. "This is not a request, Dr. Johansson. This is a matter of national security."

Before Inger could respond, Joseph stood up. He placed a hand on her shoulder, his touch gentle but insistent. For the first time, he spoke, his voice hoarse and barely audible.

"It's okay, Dr. Johansson. I'll go with them."

Inger watched in stunned silence as the agents led Joseph away. Whatever secrets lay buried in his past were entwined with a much larger and more dangerous mystery. She couldn't let it go without some explanation.

She excused herself and followed their trail. The empty hallway, with a few benches and light pink walls, greeted her. Her ears caught the dinging bell of the lift down the end, and she hurried in its direction. Its doors slid open jerkily, allowing two staff members and a patient out onto the floor. She reached the doors in time to see it otherwise empty. With a puzzled look, she turned to examine the other exits, but there were no other places they could have gone.

Inger's head crowded with more questions about the man whose name she had only just learned. Her best clue lay with the Australian named Anthony Nowland.

Afterword

The Titanic Connection directly follows Paradox of Buck Nowlan, a sequel to Bootstrap's Journey, yet I have taken pains to make it a standalone book as well.

Operation Barbarossa was real. Hitler originally held a non-aggression pact with the USSR, known as the Molotov-Ribbentrop Pact, which stated that they wouldn't interfere with each other during war. However, Hitler was deceptive and chose to turn on the Russians. In my opinion, he had always planned to take Russian lands for Germany. I believe he had a similar plan for Japan, the other member of the Axis powers, in line with his view of the Aryans being the master race. Thankfully, he never reached that point in his plans.

If Operation Barbarossa had succeeded, Hitler might have won the war. As it turns out, the Russian winters worked against him, as they had for others who had fought them. The campaign took too long, cost too much, and divided his forces.

And of course, linking it to the Titanic seemed the most logical thing to do. Tony had seen Stan with a Nazi officer during his first visit to the Titanic. We don't know the exact nature of that meeting between the enemies; I imagine it was part of Stan's plan to win the Germans to his cause.

Have we seen the end of Stan? And who is Patient X or Joseph Nowland? Before you ask, the difference in name spelling between Nowland and Nowlan is intentional, something half-explained in Bootstrap's Journey. You will probably remember that Tony Nowlan adopted the name

Nowland as an alias when he travelled back to 2017. Since marrying him, Erin chose to adopt the Nowlan name, but I wonder what would happen when they find their own place away from it all, and in what time?

I'll let you ponder this as I write the next volume.

Happy Reading!

Chris Johnson
27th May, 2024.

About the Author

Chris Johnson's thrillers blend science fiction, light modern fantasy, the supernatural, and action and adventure, with a dash of quirky humour. He loves to include wise-cracking heroes and heroines who are stuck in strange situations from which they have to escape. Most of his novels and stories are based in his home country of Australia -- but don't be surprised if you find yourself in another far-flung international city too.

If you'd like to know when the next book comes out, please sign up for Chris' newsletter at

https://www.larrikinbooks.com

You will receive a free gift, and see behind-the-scenes looks at the new books before their release, and more.

Other Books

The Craig Ramsey - Occult Detective series

Deja Two (2022)

Dead Cell (2016)

Demon Blade (2018)

The Universe Crack'd (2021)

ChronoSpace series

Bootstrap's Journey (2017)

The Paradox of Buck Nowlan (2023)

The Titanic Connection (2024)

Standalone Books

Twelve Strokes of Midnight (2016)

While He Was Sleeping (2020)

The Trick (2016)

Grantley's Last Laugh (2023)

Read more at Chris Johnson's site *https://payhip.com/ChrisJohnsonAuthor*